Such Happiness As This

LAINA VILLENEUVE

Bella
BOOKS

2015

Bella Books, Inc.
P.O. Box 10543
Tallahassee, FL 32302

Printed in the United States of America on acid-free paper.

First Bella Books Edition 2015

Editor: Cath Walker
Cover Designer: Sandy Knowles

ISBN: 978-1-59493-464-3

Other Bella Books by Laina Villeneuve

Take Only Pictures
The Right Thing Easy

Acknowledgments

The years I spent in Arcata gave me so many gifts. Michael, thank you for sharing your home, craft and knowledge of the coast with me. Heather, thanks to you and your family for help with military details and recollections of Arcata hotspots. Thank you, Ruth, for reading my thesis project so many years ago and saying it was good enough to send to Naiad and for letting me use your poetry here. Susan, thanks for introducing me to Freshwater and for your notes. I am truly honored to be your colleague.

Thank you, Marilyn, for every walk we shared and for playing violin. The music in the book is here because of you. Dad, I hope that I got the music right. I will always treasure the conversations we had that contributed so greatly to character and plot.

To my sisters-in-law: Theresa, thanks for fashion advice. Katrina, your *Queering Marriage* inspired me greatly.

Idalia and Vasthi, thanks for help with character diversity.

Tamara Bertolini, you helped me understand when things need to be tossed overboard.

Everyone at Bella, thank you for making this book awesome inside and out. Cath, thank you for not only spotting the plot holes but helping me find ways to fill them.

Mom, thank you for the title.

Readers will want to thank my wife for having a better sense of where this story was going than I did. I am forever grateful that she always had an answer to my question, "what happens next?"

Finally, I am thankful for the spark lent to this story by Caemon Patrick Marston-Simmons, a boy I had hoped to one day meet. I was devastated when leukemia took him just after his third birthday. His moms generously allowed me to use his name which in turn brought so much more. The life he brought to this story surprised me. He snuck his way into scenes and shaped the lives of my characters. He has touched my life deeply, and with this story, I honor his legacy. More about him is available on the blog C is for Crocodile.

About the Author

Laina Villeneuve and her spouse first registered as domestic partners in the spring of 2005 by getting the document notarized at a local copy shop and still wonder if the clerk had any idea she played a part in their commitment. A year later, they married illegally at their church surrounded by family and friends. In 2008, they remarried after California legalized gay marriage with their first son as a witness. They will celebrate ten years this summer by touring some of California's natural wonders with their three children.

Dedication

For Timaree and Jodi
In admiration of your strength and resilience

Then he rustled his feathers, curved his slender
neck, and cried joyfully, from the depths of his heart,
"I never dreamed of such happiness as this, while I was
an ugly duckling."
-*"The Ugly Duckling"* Hans Christian Andersen

CHAPTER ONE

Opportunity sat in the palm of Robyn's hand.

She'd pulled it from the bowl of small pewter stones that she kept on a low table by her bed. Every morning before she rose, she sifted through the cool stones, each inscribed with a word, mixing them in their shared bowl before selecting one. A second smaller bowl held her choice for contemplation or inspiration throughout her day. She accepted what the bowl gave her.

That wasn't actually true. She'd grown tired of how often *Tears* sat in the second bowl and had started avoiding the small stones, shifting her fingers to a second stone if she happened to feel the almost round one between her thumb and forefinger. She wasn't one to cry and took it as some cosmic suggestion that she might feel better if she did. But she was stubborn, not that there was a stone for that. *Promise. Loyalty.* Many of the stones reminded her of the commitment she had made to heed their message and inserted themselves into her fingers, bowl and consciousness.

Her decision to lease a horse after more than twenty years away had given her something different to think about each day. Finding another way to invest her energy gave her days new purpose. Instead of reminding her of her failed relationship, they seemed to be pointing Robyn back toward herself.

* * *

Once she arrived at the barn for her morning chores, Robyn ran her hands along the bay mare's neck before grabbing a brush. She worked her left hand in small circles with the black rubber curry before brushing the dust and hair free with her right, this ritual her meditation. Thinking about this morning's offering of *Opportunity*, she wondered if the stones were nudging her to buy this mare she'd been leasing. The barn and the routine that came with it were good for her, an opportunity (there was that word again) to focus her thoughts on the present instead of over-analyzing the past and worrying about her future.

Before these horse chores had pulled her out to the barn, she'd become a hermit, leaving the house only to roam the beaches alone or scour estate and garage sales. She was alongside people but never interacting with them, her eyes keen to find a hidden treasure.

When Barb had first noticed her, talked to her and pulled her out of her shell, she'd felt like it was she who had been pulled from the discards. She had felt valued, polished up and finally seen. Their first years had been full of love, laughter and joy, stones that had once felt wonderful but now mocked her when she saw them in her palm.

She closed her eyes and leaned against Taj's barrel, feeling her warmth, matching her breathing to the rise and fall beneath her, trying to pinpoint how long things had been cold with Barb. When had they stopped touching? Once, she had always turned to spoon her lover and savor the moments before they separated for the day as she came up to the surface of wakefulness.

But that was back when they had shared Barb's massive four-poster in the master bedroom that Robyn's grandparents had shared for sixty-six years. When she and Barb went to bed together, Robyn could convince herself that it was their room. When Barbara started to come to bed hours later, Robyn spent too many nights lying alone comparing the love and respect her grandparents had for each other to her own relationship. She and Barb were such a failure in comparison that she escaped to the loft her papa had built in the attic above the room that was hers each summer. She lay on the simple queen mattress and stared at the stars, telling herself that she didn't want to disturb Barb's sleep.

They were barely roommates.

Forgiveness.

The stones were always reminding her that no relationship is perfect. They had eight years together. That was surely worth something.

But it wasn't *Forgiveness, Loyalty or Promise* she'd pulled from her dish of stones today. Not *Patience, Courage* or *Worrier.*

Opportunity had come to her.

CHAPTER TWO

Indirect

"Can't catch me!" a child's voice boomed in the aisle, breaking the peace of the morning.

"No running, Caemon," a woman's voice answered. "We don't want to spook the horses."

Robyn peeked from her horse's stall and saw a tall woman and young boy stop at the neighboring stall. Both wore plaid shirts, jeans and boots. They worked on the combination lock of the tack shed together, the youngster keeping up a constant stream of chatter. Robyn's blue eyes widened in surprise at his loquaciousness. Before either saw her, she ducked back into her stall.

To her, quiet was peace. She'd never been one for a lot of words, always preferring to just listen. In college, she'd been the student who sat in the back without uttering a word all semester. She soaked everything in but never felt the need to participate.

Barb was always pushing her to open up more, but it never went well when she did share what was in her head. So she typically kept her words to herself.

She stilled when the chattering ceased. Curious, she inched toward the door to see if the pair was already leaving.

"You Penapea's friend?" the tow-headed youngster asked quizzically.

Robyn stepped closer to the door and peered over and into two keen blue eyes. How had he even known she was there?

Seemingly unconcerned by Robyn's confusion, the boy continued. "My Mommy has a baby in her belly. I have one too. See?" He pulled out a stuffed cat and held it out for her to examine.

"Caemon, come help me with the rake, please. Let's not bother the nice lady."

Robyn studied the woman, looking for shared traits with the boy. While their coloring didn't match, the sharp line of his jaw echoed hers. "He's no bother," Robyn surprised herself with her answer, and her words stopped the woman across the aisle. After a moment of hesitation, she approached to stand by the boy, tucking her light brown hair behind her ears.

"Baby Kitty cared of horses, so he tay in here," Caemon said, bringing her attention back to the boy as he tucked the stuffed animal back under his shirt.

"Baby Kitty is scared," the boy's mother translated, walking over to scoop him up into her arms. He promptly grabbed the half-door and pulled both of them to where he could look in to see Robyn's horse.

"But it doesn't look like that one is scared," Robyn observed.

"Of anything," the woman said. "I'm Kristine, and this is my big boy, Caemon."

"Caemon Owens-Fisher," the boy said, puffing out his chest.

Robyn straightened her posture. "I'm Robyn Landy. Pleased to meet you both." Seeing no baby bulge on the woman in front of her, she guessed that she was talking to Caemon's other mom.

"I a big helper," Caemon provided. "I can do the rake and ride in the wheelbarrow. Sometimes I ride the tractor. Do you have a tractor?"

"I don't."

He looked disappointed.

"You no like tractors?"

"Oh, I love tractors, but my garden isn't big enough to use a tractor."

"I want to see your garden!" he exclaimed.

"Caemon, we came to see Bean. You're going to help me clean his stall, remember?"

"I get the rake!" he squealed, wriggling from his mother's arms.

"How do you keep up?"

"Not very well," Kristine said. "And my wife's in the last trimester of number two."

Robyn was pleased to discover she'd deduced correctly and liked the way Kristine talked about her family so openly. It could be that Kristine already intuited that Robyn herself was "family." Her short hair could ping people's gaydar, but then people had often commented that she seemed too feminine to be gay, which Robyn attributed to her Japanese ancestry. Something about the way Kristine carried herself made Robyn suspect that Kristine would have mentioned her wife to anyone she was talking to, gay or straight. Robyn had spent many years wishing she could speak so candidly.

"Mama! The rake tuck, Mama!"

"I'm coming," Kristine called, but she didn't leave the stall immediately. She studied the horse behind Robyn. She took a carrot out of her pocket and snapped it in half, immediately capturing the animal's attention. The mare promptly stepped to the door to take the carrot. Kristine slid her hand along the horse's jaw and continued to stroke her neck. "Did you buy her?" she asked, her eyes shaded with sadness.

"I'm leasing her. Her owner doesn't seem ready to sell, and I'm okay with that. It's been a long time since I've been a barn rat. It's probably good to come back slow."

Caemon came racing across the barn, noisily dragging the rake he'd found. The horse ducked away from the stall door. "Drop the rake," Kristine barked.

Caemon froze and followed his mother's order.

In a softer tone, Kristine explained that they didn't want to spook the horses.

"I give Taj carrot?" Caemon asked. "Where Penapea?"

Kristine gave the other half of her carrot to Caemon and lifted him, and he expertly fed it to the horse. "Robyn is taking care of Taj while Penelope gets better, Sweet. Let's go give some carrots to Bean before he gets jealous." She squeezed him tightly before setting him down. Robyn caught her swiping a tear from her face as she stood and offered a smile. "Hope to see you again."

"Likewise." Robyn watched Kristine follow Caemon back to their horse's stall. She wondered again about the arrangement she had with Taj Mahal's owner, Eleanor. Though Eleanor had seemed as at home in the barn as anyone, she was clearly relieved when Robyn had decided to lease the horse. Robyn had already puzzled over whether the horse might have belonged to Eleanor's child, but she hadn't said anything about a Penelope or what she was recovering from.

Robyn quickly saddled and bridled the horse in her stall, waving to Kristine and Caemon as she led Taj out, surprised when the mare started heading toward Bean's stall. Giving Taj a tug, she turned her toward the arena, feeling Kristine's steady gaze on them as they made their way down the barn aisle.

CHAPTER THREE

Hard Work

Wind off the ocean blew wet and cold, forcing Robyn to trudge along with her hood up and head down to keep warm. Most people thought of the beach as warm and welcoming. They had no experience with the shoreline on the Northcoast where rock formations jutted from the cold water and steep cliff faces topped by tenacious evergreens. Some beaches had a wider stretch of sand with ever-shifting dunes. As she walked, she scanned the shore, hoping last night's storm had kicked up some good wood she could work in her shop.

So far, the offerings were beautiful pieces but either much too big or small and splintered. She had found a manageable chunk that wasn't the redwood or madrone that typically washed up. Based on ocean currents it was likely lumber lost from a Japanese freighter. She looked forward to getting it back to her shop to clean it up and determine whether it was mahogany.

She walked the full length of Clam Beach, stopping at a huge redwood stump she'd had her eye on for some time. She rubbed her gloved hand across it. Even with more of the stump freed by the latest storm, she knew that she could not roll it without help, and she had no one to ask. It would have to be cut into pieces to work it, and she'd hate to make the choice of how to cut it up out on the beach before she could get a look at it from all sides.

Hard Work.

The stone she'd warmed in her palm that morning had given her a good feeling for the day, but this work was beyond her. Maybe if she hitched it to a horse. She turned and scanned the beach. A few walkers stayed close to the waves on the more firmly-packed sand. There were no horses on the beach today. Not like the one she had seen galloping effortlessly along the shore months before which had reminded her of her childhood promise to herself. It had prompted her to visit the bulletin board at the barn she frequented for manure for her compost, to look for a horse to lease.

She'd been in the fourth grade when she convinced her parents to let her take riding lessons. Saturdays, they would drop her at the barn in the morning, and she'd spend the entire day with her beloved animals. Most of the riders at the barn were around the same age, and they all laughed at the old ladies.

Old. Robyn laughed at herself. More than a few years into her forties, many of the women she remembered were probably years younger. She saw herself in them now when she brushed down Taj, returning to riding after too many years away. As a youngster, she had promised herself that she would always have a horse. She would never lose sight of something that grounded her so well.

Yet she'd sold her childhood horse when she went away to college and forgot all about riding while she served in the coast guard. No horses at sea. But then she'd seen the horse and rider on the beach and remembered the unbridled joy she had felt at that breakneck gallop, as if she could outrun any problem.

Could Taj help her outrun the problem she found herself in now? She twisted the band on her left ring finger, wondering what Barb thought of when she looked at its mate on her hand.

Two female figures curved, arms above their heads to grasp a garnet. Barb had found them at the North Country Fair, and they were perfect.

They had been for eight years. Most of those years…Some of them? She was so tired of living unhappily ever after. When had being with Barb become such hard work? More importantly, when had she begun to look at it as work she was not capable of handling?

She looked out to the horizon where gray met gray, the line between water and air obscured by the low-hanging clouds and mist. Her answer was not out here in the cold. It wasn't in the warmth of the barn either. Taj helped with her friendly nicker and the way she butted at her pockets for hidden carrots. The mare had raised her spirits considerably, but now she could see how far she had fallen. The cold gray had never affected her. It had always felt invigorating, inviting hard work to warm her.

But lately it had invited the darkest of solutions into her thoughts. It would be so easy to crawl away from the cold and just sleep, sleep past all the fights and worse, the silence that hung about them.

She looked back at the stump. Something beautiful waited to be born from it, but it was going to take a hell of a lot of work.

But not today. She slung her adz over her shoulder. On some large hunks of wood she used the ax-like blade to clean sandy grit away so she could saw the wood into manageable pieces to carry off the beach. With this stump, she couldn't see enough of it to know where to start. "Don't go anywhere," she said, rubbing the sandy surface again. "I'll figure out a way to get you home."

Speaking to a piece of wood throughout the process of finding it through finishing it wasn't unusual for her. But these words brought her pause realizing that she was trying to figure out a way to get herself back home too.

CHAPTER FOUR

Discovery

Robyn turned on her heel, quickly shifting her trajectory from the stalls to the covered arena to avoid interrupting the women standing by her stall. She'd recognized Kristine and saw that the sobbing woman she had her arm around was Taj's owner, Eleanor. Her presence surprised Robyn since she had not seen the woman since she'd signed the lease months ago.

She sat down on the bleachers and watched the riding lesson in the ring, a young girl on a fat, furry pony struggling to maneuver the stubborn animal into figure eights at a trot. When she was only eleven, the barn where Robyn had ridden would have put her on this pony to get it behaving again. She spent most of her weekends riding the lesson ponies. Her slight build allowed her to ride even the smallest of them and her strength, both physical and mental, kept them from believing they could get away with anything. In those days, she resembled her Japanese grandmother.

No one would match that little girl who never could find jodhpurs to fit snugly with who she was now, her Caucasian genetic majority having kicked in at puberty to stretch and broaden out her frame. She wasn't self-conscious about how the fabric now fit around her thighs and rear. Still strong, she knew she was sturdy, not skinny, and that suited her fine considering the labor-intense work she had chosen.

She wouldn't say she breezed through basic training in the coast guard, but she had no trouble compared to others in her group. In fact, she had excelled. She was granted any mission she wanted, as it was well understood she threw herself into her rescues a hundred and fifty percent. When she had announced her retirement two years ago, her superior officer initially refused to accept it, arguing that she had a lot of good years of active duty left. Perhaps her current melancholy was directly proportional to the plunge in physical day-to-day exertion.

Her mind returned to the stump she wanted to turn. Since it didn't feel right to interrupt Eleanor and Kristine, she pulled her cell from her pocket and scrolled to a number she hadn't dialed in a while.

"I cannot believe you are calling," Isabel said. Robyn couldn't help but smile, convinced she'd never heard her childhood friend answer the phone with "Hello." "I was just texting you."

"I don't believe you," Robyn said. They hadn't talked in at least three months.

"I know, right? But it is true."

"What were you texting me?"

"You know, how I am the worst friend ever. I never visit. I never call. I lost it all when I accepted your call, though, so do not ask me to send it."

"I'm the terrible friend," Robyn said. "You've got a family to take care of. How are the kids?"

"They are know-it-all nine-year-olds. They do not need me anymore. What is with you, mija? You do not sound like you."

Robyn didn't answer immediately, her voice constricted by her friend's ability to read her from hundreds of miles away. She cleared her throat and answered that she had to keep it down because of the lesson she was watching. They reminisced about the problem ponies they'd ridden as children, and Robyn told her about Taj.

"This is amazing!" her friend said. "I am so jealous! I cannot remember the last time I went riding."

"So fly down and go riding with me," Robyn said. "I'm sure I could borrow a horse, so we could go out."

Isabel took so long to answer that Robyn checked her cell to make sure she hadn't lost connection.

"Are you sure you are okay, mija?" she finally asked.

"I'm sure. I just don't want to tell you my ulterior motive which includes some heavy lifting." She smiled as Isabel's laughter boomed. She could hear her friends' twins shushing her from the other room.

After Robyn explained the stump retrieval she was planning, Isabel's tone changed. "*No sé.* If you want help like that, maybe I should just send Craig to help you."

"Don't you dare," Robyn answered. Though she liked him fine, the stump wasn't the real reason she suddenly longed to see her friend.

"I will call you tonight after I get permission from the family, *bueno?*"

"*Hai, matane,*" Robyn replied, tapping back to her obaachan's Japanese to tell Isabel she'd see her soon. She signed off and snuck back toward her stall, relieved to find Bean in the crossties, and the women gone. She strode to Taj's stall and pulled her out.

Kristine greeted her warmly when they emerged.

"No Caemon today?"

She swung around as if looking for her shadow and then laughed. "He's with his grandparents for the afternoon, and I'm taking advantage. I don't get Bean out as much as he needs it."

"Hard to get in a ride when you've got young ones at home," she acknowledged, remembering that Isabel sold her last horse shortly after she'd had the twins. She whisked a stiff brush along Taj's coat.

"I pick him up from preschool when I'm finished with my afternoon class. That's when I used to get my evening ride in. I feel guilty having Bean sit in his stall so much, but I sure don't want to give it up."

"I just talked to a friend of mine who did that when she had twins nine years ago. She really misses it."

They fell silent as they moved in and out of their tack sheds to saddle up. Robyn's thoughts turned back to how Kristine seemed to be comforting Eleanor when she arrived. She wasn't one to pry, but she couldn't put it out of her mind. Kristine's response to the horse the day they'd met made it clear she knew the story behind Eleanor's leasing Taj. As Robyn unsnapped her mare from the crossties, Kristine glanced at the bay. She looked sad again, piquing Robyn's curiosity. The look had to be because of Penelope, whoever she was.

"You used to ride together?" She worried about pressing what was clearly a delicate subject, yet her mind still spun through scenarios of what had happened to Penelope.

Kristine's gaze snapped away from Taj to Robyn, and she nodded. "Sorry. We rode a lot when my in-laws could watch Caemon for us. Last year my mother-in-law came out of remission and it got too hard for them to keep up, so I couldn't get out at all. Then Penelope volunteered to play with Caemon while I got in a quick trail ride. They had such a good time together, and we got to do what we like best, didn't we?" She patted her mount. She swallowed hard a couple of times. Robyn didn't know whether to step away from the layers of sadness Kristine had exposed. Before she could make a decision, Kristine spoke again. "Do you want to join me and Bean on the trail?"

Robyn briefly wondered whether she should decline, if Kristine really needed the time alone with her emotional chaos. She still got the impression that Kristine was a straight shooter and would not have invited her if she didn't want the company, so she accepted.

They exited the rear of the barn and mounted. Robyn's belly felt tight with anticipation. She had yet to explore the trails near the stable, limiting all of her riding to the arena as she retrained her muscles and got to know her horse. Taj knew the routine and fell in behind Bean. Within minutes, the redwood forest swallowed them, hoofbeats muted by the soft forest floor.

Sunlight streamed through the canopy of the majestic trees. They had entered a cathedral. A sudden desire to confess her sins overcame Robyn, though the military was the only religion offered by her family when she was young.

If Isabel did come to visit, she'd soon discover the catch in Robyn's voice that had nothing to do with sitting in the covered arena and everything to do with a poem she'd found in the papers scattered on Barb's desk. Robyn had been hunting for Barb's paycheck so that she could deposit it for her. They'd been arguing about why Barb wouldn't simply walk down to payroll and set up automatic banking when the poem caught her eye. Nearly another month had passed, inviting Robyn to not only think about whether Barb would remember to deal with her check herself but also whether she'd tucked the poem away.

She watched Kristine's back, her posture easy, shoulders swaying to the cadence of her mount's gait. It wasn't her place to invite grief back into the woman's window of freedom.

She tried to relax into her horse's movements and enjoy the trail, listening for any other life in the forest. Taj, however didn't invite too much relaxation, every muscle taut underneath her, head high and ears pivoting on high alert for the unexpected.

Robyn thought about how relationships were the same. The beginning of a relationship awakened her senses. Those were the careful days of really paying attention to learn the other. Inevitably relationships slipped into the comfortable, relaxed place where partners didn't worry so much about every little thing. Once their life together had become familiar, she had stopped paying such close attention. When was it that she had relaxed to the point that she could be so easily unseated, thrown so unexpectedly?

The poem on Barb's desk had certainly unseated her. She could only remember the opening lines, but they were enough.

Make yourself at home
take off
your clothes.

Whoever had written it fully explored the Freudian slip in painful poetic form. Who was she fooling. This was a conversation with her own subconscious, so she should be honest with herself and acknowledge that Barb's friend Daniel was surely its author.

Daniel with the nightmare wife and marriage. Did they commiserate, Barb comparing her own relationship to his? Did they both demonize their wives, listing unfavorable attributes? What kind of comfort did they offer each other?

As suddenly as the forest had swallowed them, it spat them back out into a clearing.

"Clear-cut," Kristine said unnecessarily, pulling Bean up. "I don't get how they are allowed to leave it trashed like this."

Robyn sat stunned, her gaze searching through the wreckage the loggers had left behind, the tractor tracks that gouged the muddy hillside littered with broken branches stripped from the trunks. The clearing let in too much light. Unchecked by the feathered branches of the redwoods, the sunlight reflecting off a solid mass of clouds made her feel like they were sitting under a spotlight. Robyn's heart hurt.

"I didn't know they were cut like this; so close. Naïve of me." In more ways than one she realized, thinking that her relationship had been stable, immune to such damage. She turned her gaze to Kristine whose face mirrored Robyn's pain.

"Taj's owner, Penelope, is in a coma."

The words sucked Robyn's breath away.

"I know her mother, Eleanor, didn't tell you. I thought you should know and I asked her if she'd told you. She said she wanted to but couldn't bring herself to say the words."

"How long?"

"Almost six months."

"That explains the lease." Robyn closed her eyes, picturing the family holding onto the horse and the hope that their daughter would recover to ride once again. Kristine opened her mouth like she was going to say more but shut it again and reined Bean back toward the trees.

"Kristine," Robyn said. She stopped. "Was the horse involved?"

Kristine looked away before nodding. "Penelope had taken her down to the beach. Some beachcombers found Taj pacing by the tributary and found Penelope in the water. They were able to resuscitate her, but…" She shook her head.

"She never regained consciousness." Robyn couldn't understand how she could have missed the details of the accident. Where had she been six months ago? So far down the hole that she had stopped registering what had been central to her professional life. Not that she wished to be in the rescue team's position. Those were the hardest for her, arriving on the scene to panicked faces so hopeful to see help arrive. If they'd found her, there would have been so many unknowns—how long she'd been unconscious, how long she'd been in the water. But it was already too late. The extended coma confirmed that Penelope had never had a chance.

Kristine met her eye. "But I know this horse. Whatever happened, it was a freak accident. I wouldn't want you to think that she's dangerous, but I think you have a right to know. I told Eleanor as much."

Robyn's eyebrows pulled down in concern. "That's terrible. But thank you for telling me. I don't feel differently about Taj."

"I didn't think you would." She smiled warmly. "I'm so glad you joined me today. And happy that Taj has you." She checked her watch, sighed deeply and inclined her head in the direction they'd come.

"Back the same way?" Robyn asked.

"Back to responsibility," Kristine quipped.

The information about Penelope should have occupied her thinking, but Kristine's final words had guided her thoughts back to Barb and the poem and her responsibility to confront the wreckage in her own life.

CHAPTER FIVE

Loss

Isabel and Robyn worked around each other in the kitchen clearing and washing the dishes as if they did it all the time. After a final wipe-down of the counter, Isabel stretched with a loud moan. "I might be broken."

"Good thing I fired up the hot tub when we got home then."

"You owe me after the workout getting that stump off the beach. Too bad Barb could not stay," she added.

"Yeah," Robyn said without feeling. She kept her attention on the towel she held in her hands.

Isabel wound her thick black hair into a knot, studying Robyn. The way she squinted, Robyn knew she suspected something, but she let quiet settle between them as she had all weekend. Her heart rate spiked, knowing she was running out of time to voice what she had to. Isabel's flight back to Spokane, Washington, left in the afternoon, and Robyn knew she wouldn't be able to confess to her friend right before shoving her on a plane. Every lull in the conversation, Robyn had inwardly rehearsed the words she needed to say, but she had yet to work up the courage to deliver them.

"I do not feel like I got to see her at all this weekend," Isabel prompted.

"John Prine is at the Van Duzer Theatre tonight. She said he had a crazy list of demands."

Isabel raised her eyebrows, encouraging Robyn to elaborate, and when she didn't comply, her visage shifted into her disappointed Frida Kahlo glare.

Robyn pushed away from the sink. "Let me give the tub one more stir and make sure we're up to temp. You want to grab us some towels from the bathroom cupboard?"

"Fine, but then you talk."

Robyn conceded and stepped out into the cool night. She lifted a paddle from the patio and stirred the steaming water in the old oyster tank she'd picked up years ago and rigged into a hot tub with a submerged woodstove. Preparing a soak helped her clear out the left over hunks of wood she cut off stumps and burl as she shaped blanks she would later turn into platters and bowls.

After stirring, she checked the thermometer. It tipped just above a hundred degrees. Just right to soak their tired muscles. Robyn stepped inside and found Isabel wrapped in a towel. "The water's perfect. Ease on in. I'll be right out."

In the bathroom, she stripped off her clothes and covered herself with a towel just in case one of her three renters chose that moment to return home. She slipped into the water next to Isabel, an appreciative hiss escaping her lips as she carefully lowered herself into the deliciously hot water.

"When are you getting jets in this thing?" Isabel said, her whole body immersed.

"Shut up. I made this…"

"Out of an old oyster tank, I know. I know. But I miss the jets."

"So get dressed and go pay for them down at the Café Mokka."

"But then I would not be naked in Northtown. Have your neighbors caught you yet?"

"Nope. At least I haven't heard anyone screaming or anything, so I figure it's still pretty discreet."

"I love the way the cold mist settles on my skin. It is like butterfly kisses. If I lived here, you would fire this up for me every night," she said with a dramatic wave of her arm.

"Another reason we never would have worked," Robyn laughed. She stopped abruptly when she realized what she'd said.

"What?" Isabel asked.

"Barb and I don't work anymore," she said, deciding it was better to jump in after all the internal festering. She felt the water ripple against her chest as Isabel shot up from her slouch, her mouth agape.

"What? But you guys are good. You are always good. I thought you said that you got all of the hard stuff out of the way before you got married and that it was smooth sailing after that."

"We never got married," Robyn said, remembering when she had stopped asking Barb to file as domestic partners.

"After you got, what is it you say? Committed?"

Robyn laughed, thinking that being caught in a straightjacket was exactly what her relationship had turned out to be. "It was for a while."

"But you retired for her, no?"

"The arguments about whether I was trying to kill myself on the job stopped, but then it turned out that we stopped talking period."

"You said that Barbara was always too dramatic about your job. Were you trying to kill yourself?"

Though Barb had asked her the same thing, Robyn had always steadfastly denied it. Not until Kristine had told her about Penelope lying in a coma had she considered why she had been so willing to take risks at work. She thought about the things that Penelope would miss, all the firsts that set life's logical goals: graduating, dating, landing the perfect job. Once she'd accomplished her goals, she had expected to feel happy. Proud. Satisfied. Not hopeless. The only joy in her life was her job so she believed that she might as well give it everything she had, even if that included her own life. "Yes," she admitted. "I thought it would be so much easier to die than face how unhappy I was at home."

"*Mija*. I never knew it was that bad. How long was it like that?"

Robyn shrugged. "A few years."

"A few YEARS? *Ay caramba*! You never said one thing." She looked at Robyn with reprimand and concern.

"You had your own hands full," Robyn said, thinking about how stressed Isabel was when she'd had two infants to care for.

"Never that full, *mija*. You could have told me."

"I know. I've been holding on to the possibility that we were just in a rough patch."

"How bad are we talking? How is the sex? Better with her or by yourself?"

Her face, though already red from the heat of the tub, flushed at the question. "Isabel!"

"What? If you are more excited to masturbate than you are to have sex with her, then that is it."

"I'm pretty much on my own," Robyn admitted.

"For years you have been on your own?"

Robyn nodded. "The last time we had sex, you know what she said to me? 'Why don't we do that more often?' Can you believe that?"

"Well," Isabel said as the silence stretched. "Why don't you?"

"I got tired of asking, of initiating, of feeling like I was imposing on her with my demands. Three years ago, I told her that I was going to stop asking but I was always interested. All she had to do was let me know, and I'd be game."

Isabel pushed air through pursed lips, clearly annoyed. "That is pretty harsh. You cannot wash your hands just like that."

Robyn shrugged. "It just made everything easier. I didn't get my hopes up, so I didn't get disappointed, and the years went by. I kept telling myself that we'd reconnect when I retired."

Isabel reached for her hand. "I just spent the weekend with you two, and you seem the same as always. You found Barb the year I met Craig." Isabel paused uncomfortably, looking at their joined hands. "Robyn, this isn't about…"

Following Isabel's train of thought, Robyn was suddenly awkwardly aware of her friend's nakedness. She shoved at her shoulder, breaking the tension. "I don't have a secret unrequited love for you if that's what you're going to ask. I met Barb. I fell in love with her. I thought I'd spend the rest of my life with her watching the gay pride parade go by the house every year from our porch swing."

"Is this the problem, that you are always on the swing and not marching in the parade?"

"Maybe that's her problem." Robyn thought again about the poem she found, wondering if she should share that revelation with Isabel. She didn't want to tarnish her friend's view of Barb.

"Does she want you to be more of an activist, shout out your gay pride?"

Robyn laughed, appreciating her friend's humor. "No. The parade makes her uncomfortable. She doesn't get why anyone feels the need to get out there and march or make any kind of announcement about it."

"Is it really necessary in Arcata? I thought all the ladies in this town were into each other. Lesbian beer, lesbian mayor, lesbian president for your college. Isn't everyone lesbian?"

"And Craig let you visit all by yourself."

Isabel glared at her friend. "I am just trying to understand. You never say one thing about the two of you not working, and all of a sudden, what? You are going to split? Have the two of you talked about that?"

They'd talked about it before Robyn had offered to stop asking Barb if she wanted to have sex. Barb had fallen apart, sobbing, arguing with Robyn about how a relationship was so much more than sex. She'd said she didn't know what she would do without Robyn. "We haven't talked about it lately."

"So why do you think you do not work anymore? What changed?"

Robyn had to tell her about the poem, she realized. "She's invested her energy in someone else. I thought that we were developing other friendships to strengthen ourselves, to have more to give to each other, but then I found a poem she received from one of her friends."

"And it was not innocent."

"That's the thing. It could have been. From the contents, I got that one evening, instead of saying 'take off your shoes,' he said 'take off your clothes.' He was exploring the powerful emotional connection two friends can have."

"He."

"He," Robyn confirmed.

"*Dios mío*. I must read this poem. Where is it?" Isabel asked.

"Are you kidding? I didn't keep it. I left it on her desk. On top," Robyn said.

"So she knows you read it."

"Yeah, but it's not evidence that she's having an affair."

"So she doesn't understand pride parade because she is not gay? She has been with you what, eight years? And she has not figured it out yet? Did you two go to a counselor?"

"I tried," Robyn said. "She picked the first therapist, some hippie-dippie 'push your hand against mine, and I'll tell you what's wrong' lady."

"Hand pressure?" Isabel repeated skeptically.

"She had this theory that as she asked questions, she could tell what was going on with you by the amount of pressure you offered. She was horribly expensive—she didn't take insurance—and I didn't feel like she actually had any useful strategies for us to change how we were. I found this other guy who we saw a few times. He got right to the problems with intimacy that we were having and gave us stuff to work on."

"Barbara didn't like him?"

"She said that he was homophobic and that the homework he gave proved that he was just trying to break us up."

"*Serio*? Did you try anything else?"

"I went to that guy by myself for a while, but I didn't feel like I was the one who needed to be there. I don't want you to think this is all Barb, but it didn't feel productive going to therapy to hear what I already knew. If she's not gay, we shouldn't be together, but she's the only one who knows whether she is or not."

"*Mija*, you deserve better than this."

"I'm forty-three, Isabel. Who dates in their forties?"

"Plenty of people. You are not dead. You pushed a—how many pounds was that stump, anyway?"

"Six, eight hundred pounds, maybe."

"You pushed an eight-hundred-pound stump across a beach today. This is nowhere close to over the hill."

Robyn laughed, appreciating that her friend automatically took the higher number. By the time she got home, she'd be telling her boys that she'd rolled a thousand-pound stump across the beach while Robyn ate bonbons. She laughed harder than called for and felt tears form. That was all it took to open a floodgate that fell freely into the hot tub. She buried her face in her arm. Isabel laid a hand on her shaking shoulders to comfort her.

"So you split up. You find someone who wants to ravish you so much you have to turn her down once in a while. What keeps you with Barbara?"

"I don't even know where to start. I don't want to give my parents any reason to say 'I told you so.' And all of our stuff is mixed together. What do we do about the bank accounts, the credit cards? I get so overwhelmed, I just hole up in my shop and turn bowl after bowl."

"You cannot stay together for stuff or for accounts. If it is that bad, I can fly back down and help you sort. I can do that."

"You're good to me."

"You are my oldest friend in the world. Forty-three. You really are old, you know?"

"Only four months older than you."

"Still, you will always be older."

Robyn rested her forehead on Isabel's shoulder enjoying the laughter she brought to her life. Then she sobered. "I don't want to disappoint you," she whispered.

"I only want for you to be happy. If you and Barbara do not make each other happy, the disappointment is going to come from you torturing yourself by staying in a dead relationship."

"So you'll break it to everyone?" she asked hopefully.

"Sure. I think that's in the duties of the best friend, way down in the fine print that nobody ever reads."

"You'll start with Barb?"

"You're on your own with that, *mija*," Isabel laughed. "Get me out of this tub and show me your new creations. Let's see if misery has sharpened your genius."

CHAPTER SIX

Trust

Talking to Isabel made Robyn acutely aware of how few friends she had. She socialized with Barb but never completely felt like she belonged. In the days after Isabel flew back home, instead of shrinking back into her shell, Robyn timed her afternoon horse feeding to coincide with Kristine's, enjoying their easy conversation. They had been on a few more trail rides, but mostly Kristine turned Bean out in the exercise ring while she mucked out his stall, brought him back for a quick brush and apologized for not having time to ride. Her life seemed full to the brim with a lot to juggle in a tight schedule.

A smile jumped to Robyn's face when she heard Caemon's voice ringing in the aisle. Since it was a weekday, she hadn't expected him to be with Kristine.

"Please I ride with you? Mama say Bean like the forest," he pleaded.

"I know you're a big boy," Kristine said, "but it's too dangerous to take Bean on the trail. You can ride him to the turn-out corral, okay?"

"This is a treat," Robyn said, squatting so she was eye level with Caemon. "I don't usually get to see you."

"Mommy needs a nap today," Caemon supplied happily.

"Someone isn't sleeping well all of a sudden," Kristine said, tipping her head in Caemon's direction. Her tired eyes supplied evidence that both moms were suffering from lack of sleep.

"You look like you could use a nap too," Robyn said.

Kristine laughed. "Back when I was riding trails in Mammoth, before Gloria and I met, I could nap in the saddle. Sometimes it's tough to not miss those days."

"Up," Caemon said, extending his arms. He burrowed his head into Kristine's chest, eyes sparkling and lips hinting a smile.

"Looks like someone knows how to make up for it, though."

Kristine buried her face in her boy's hair, drinking him in. When she tipped her head to rest her cheek against his crown, her posture relaxed, and Robyn envied the synergy between them, the absolute and unquestionable love. She and Barb had breathed in each other like that once, but love between partners wasn't the same. The tensions between them had drained her emotionally, and she couldn't remember the last time she had been able to turn to her to draw any comfort.

"Last time we talked, you said you were a fan of tractors," Robyn said to Caemon. "I go to estate sales all the time, and you wouldn't believe what I saw yesterday."

"What?" he said, the question punctuated as his body shot straight up, jarring Kristine.

"A John Deere tractor."

"An excavator?" he shouted.

Robyn scratched her head. "I don't know. Do excavators have a wagon on the back?"

Caemon looked at his mom. She shook her head. He crinkled his brow as if he was searching his database of tractors. "No. Excavator has a bucket."

"Maybe you could tell me what kind it is," Robyn said, slipping out of the stall. Kristine tipped her chin in question, so she whispered, "I hope it's okay I picked something up for him."

She opened the door to her tack shed, blocking their view of the child's tractor that pedaled like a tricycle. Caemon and

Kristine wore identical expressions of wide-eyed wonder that lit up in unison when she pushed the tractor out into the aisle. Caemon squirmed down from Kristine's arms. "Please I ride?" he asked his mom.

"You'll have to ask Robyn."

"You bet. I got it for you, so you can help me muck out my stall."

His gaze shot between the two adults.

"Go ahead," Kristine said, guiding Caemon to the small tractor's seat. He fit perfectly and with a small nudge was able to start pedaling, slowly making his way down the center of the aisle.

"I hope it's okay," Robyn said. "I was going to check with you today, but then you had him, and I couldn't resist."

"It's amazing. Look at him. He's in heaven right now. You have to let me pay for it."

Robyn shook her head. She couldn't explain the impulse to buy the tractor after the brief exchange she'd had with the boy, but seeing him leap off it to turn it around and pedal back to them with a grin that took over his face made her feel more alive than she'd felt in a long time. "I was serious about him helping me muck. I figure we can put some manure in that wagon, and we can see if we can make it out to the pile. I bet it would take long enough for a ride if you trust me."

"Robyn…"

"I know you barely know me, but…"

"No. It's not that. It's just…" Robyn was surprised to see tears forming in Kristine's eyes. "You don't know how much I need it."

"You want to see if you have permission?"

"I think you sealed that with the tractor," she said, squeezing Robyn's shoulder before she jogged over to Caemon to talk to him.

Robyn put her hand over the spot Kristine had touched, remembering how good it had felt when Isabel had put her arms around her. How had she missed noticing how long it had been since she'd had contact with another person? Kristine turned with a smile as big as Caemon's, and they both gave a thumbs-up. The two looked like peas in a pod. "You don't mind a little work?"

He shook his head vigorously. "I working man."

"Okay," Robyn said, winking at Kristine who slipped into Bean's stall to saddle him up. Robyn guided Caemon back to Taj's stall. She had him sit on the tractor while she put the mare in cross-ties, so they could work with the barn door open, scooping up piles of manure to put in his wagon. He started talking about different John Deere tractors and was completely immersed in his work when Kristine waved to Robyn, mouthing *thank you* as she slipped away.

The half hour Kristine took to ride slipped by in a blink for Robyn. They only made one trip to the manure pile with the tractor because Caemon's legs looked like jelly on the way back, but he was happy to play on the tractor while Robyn filled the wheelbarrow. When it was full, he insisted that his mom always let him ride on top of the muck in the wheelbarrow after she put a tarp on. Since he was able to supply the tarp from their tack room, Robyn obliged, and they continued working happily together.

They mucked out both stalls and had moved to grooming Taj when Kristine returned.

"You're an angel," she said when she saw the stall mucked. "I don't know how to repay you."

Robyn didn't know how to tell her how much she valued their currency of love. She didn't want to scare her by admitting how very much she needed it. "I'm pleased it worked out," she said. "And I hope you'll be around to help me again, young man. I'm an old lady and could sure use it."

Caemon laughed. "Mama, you old lady, too?"

"Sometimes I feel like it, mister. But I'm no old lady yet, and neither is our friend Robyn. She's just happy to have such a good helper."

As they left, Kristine stopped to run her hand along Taj's neck, and Robyn knew she was thinking about Penelope. She felt a pang of guilt that the shift in her life was connected to the accident and wondered if there was any change and whether Kristine ever visited her. The crazy idea of visiting Penelope herself flashed through her mind, but she discarded it. What would she say, that this new lightness she felt, a first inkling of hope, was like coming out of a coma herself? That hardly seemed appropriate. Still, it felt like she owed the young woman a thank-you, one she had no idea how to deliver.

CHAPTER SEVEN

Tears

An empty house shouldn't have felt any different. Robyn was used to Barb working late hours at the university where she booked acts for the theater, especially on a night there was a show. Yet in the week since Barb had walked out the door with a duffel full of her essentials, Robyn had spent more hours at the barn or out in her shop avoiding the house.

When Barb had first moved in, the newness of her presence had thrilled Robyn, sounds of her showering, drying her hair and putting on makeup, talking to herself about things she needed to not forget. The jackets that hung next to hers in the front hall closet. Her books shuffled in with Robyn's in the living room.

The sweet smell of the coffee she brewed. Her hazelnut grounds still sat tucked into the door of the freezer, mocking Robyn every time she opened the door. Now the shop was a safe haven where she would not uncover another item of Barb's and wonder if and when she was going to come retrieve it.

Her hands spun the almost-finished bowl she'd been sanding, feeling for any uneven surfaces. Worked with the finest grade of sandpaper, it was nearly ready for rubbing with mineral oil to reveal the true character of the grain. The nice chunk of walnut had given her many bowls, so she could anticipate the rich hue. She ran her thumb along the base of the bowl. She'd given it a new flare that Isabel had admired when she'd pored over the work in various stages of completion.

If she asked, Isabel would be on the next flight down to help her face life as a single woman, but she hesitated. Isabel would want to know all that had happened, details like whose idea it had been and whether Barb had left her for Poem Boy.

Robyn didn't want to report how well Barb had taken it. She'd tiptoed around their failing relationship for years, scared to trigger a breakdown, yet after Isabel's visit when she finally asked about the poem, she'd been floored by Barb's response. The way she sat and leveled her gaze at Robyn had told her they were over, that they had been for some time, and that she had simply been treading water until the time to leave was right for her.

She had her own questions but had been unable to ask them. Like why Barb hadn't just said it was over whenever it was she had stopped trying and how much of her deciding not to try any more had to do with Daniel? Was he leaving his wife? Was she going to live with one of her friends, or was she going to get a place with him? What had happened to her being a lesbian?

Barb hadn't fought for them. Not once did she talk about them working things out. Barb's tearful responses to earlier attempts to discuss their relationship had kept Robyn from broaching the subject later. But something had shifted between them, and now Robyn realized that it was some*one* who had made it possible for Barb to leave. It hurt to realize that Barb had just been marking time until something better came along.

She heard in Barb's voice what she had already felt, *We've been roommates for a while*. Robyn was still flabbergasted that Barb had neutralized the end of their relationship and treated that last night like a tenant deciding to leave. Robyn had felt like demanding months of past rent or threatening to keep the deposit for the emotional damage she had caused.

Her mind returned to the stuff of their shared life. The enormity of the task ahead of pulling their lives apart overwhelmed her. She'd have to call credit card companies, the bank, the utilities, figure out how to get herself removed from the title of Barb's car. She would have to call Barb.

She wanted to be free of it, free of everything. For months, ever since she'd begun riding, she'd felt that the relationship was about to crash. She'd known that it was over and just didn't have the energy to confront the emotional wreckage. Barb had moved them from the abstract of negotiating their failing relationship to the concrete of dismantling it but true to form did not want to contribute to the hands-on work. Robyn eyed the light blue two-story house and felt the weight of clearing up the debris of their past life together. Yet she was also ready to have it feel like her place again. Once she was completely free of Barb, she would be able to admire it again, seeing the original frame as well as her grandfather's various additions instead of the "shipwreck" image that Barb had imposed on her.

Robyn set down the bowl. This she could do.

She stopped at the shed where she stored the items she picked up at estate sales and out of the garbage at the end of the college semesters, desks stacked top to top, boxes of kitchen accoutrements, lamps and other small electronics college students discarded rather than fix. She kept it all for the yard sale she held when they returned en masse before the fall semester desperate to furnish their off-campus apartments. She grabbed a few empty boxes.

The first ones she parked on the table, filling them with Barb's kitchen utensils, fancy coffee press and the serving dishes she had insisted on buying when she'd been happy nesting. As Robyn wrapped these items in old newspaper, it occurred to her that she could feel thankful that Barb had never agreed to registering as domestic partners. One less thing to put on the list, she thought pragmatically. Before carrying out the first full boxes, she pulled the hazelnut coffee from the freezer and deposited it in the garbage.

Room by room she reclaimed her space. At the bottom of the stairs, she regarded the downstairs living room, her office desk tucked in one corner. Barb kept nothing there or in the bathroom. Robyn rented the one bedroom on the first floor to a university student, one of three she housed to supplement her retirement income. Her work awaited her at the top of the stairs.

The upstairs hallway had three doors. Her childhood room to the left, a renter's room to the right and straight in front of her the master bedroom. Two large picture windows filled the western wall, showcasing the evening's red and orange sunset. The eastern side of the room had an enclosed porch that served as a private small living room since Barb hated sharing space with the renters. She paused at the door she had made especially for Barb, running her hands over the smooth glass she had inlayed to pull down the stars for her lover. How often had it been closed between them when she slept in her loft while Barbara slept diagonally in the king bed down below?

As day eased to night, Robyn weeded out Barb's books and CDs, deciding which movies to keep and which to pack. What would flash through Barb's mind when she found *Kissing Jessica Stein* in her box? She imagined her watching the movie with Daniel, the two of them satisfied with Jessica's renewed interest in her old boyfriend at the movie's closing.

They'd talk intellectually throughout the movie, analyzing the difficulties Jessica had being lesbian. They'd discuss whether the two women flirting in front of men at the bar was hot. Who was she fooling? By the time Jessica and Helen sleep together, the movie would be long forgotten, Daniel and Barb...She did not need to be spending time thinking about her ex tangled up in sheets with a man. She quickly buried Jessica Stein with every subtitled film she'd suffered through.

Once she started, she could not stop, always picking up an empty box from the shed after she deposited a full one, working straight through dinner into the night. Her heart caught when she heard the door open. Intellectually, she knew it was one of her tenants returning, but her body was still conditioned to expect Barb. She sunk down on the stairs that led to her loft and curled into herself, elbows on knees and head in hands, suddenly exhausted.

As a child, her room had been the smallest in the house, barely big enough to hold a single bed, her simple pine dresser and the shelves that held treasures she had collected throughout the summers spent with her grandparents. Since both of her parents worked full-time, once summer hit, Robyn and her older brother, Jeff, lived with their grandparents who were happy to spend days combing beaches and hiking in the redwoods. After three summers of complaining that Jeff got the bigger room, her grandfather surprised her by creating a loft to give her a private play space. She'd surprised him by insisting that they move her mattress up to the attic room, arguing that she wanted to sleep in the room that held her toys.

After that, she had never complained again. Her room felt spacious and inviting. Barb had changed that when she moved in and claimed it as her office, filling her special shelves with unfinished projects and mountains of papers she had promised to organize someday. With all of that now crammed into trash bags, Robyn felt the room come back to her. She had hoped to reclaim the space with her collection of shells, but she was utterly spent. Even if she could convince one of the renters to lend a hand, there was no way she could move Barb's hulking desk that night.

A soft rap at the doorjamb pulled her upright. Jen stood in the hallway, home from her rehearsal with the community orchestra. The stylish youngster had rented the room across the hall since beginning her undergrad in music and through her master's in education. She seemed to have spent those years in flannel pants and T-shirts. Since she had graduated and begun searching for a job teaching music, she'd started buying slacks and blouses.

"You okay?" she asked, holding her long black curls up to unwind a scarf from her neck.

"Super," Robyn said, knowing that her tone suggested otherwise.

"You and Mom are getting a divorce, aren't you?"

Robyn couldn't help laughing. When Jen had come out to

unenthusiastic parents in Tennessee, she had announced that she was adopting Robyn and Barb as her gay moms. "Mom's playing for the other team, dear."

"Oh, ouch. Didn't see that coming. I thought I was going to grow up and be just like you two."

"Don't marry a straight girl. That's my mom advice for you."

Jen laughed, but she looked concerned. "You seem to be taking it well."

Robyn gestured to the boxes, "I've been at this so long, I think I'm just crazy. Sorry."

"Have you eaten anything?"

"I maybe forgot."

"Come on. I've got some yukki soba we can share." She flung her scarf into her bedroom and bounded down the stairs.

Touched by Jen's motherly gesture, Robyn sighed and followed her down the stairs to the kitchen, a reminder that kids grow up and start taking care of their parents, payback for the years of exhaustion. She pictured how drained Kristine often looked but could project an adult Caemon caring for her someday. Eleanor would have enjoyed that with Penelope. She poured herself a glass of water and drank the whole thing. She hadn't even realized she was thirsty. She filled the glass again, blinking back tears prompted by the sorrow she felt for what Eleanor had lost.

"I need a beer. You just shattered my perception of happily ever after, you know."

"Sorry about that," Robyn said, accepting a plate of soba noodles, tofu and vegetables.

"*Itadakimasu*, right?" Jen said.

"Yes, *itadakimasu*." Robyn repeated the phrase her obaachan had taught her, knowing she would be pleased that they still voiced gratitude for each meal received. "How was rehearsal?" she asked, needing to deflect the conversation.

"Okay. I wish it paid. My parents are right. I'm never going to get a job in education up here. But I just can't imagine living anywhere else now."

"But you can't imagine working at the hot tubs forever either?"

"Exactly." She sighed deeply, tucking another mouthful of noodles in with her chopsticks.

"Why don't you give lessons? You could start pulling in students when you're not down at Café Mokka. Eventually, you could have enough to quit working down there, don't you think?"

"How many kids want violin lessons?"

"You could teach more than violin, couldn't you?"

"I'd need some instruments."

"We've got a piano upstairs."

Jen furrowed her brow.

"It's in the master bedroom," Robyn said. "Come see," she said, carrying her bowl. Though her muscles ached from her long day, having an excuse to move out of the bedroom she'd shared with Barb energized her.

Jen followed her up the stairs to what she had only known as Barb's domain. Robyn and Jen stood in front of the upright piano.

Taking a step closer to the piano to look at a portrait of a young blond woman Jen said, "She's a hottie. Did you date her before Mom?"

"That's *my* mom," Robyn corrected.

"Seriously? She looks like the all-American cheerleader, nothing like you," Jen observed, a guilty look crossing her face.

"My paternal grandmother was Japanese." Robyn pulled a photograph of her grandparents from the bookshelf behind her, a sturdy Midwestern man in his naval uniform and his petite bride in front of the house now Robyn's.

"You got their house? That's awesome!"

"It has a lot of history. Since I spent every summer of my childhood here, they left the house to me and my brother, Jeff. He lives in Japan, so he was happy to sell me his share."

"Was the piano theirs too?"

"No. I bought it for Barb, not that she ever played it. I had it tuned once. Does it need it again?" she asked, motioning Jen to the keyboard.

Jen set her bowl down beside her on the bench and tapped out a simple tune.

"Even I can tell that it needs tuning," Robyn said, apologetically. "But if you get it tuned, you have a piano. I can keep an eye out for instruments at estate sales if you want others to offer students. But it seems to me that if a parent wants their kid playing any other instrument, the kid will come with it, wouldn't they?" She couldn't help feeling excited at the prospect of helping Jen realize her dream.

Jen nodded, assessing the space again. "It's got a nice high ceiling, no carpet. This is a perfect studio space. She chewed on her lip. "How much would you want for it?"

"What do you mean?" Robyn asked.

"Rent."

Robyn waved dismissively. "You already pay rent."

"But you could put another tenant in here and charge twice as much as what you charge me. That's not fair."

"I'm making enough with the three tenants I have and don't feel like interviewing to fill up another room. You'd be doing me a favor." She smiled.

"How am I suddenly the one doing you a favor?" Jen asked.

Robyn had only taken over her grandparents' space as the master bedroom at Barbara's insistence and reflected on how uncomfortable she had always felt there. "You're helping me redefine the room. It isn't the master bedroom anymore. It's your studio. It's your music school. I can't wait to hear you teach." Robyn felt new energy coming into her home, a breath of new life.

"Maybe we should put that in writing before you're exposed to hours of kids sawing away out of tune."

"And you'll teach them to sound like you." She rubbed her hands together. "I'll pull the pictures off the walls, and then it's all yours."

"I'm sorry about the divorce, Mom."

Robyn paused, acknowledging Jen's words with a sad nod. "Me too."

Jen took their bowls and disappeared down the stairs. Robyn took down Barb's prints and carried them to her room. She and

Barb smiled at her from the cover of a photo album in the open box. Robyn folded the edges of the box over and carried it out to the shed, the evidence of that life now stowed and ready for Barb to pick up.

Closing the door to the shed, she felt the satisfaction of truly moving forward with her life.

CHAPTER EIGHT

Patience

"Did she come to get her shit yet?"

True to character, Isabel didn't say hello. "No. It's still out in the shed."

"Are you kidding me," Isabel exploded. "How many weeks ago did you pack it all up? Did she even thank you for sorting it all out?"

"Three, and no."

"That is it. I am coming down there to kick her ass."

"That's not why I called you."

"I'm sorry. What is it?"

"I was just looking for a pep talk."

"Is it raining?"

"I'm in Arcata. Winter is right around the corner. Of course it's raining."

"You should come inland get away from the gloom. You know here in Spokane, we actually see the sun. Come see and spend some time with my house of crazy, and you will go home happy to have your peace and quiet."

Robyn sat in her too-quiet house, consumed by dark thoughts and loneliness. Breathing felt like an effort, so much so that she pushed her breath out as slowly as possible, wondering what it would be like if she could order her body to simply not inhale again. She wouldn't have to deal with a single thing ever again. Only when her body screamed at her did she fill her lungs again, accepting with it the sadness she couldn't escape.

"Ah. I get it. You want crazy," Isabel concluded. "You want one of the twins? You pick. You want the white one or the brown one? Might as well take the white one—everyone thinks I am his nanny anyway. I will pop him in the mail first thing in the morning."

"You're awful, you know that? I don't know why I call you."

"Because I make a smile on your face. I can hear it in your voice," Isabel said.

Robyn could picture her in her home, phone pinched between cheek and shoulder, folding clothes, stirring supper or doing dishes. Her hands were always busy. She never had time to sit and let her mind wander, and knowing her friend, even if she did, she would not be pulled into the spiral of melancholy that had such a strong grip on Robyn.

"Have you been to the barn? Maybe you just need a ride. Go take a long ride in the rain and get soaked. This will be a rebirth for you."

"Right. Very symbolic," Robyn groused. "It kind of loses meaning when it rains most of the year."

"Too much rebirth. You never get the chance to mature. I can see the problem. No wonder you enjoy that little boy at the barn so much. You are like the big sister."

She did miss Caemon and had already told Kristine that she'd be happy to help out with him when the new baby arrived in three weeks or so. "Are you sure this is not your clock starting to tick-tock?"

"I never wanted a kid. You know that," Robyn said, watching rain roll off the skylight above her, her loft dim with the dark gray sky stealing the afternoon light.

"You just wanted Barb?"

"I wanted my person. I thought *she* was my person, and it turns out I was wrong. Eight years wrong."

"So you keep looking. But you've got to get out there. You're not going to meet anyone lying around in your loft all day."

"I'm not lying in my loft," Robyn lied.

"Do not test my powers," Isabel said.

Robyn could see Isabel, arms crossed over her chest. She swung her feet over to the ladder and eased down into the room just as Jen passed with someone short behind her. She gave a thumbs-up as she closed the door of her studio. "I think Jen has a student," she said.

"Oh, this is great news! Rebirth, just like I said!" Isabel chortled.

"How is her student an example of rebirth?" Robyn asked, listening to Jen play a note on the piano and tune the violin to it.

"Here is my prediction. New student has a mom, a beautiful single mom who waits while her kid is getting musical instruction. You offer her a cup of tea one day, and the next thing you know, you are a happy little family."

"You sound very proud of yourself."

"I am trying to be helpful. Am I not helpful?"

The first tentative notes of a scale crept from the studio. "I don't want a kid, remember?"

"Go ride your horse, then."

"Thanks, Isabel. You really are helpful," Robyn said.

"I know."

"You could come see me," Isabel's voice was gentle on the line, and Robyn knew she was thinking about the years that Robyn had kept her pain hidden.

"Maybe I will. Your boys probably don't even remember who I am."

"No. Craig keeps asking about my new friend."

Her spirits rising again, Robyn laughed. "Maybe I will come up for a few days and tell Barb that anything left in the shed when I get back will go to the curb."

"This works. It will save me from coming down there to kick her ass."

Robyn pocketed her phone. Isabel was right. She couldn't move on when she had to pass the shed full of her boxed-up past on her way to her workshop every day. When had she become so passive? In the coast guard, she'd been all purpose and decisiveness. Without her job she felt adrift.

Another reason leasing Taj was a good idea. She had something dependent on her. The little musician next door had finished warming up and had moved on to a tune. Robyn paused at the top of the stairs recognizing the halting notes of "You Are My Sunshine."

She began humming along as she descended the stairs and headed off to the barn.

CHAPTER NINE

"Hand over the baby and nobody gets hurt," Grace said, pushing by Kristine.

"She's asleep."

Grace Warren turned her Administrative Director glare on Kristine and hung her black MYCRA PAC slicker by the door. She wore her shoulder-length curly red hair in an attractive French roll in an attempt to tame the mass it became with the coastal dampness. She looked every inch the professional in her standby plum Elie Tahari suit.

"Right. One sleeping baby coming up. Wash your hands."

They met back at the couch, Grace's clean hands extended for the days-old baby. Grace sank back into the couch, nestling Kristine's newcomer to her chest. She closed her eyes and breathed in the first peace she'd felt all day. "No Caemon?"

"He's on an outing with his Grandpa."

"I got the baby if you want some wife time."

"Gloria's asleep too. Sleep when the baby sleeps, you know?"

"I think it would be better if you went to feed your horse, and I held the baby."

"It was that bad?" Kristine asked, worry in her voice.

"Have you not seen my feet?" Grace waggled her beige suede Stuart Weizman pumps that would never be the same. At five eight, she did not need the added height, but she knew part of her authority came from her stature and she exploited it to its fullest.

"Oh."

"Yeah. You're lucky they weren't my favorite."

"I've got some saddle soap. I could clean them up for you."

"Like you don't have your hands full. How's she sleeping?"

"Okay. She goes about two hours, but I try to hold her off for a while, let Gloria get in another hour before she nurses."

"So. What? You're out here walking the halls?"

"She likes the bouncy ball," Kristine said, pointing to the exercise ball in the corner.

"If she's hungry, why not just feed her?"

"She's not really hungry, so she just nurses a minute and falls back asleep. If she goes longer, she really eats. Then we can both sleep longer. If Caemon's not up."

"You've got the life, sister."

Kristine curled her feet up underneath her and rested her head on the back of the couch. "Was it just your shoes?"

"Your horse also provided me with a shower. We had a misunderstanding about how the green stuff was supposed to go in his stall, not all over me."

"You didn't open the door to put it in?"

"Have you seen how big that thing is? I thought it was safer to chuck the hay over the door. His face wasn't there when I threw it, but then suddenly it was coming right back at me." Kristine laughed, and Grace slapped her. "The one across the aisle is much more civilized. And you said that your friend will be back tomorrow to take over?"

"Yes. When we made the plan for me to take care of Taj this weekend while she's up in Spokane, I thought I had wagons of time till the baby came. You really saved my tush."

"What did you do yesterday when Gloria was still in the hospital?"

"Yesterday was easy. Gloria had the nurses to take care of her and Eliza. I spent the day with Caemon, and he loves to play at the barn."

"Any cute single nurses?"

"Not your type."

"You don't know my type."

"I assume your type isn't male."

Grace laughed. "You got me there. Well, I was happy to help, but I'm off the hook tomorrow?"

Kristine's face fell.

"What?"

"I just realized I don't have Robyn's number. I should have had you leave a note for her with my number. Baby brain," Kristine apologized.

"Don't worry about it. As long as I don't have to muck, it's not that big of a deal." Grace brushed the soft down of Eliza's brown hair with her lips, drinking in her baby smell. Wrapped in a luxurious yellow velour blanket, Eliza radiated warmth that soothed Grace's soul and made the added trials of her day worth it. She looked over at Kristine, who had fallen asleep sitting up.

Grace admired the baby's delicate eyelashes. Under Grace's intense stare, Eliza's eyes fluttered open. "Hello dear one," she whispered. "Your mommies are sleeping. You don't mind hanging out with Auntie Grace, do you?" Eliza opened her eyes, two wide almonds. Her lips formed a rosebud O. "You're a lucky girl, you know that? You have the two greatest moms ever and a fantastic big brother. And you've got me for fashion advice. That cowgirl thing works for your mama, and your mommy's got a great relationship with green thanks to her Fish and Game ranger uniform, but there are other things to wear. I'm here for you."

She chatted with the baby about picking shoes for style rather than comfort and about how there are rules about colors and seasons. The baby listened, focused raptly on the cadence of Grace's low-pitched voice. Prodding at Eliza's fist,

Grace delighted when tiny fingers wrapped around hers. She marveled at each slender digit and the delicate fingernails. "I'll make sure your moms get you violin lessons when you're older, or you can play cello. Lots of people think the violin is more versatile, but I love the cello's voice." She told Eliza about her favorite compositions, and by the time Gloria emerged from the bedroom, flushed with her blond hair sleep-rumpled, Grace had moved on to listing the trials of her day.

"Who's in the doghouse?" Gloria asked, putting one of Kristine's flannels on over a stretchy tank top.

"Ceramics. I had them set to show in Old Town, but now Ferguson isn't happy with half the pieces his seniors have done."

"You'll whip them into shape, I'm sure."

"That's right," Grace said, speaking again to Eliza. "No one messes with me, not if they want a future in art."

Gloria held her arms out for Eliza. "My boobs say it's time to eat."

"Mommy's playing the boob card. I can't argue with that, kiddo," Grace said, handing Eliza over. "You're back in your pre-pregnancy clothes already?" she noted.

Gloria snapped the waist of her gray yoga pants. "They're elastic and have a lot of give. A lot. I still feel like a broodmare." She easily maneuvered the tank top out of the way to let Eliza nurse.

"Broodmares are important," Kristine mumbled.

"You're not supposed to agree with me," Gloria said.

"You're still sexy. Grace, isn't my wife sexy?"

"I am so not answering that," Grace said, pointedly not watching her nurse. "I thought you were out cold."

"I got scared that if I opened my eyes, you'd get on me about the prints I owe you. The only other person as persistent as you is Gloria's mom, and once I smartened up and took the teaching job here…"

"Smartened up and chose true love over your career," Gloria inserted.

"As I was saying, when I chose Gloria over a promising career in nature photography, my now mother-in-law eased up on her demands for new prints."

"I cut new moms *some* slack." Grace perched on the edge of the couch, knowing she should go but was enjoying their banter too much. She'd had her baby fix and should leave the couple to their quiet evening, but she couldn't make herself stand. The couple never made her feel like the third wheel, always welcoming her into their home.

She'd accepted their hospitality, and then their friendship. From the moment Grace had joined the staff at Humboldt State, Kristine had pulled her into their circle. As colleagues they worked well together, and when Grace spent time with them it was easy for her to picture finding someone who could fit with her the way Kristine and Gloria naturally fit each other.

She adored their boy Caemon and lived vicariously through them. She'd never been interested in having her own family—she knew she didn't have the patience for it—but she found that she really enjoyed the toddler. It felt like a gift to be able to stop by to take him on a walk, and his moms always seemed happy to hand him over in hour-long increments.

They had become her family, but she couldn't help envying their partnership. She wanted to feel the peace of Kristine and Gloria's home. Their space had a settled quality, even with kid stuff scattered all about. Grace was seeking what they had found.

Even when she was comfortable, she heard a voice in the back of her head that continuously urged her to keep busy. It reminded her that she still had to cook dinner and that she ought to stop by the store to pick up more bread for breakfast. Once the list started, she couldn't stop it. She pushed to her feet.

"You have to go?" Kristine asked, opening one eye.

"I can't take the smell of these shoes any longer. I promise to give you space to settle in, but Kristine, I'll see you in a week."

Kristine groaned. "Don't even talk about next week."

"I control many things but do not recall you ever asking for my advice about whether to have another baby in the middle of the fall semester."

"Thanks for your help, Grace," Gloria said, moving the baby to her shoulder for a burp.

"Anytime," Grace said. She was happy to be able to offer help so easily, but at the same time, being able to do so made her aware of how empty her own life was.

CHAPTER TEN

The hiking boots she'd pulled from a box in the garage clashed horribly with her black Calvin Klein skirt suit but were far better suited for the puddle-riddled drive and dusty aisles at the barn. She slid into a raincoat and zipped it against the fine mist hanging in the air.

Her stride was long and confident even though she hadn't been in a stable since she'd followed her father from stall to stall as he mucked. It hadn't been her thing then, and she was no more comfortable now, but Kristine had given her so much and she was pleased to be able to extend a kindness to her. She was much more at home on city streets looking for a boutique restaurant, or finding an exciting show or exhibition. The few people she saw at the barn grasped travel mugs steaming with coffee probably poured from an old stained coffee carafe. If she drank coffee, it was foam-topped and syrup-sweetened and enjoyed in a comfortable chair with a good book, not standing in the middle of a round corral flicking a wickedly long whip with one hand and taking sips of her coffee with the other.

She was merely a visitor in Kristine's world, one she had only heard about in the office and occasionally seen in her photographs, and would be happy to hand off the assignment to Robyn. No sign of life around the stall across from Kristine's, Grace turned her attention to the lock on Kristine's tack shed where she kept the horse's food. Bean swung his neck out over the partial door and nickered for the flakes of hay she had peeled from the bale.

"Step back," she ordered, sliding the latch to free the door. "Your mom says this will save me from another alfalfa shower." She placed a tentative hand on his chest, blocking the doorway with her body while she maneuvered the hay into the stall. He dropped his head and ran it the length of her body, turning her into a scratching post. She hurled the hay into the stall and stumbled out to slam the door.

After she secured it, she turned to check her skirt. "Damn," she muttered, finding that he'd lifted her raincoat and used her as a tissue as well. She looked for something in the tack shed to remove the slimy trail he'd left on her skirt. Her watch confirmed that she didn't have time to double back and change before she was due in her office at the Art Department. Growling, she grabbed a brush from a bucket and whisked it across the fabric in an attempt to be presentable.

She looked around once more for the woman Kristine had sworn would take over Bean's care and still saw no one. She would have preferred checking in with the woman in person to leaving a note. Her busy brain worried that if Robyn had to extend her trip for some reason, the horses would go hungry. She shooed away the nonproductive concern, knowing that a barn manager would keep such a thing from happening.

Just as she slid Kristine's padlock back on the tack room door and the note she'd prepared in her hand, Grace spotted a striking woman approaching the stall across from her. Kristine had said Robyn must have Asian ancestry which Grace could clearly see in her coloring, sculpted eyebrows and dense closely-cropped black hair.

"I hope you're Robyn," she said, pocketing the note. The woman looked surprised, so she quickly added, "Kristine's at home this week with the new baby. She said she'd talked to you about caring for the horse but never got your number."

Grace felt the woman's gaze shift from her to the stall behind her and back again. She smiled. "Boy or girl?"

"I think it's a boy." Grace glanced into the stall. "Does it matter?" Her puzzlement added a terseness into her voice.

Robyn looked puzzled. "The baby?"

"Oh, god!" Grace brushed a few tendrils of hair from her forehead with her forearms, not trusting her hands to be clean. "The baby is a girl. Eliza. Cutest little thing. Seven and a half pounds, almost twenty inches, ten fingers and toes."

"How long does she want me to look after Bean?"

"The rest of this week, at least. She's back to work on Monday," she said, surprised by how quickly Robyn turned the conversation back to the horse.

"Has he been out?"

"You're kidding me, right? I only signed up for putting food in."

"Not a stall mucker?"

Grace thought the question might have carried a hint of a tease, so she lingered longer than she had intended.

"And get dirt under my nails?" she asked, studying them.

"Let her know I'll take care of him. The works," she said pointedly.

"You're a kinder woman than I."

Grace studied Robyn for a moment, taking in her calm. There was a precision about her, no hint of excess in her speech, her practical attire, even in how her hair feathered back from her makeup-free face, nothing to accentuate the palest blue eyes she'd ever seen. She felt time slow for a moment as she tried to place the color. A shallow ocean with white sand…aquamarine… the water only barely reflecting the blue of the sky.

Satisfied, her brain turned back to the long list of things to do. Now that she'd met Robyn, she could check barn duties from it. "You'll want Kristine's number," she said, reaching for the note she had stowed. She hesitated and pulled a business card from her purse instead. It never hurt to give a beautiful woman one's number, she thought, quickly writing Kristine's number on the back. "That's her cell, so don't worry about waking the baby."

Taking her leave and utterly caught up in her own schedule, she realized she hadn't thanked Robyn. Turning back, she found those keen blue eyes glued to her. The corner of her mouth ticked up. "Thank you," she said. Her body suddenly feeling alive, she adjusted her posture and stride to invite Robyn's continued appraisal.

CHAPTER ELEVEN

Helpful

That evening, Robyn turned the card over in her hand, alternating between Kristine's number and the contact information for the woman from the barn. Grace Warren, Administrative Director. Art Department, Humboldt State University. Simple and professional with the school's colors featured in the forest green of the lettering and the gold of Founders Hall, the building which had once been the entire campus.

She pursed her lips, considering whether this Grace was a friend or simply a colleague. She'd be surprised if they were more than work acquaintances. Even though her elegant business attire, absurd for the task at hand but nonetheless very attractive, the cut and style suggested that fashion, not function, came first for her. As an administrator, her closet was sure to look more like Barb's than Robyn's or Kristine's. Workday or weekend, Kristine's attire never wavered from her cowboy boots, jeans and tidy plaid shirts.

That the administrator would help out one of the adjunct employees had warmed Robyn, making her appreciate, again, the tight-knit community that was Arcata. People took care of each other here. The neighbors had noticed when she'd taken up residence in her grandparents' old place seven years ago. Until she'd been able to secure a coast guard assignment at Sector Humboldt Bay and move back to Arcata, she had rented out the two-story house in Northtown Arcata.

Like distant relatives, the neighbors recognized her from the summer vacations she spent there as a child. Still, the number of them who had stopped by with fresh-baked goods or fruit in hand had floored her. It had been years since she'd been at the house and she was the sole member of her immediate family who had chosen to reside permanently in Arcata. Her brother had been called by their grandmother's homeland and her parents had eventually followed him to be with their new grandson. She still felt her grandparents' presence in this community of theirs that had welcomed her so openly. She knew that if she found herself needing a helping hand, there were many around her to give her just that.

She called Kristine to let her know she'd run into Grace and was happy to take care of Bean. "Is Caemon enjoying being a big brother?" she asked after they'd checked in.

"He is, but it's tough for him to have our attention divided. That's one of the reasons I asked Grace to take over Bean for me. I don't want Caemon to feel sidelined."

"He loves coming to the barn, though."

"I know, but he's getting big enough now that he isn't entertained by mucking and waiting for me to give Bean a decent workout."

"He's entertained when he's working with the tractor. If you bring him when I'm there, I'm happy to have him help with that again."

"That's nice of you to offer. Maybe I'll try to bring him on Saturday and sneak in a ride too. If you're sure."

They agreed on a plan to coordinate Saturday afternoon, and Robyn heard Kristine stifle a yawn. "Have you got anyone in town to help out?"

"Gloria's parents are here in Eureka." She was quiet for long enough that Robyn wondered if she'd been distracted by the baby in the background. When she spoke again, she sounded even more exhausted. "They help as much as they can. One of these days, I'm going to have to be the grownup and cook supper again."

Impulsively Robyn asked if they had a dinner set up for that evening.

"I'm just going to scrounge some kind of leftover together tonight, I think," Kristine said. "Or order in."

"No, you're not. I'll bring something by when I'm finished at the barn."

"You're already taking care of Bean."

"It's no trouble. I'd like to. When my brother and his wife had a baby, my parents went to Japan to help them get settled."

"That's amazing. How long did they stay?" Kristine asked.

"Nine years."

Kristine's laughter rang through their connection. "And you never had a kid to bring them back here."

"Nope, and if they're waiting for that, they're never coming back." Robyn waited out Kristine's laughter before continuing. She smiled remembering how good it felt to make someone laugh. "I feel guilty for not being there when my nephew was born, so you'd be helping assuage my guilt."

"I never say no to food."

"Good," Robyn said, feeling excited to plan a meal for them. After checking for allergies and preferences, she signed off and rubbed her hands together. She pulled some potatoes out of the pantry and harvested a few leeks from the garden, frowning at her beds. If Kristine's baby had come in the spring, she could have created a salad with greens and berries from her backyard. She remembered Caemon's joy when she mentioned her garden and smiled at the possibility of having him help harvest berries later in the year. Since garden pickings were slim at the tail end of autumn, she made a list to take to the co-op.

Back inside, she rolled up her sleeves and got to work on mixing bread. While she kneaded it, she figured out the timing for the soup and salad to be done and the bread out of the oven before she went to take care of the horses. The stopover at the barn would give the potatoes a chance to absorb the flavor from the leeks. Kristine would have to reheat it, but that should be the only thing she'd have to worry about for dinner.

In her workshop, she found a large bowl she'd made out of a beautiful old oak burl. The shed also yielded a nice basket that would hold the bowl and its bread. Wiping out the bowl, she had an idea and called Isabel.

"What does a nursing mother really want?"

"What kind of greeting is that?" Isabel asked. "And since when do you have a nursing mother to care for?"

"My friend at the barn has a new baby, and I'm making dinner for them. Soup, salad and bread. What else should I put in the basket?"

"Guinness. The darkest one. It's good for producing breast milk. I lived on the stuff, and I wanted dark chocolate. Is this their first or second?"

"Second."

"Make sure you put something in the basket for him. The big one so often can feel left out."

"Thanks. I got it."

"This is good. You have a new friend who's getting you out of the house. Barb come get her shit yet?"

Robyn was quiet.

"You cannot let her steamroller you, *mija*."

"I know. I'll call her. It's not that big of a deal. It's all out of the way in the shed."

"Whatever. It's still not right how she's treating you. The least she could do is make a clean exit, so you can get on with your life."

"I'm getting on."

"I'll believe that when you're cooking for a single girl, not a family, but this is a good start."

Enjoying herself, Robyn pushed aside Isabel's observations about her dating life and Barb and went back to the dinner plans. Having someone else to focus on, whether it was cooking for Kristine's family or putting work into Jen's studio space, made her feel freer than she had in years. For too long she had allowed her failing relationship to drag at her like diving weights around her waist. Slowly, she felt herself letting each weight of disappointment sink away while she surfaced, thankful for every breath.

CHAPTER TWELVE

"This bread is amazing. Where did you get it?" Grace said, helping herself to another slice, glad she had accepted Kristine and Gloria's invitation to stay for dinner. Gloria had just fed Eliza who had promptly crashed out. The three adults had beers and steaming bowls of soup in front of them.

"Robyn made it," Caemon piped up.

"The Robyn from the barn?" Grace asked, surprised. Baking bread from scratch didn't line up with the woman who had seemed so disengaged by the baby details.

Kristine nodded and gestured to the soup with her chin. "Made this too. The potatoes and leeks she grew, and she was very apologetic that the salad fixings weren't from her own garden."

Grace took another bite of soup, letting the creamy base baptize her tongue before she chewed the perfectly-cooked potatoes. "Is she married?"

Gloria and Kristine laughed in unison. "You weren't asking that after seeing her, but her food makes you curious?"

Caught, Grace blushed. "My mother always said you marry a woman who can cook."

"I can cook," Caemon said, causing all the women to laugh together.

"That's true. You're Mommy's best helper," Gloria said.

"She expected you to marry a woman?" Kristine asked Grace.

"She expected you to be good at feeding a man," Gloria stated, a patronizing look directed at her wife. "Pardon her. She grew up on a farm and was only expected to be good with horses."

"And Gloria grew up here, so her parents expected her to marry a woman," Kristine rallied.

"Point taken," Gloria smiled, taking Kristine's hand across the table for a brief squeeze before she was pulled back to managing Caemon's soup which was starting to spread out across his placemat. She returned a square of potato to his spoon and encouraged him to use the utensil instead of his hands.

"I'm sure she's convinced that my being single is directly related to my failure to understand the basics of cooking."

"Why *are* you single?" Kristine asked. "You're gorgeous and fun. You've got a good job."

"I thought it was being in Houston. That's why I took the job here. In the city, all I could think about was the competition to get ahead. That's great for a professional life but not so much for your personal life." She did not add how she had thought the town's proximity to Oregon would improve her relationship with her sister. Shaking off the guilt she felt about not having spent more time with her family, she continued. "I was promised a lesbian mecca, but so far, it seems like all the lesbians I've met are dating each other, not waiting for me."

"Don't look at me," Gloria said. "I had to import mine." They shared one of their looks, drinking each other in like they did so often.

"That doesn't help me, you know?" Grace shot back.

"What about Robyn?" Kristine asked.

"A little rough around the edges, but she has potential," Grace mused. "I did put your number on my card."

"That was inspired!" Kristine said.

"Doubtful that anything will come of it, but it doesn't hurt to put oneself out there," Grace said, clearing her dishes. "Dishes in the dishwasher clean or dirty?"

"Clean, I think," Kristine said.

Grace inspected a glass and, satisfied that Kristine was right, began opening cupboards and finding where things went.

"You don't have to do that," Gloria said without conviction.

"I know, but I want to," Grace answered. "It makes me feel less guilty for eating your dinner."

"Have you seen how much food we have left over? We're happy to have you here to help us, and believe me, I enjoy the adult conversation," Gloria said.

Grace relaxed into the kitchen cleanup, chatting easily with both Gloria and Kristine until Kristine slipped away to give Caemon his bath.

"Don't mess with routine," Gloria commented as Caemon skipped ahead of his mama to the bathroom, trying to pull off his shirt as he went.

Grace scooped the remnants of the salad into a food saver, turning the bowl in her hands. She ran her hands over the smooth surface and studied the signature on its base, a simple circle of milky white Mother of Pearl. "Where did you get this? It's lovely."

Gloria shrugged and joined Grace at the sink. "Must have come with supper. I've never seen it before."

"I'll have to ask Kristine about it," Grace said, admiring it once more before she rinsed it and dried it carefully.

"Are you in town this weekend?" Gloria asked.

"No. I have tickets to *Wicked*."

"I envy you. It's nice to have friends who will fill me in on stuff that happens on the other side of the Redwood Curtain, but it makes me feel very homebound too."

"Before you had kids, did you make trips to San Francisco?"

"A few times. A mentor of Kristine's had a show at a high-end gallery down there, and we went for the opening. I've never been to a musical though."

"Never?"

Gloria shrugged. "I don't think I could sit still that long— Kristine either."

Grace sighed and rolled her eyes. "Could you be any better suited for each other?"

"Sorry," Gloria said.

"No, don't be. It's nice to have friends who have a great relationship, but it makes me feel very single too."

Gloria laughed. "I think you should do more here. Have you seen anything at the campus theater?"

"I've seen a few shows. They were okay."

"For a small-town university." Gloria's tone indicated that she understood Grace's disappointment.

"They just don't have the facility to do huge productions like *Wicked* or *Mama Mia*. Last year, I saw this amazing musical called *Big River*..."

"The one based on Huck Finn, right?" Grace's expression betrayed her surprise, earning her a smack on the arm. "We have degrees, missy. We know some stuff. The music in that is amazing. There's a local bluegrass band that often puts something from *Big River* in their set. The next time they play, you should get Kristine to take you. They're something else. You want to meet someone, you've got to spend more time here instead of driving off to San Francisco every weekend," Gloria said pointedly.

"So noted," Grace said, running a dishtowel over the counter.

Gloria grabbed the towel from her. "No more cleaning. You're exhausting me. Come say goodnight to Caemon, and I'll get that gorgeous baby girl you've been dying to see. I'm starting to hear some peeps."

"Now we're talking!" Grace said, taking the towel back for a few more swipes before she finally relinquished it.

CHAPTER THIRTEEN

"Grace, someone here to see you," Aaron sang from the outer office.

When she'd first arrived at the Art Department, the informality had irked her and reminded her of how her own mother's hackles went up any time she or her siblings hollered for someone across the house. Now she accepted it as part of the charm of a small campus, one of her reminders to slow down.

Normally, she asked him to direct people to her office even though it was small, but this was at least the fifth visitor to ask for her that morning. She feared that this one, like the others, was not related to business, so she stepped out into the general art department office.

"Can I help you?" Grace said in what she hoped was a friendly tone. She had no appointments, and as she'd suspected, she didn't recognize the cute baby dyke.

The young woman smiled broadly, making her look even younger. "There's a poetry jam this weekend."

Grace accepted the flyer, the third she had to add to her stack. She'd also been informed of a feminist author who was visiting and talking on campus and of the art opening at the First Street Gallery in Eureka. She wondered if the student who invited her to the art opening had any idea that she was behind the entire project and would be there to coordinate, not socialize.

"Thank you," she said. "I'm sure many of our students will be interested in attending. In the future, you can give event notifications to Aaron, and he'll be happy to post them for you."

The young woman remained rooted where she stood, and Grace could tell she was working up the courage to invite her specifically. To save them both from the awkward silence, she thanked her again and disappeared into her office. She felt a little unkind, but better to be brisk and shut down any hope these young women had about fraternizing.

"Are you the new GLBSA advisor or something? What's with the parade of adoring young women?" Aaron asked a few minutes later, merrily batting thick eyelashes that Grace envied. The public face of the office, Aaron's couldn't have been better chosen with his warm smile, carefully trimmed beard and neat, styled, close-cropped hair.

Grace rested her forehead on her palms. "I have no idea. It's a little late for the welcome wagon. Do me a favor and run interference for me? I'm not here unless it's campus business."

"You bet."

Minutes later, a rap at the door sent Grace's forehead down to the desk mumbling about Aaron's failure to protect her from the campus lesbians. Steeling herself, she sat up and without trying to hide her annoyance, barked "Come in."

"Is someone wearing grouchy pants today?" Kristine asked, hesitating at the door.

Grace slumped with relief. "Kristine."

"Who were you expecting? A firing squad?"

"All this week, I've been ambushed by student dykes."

Kristine eased into the chair opposite Grace. "What prompted that?"

"I wish I knew. I told your wife I was ready to meet someone. I guess I should have specified that I'm ready to meet someone who is well into her thirties."

"You two had a nice visit the other night?"

Grace stretched back in her chair. "Indeed. She said you know a good bluegrass band."

"Yeah, she mentioned that. I'll let you know when they play again."

"I've never been a huge fan of bluegrass, but it's got to be better than the stuff they play at the club."

"What club?" Kristine asked, leaning forward.

"The one over in Eureka, Club Triangle?"

Kristine doubled over laughing.

"What?" Grace demanded.

"There's your problem. That's the feeding ground for all the baby dykes."

"I only had one drink. A drink. That's it. Then I left. I couldn't even hear myself think."

"Well someone recognized you, and now they're probably all crushing on you," Kristine said, still laughing.

"The way everyone was glued to each other, I'm surprised anyone noticed."

"Think about how many of them probably don't know a lesbian of your stature. Successful. Professional. They admire you."

"Please don't call me a professional lesbian."

Kristine cocked an eyebrow in question.

"It's not like one can make a successful living from it." Grace reflected on Kristine's words, remembering the older established women she herself had crushed on when she was young. "If it were just admiration, I'd be okay, but they're not in here asking me to be a mentor. They're asking me out to events."

Kristine flipped through the fliers. "These are actually way more your speed compared to the club. Check out the poetry one. I've been really impressed with the events The Jambalaya hosts. And it's going to be a different crowd. They won't be sizing you up."

"Sounds like you have experience."

"Arcata and Eureka are bigger than Quincy, where I grew up, but the lesbian community here feels just like it, everyone up in someone else's business. It took me a long time to get used to when I first moved here. I went from a town where no one wanted to acknowledge I was gay to having this gaggle of lesbians in my face about what my intentions were with *their* Gloria, sizing me up, seeing if I was good enough for her."

"Guess you passed the test," Grace said.

Kristine shrugged. "We're pretty much off the radar now that we have the kids. It feels like we have more in common with new parents. Single lesbians aren't interested in potty training or sleep deprivation."

"I like hearing about how Eliza's sleeping."

"That's because you're wacked."

"Has she figured out night and day yet?"

"Getting there. We should hit a good rhythm this next month."

"Seems like you've made the transition back to work okay. Now that you're back, will you scare off all those lovely young women who are after me?"

"Aaron says it's entertaining."

"At least someone is enjoying the attention," Grace groused loudly enough for Aaron to hear. He would turn the day's entertainment into an elaborate story. This she knew from the dramatic story he told of plucking Kristine out of the High Sierras to cover the classes of an associate professor whose illness forced her to retire. Tired of dwelling on her personal life, she switched gears. "I'm sure you didn't come in here to observe the flirtations."

"No. Actually, I came in to talk about the Nature Photography class. I want to get them shooting something other than forest and beach. What do you think of me taking them to Joshua Tree or the Grand Canyon, somewhere we can play with light? Just a weekend trip."

"Not any weekend soon. You can't leave your wife alone with two kids," Grace said, her voice stern.

"No. Not until next year for sure. But isn't it better to investigate funds now?"

Grace acquiesced. "Yes, it is. I like the idea, even if it's a thinly-veiled opportunity for you to get your own shots."

"Just as instruction." Kristine feigned affront.

"Mmm-hmmm." Grace woke up her computer, happy to have actual work to occupy her time.

CHAPTER FOURTEEN

Strength

"Your mom's not having an easy time of it," Robyn said to Bean as she eased into his stall to slip on his halter. Since Kristine wouldn't be able to make it to the barn, she'd turn him out while she mucked his stall. She took her time, sobered by the devastation she'd heard in Kristine's voice when she told her that her mother-in-law had been hospitalized after consulting her doctor about a cough she couldn't shake that developed into pneumonia. It didn't feel right for the new mothers to be at the hospital, and remembering that Kristine had said that her mother-in-law had relapsed, she understood the graveness of the situation and told Kristine not to worry about Bean at all.

She looked across the barn to Taj's stall. The mare stood with her head hung out of the window, her lower lip hanging loose as she dozed. Robyn hadn't seen Eleanor at the barn again since the day she'd seen Kristine comforting her. Aside from the checks Robyn sent each month, they'd had no contact.

Even before Kristine's call, Robyn had been thinking about Penelope again, wondering if there was any change. She'd thought about asking Kristine if she ever went, but that had been before Eliza arrived. Now Kristine had her mother-in-law to worry about—she didn't need to field Robyn's questions about Penelope.

Both stalls clean, she threw her saddle on Taj and led her to the arena, grateful she was the only one using the space. They circled the arena at a walk, Taj's muscles warming and lengthening with the workout. But Robyn wasn't concentrating on Taj.

Her mind was at Mad River Hospital. So often thoughts of the tragedy accompanied Robyn to the barn, and she contemplated the possibility of visiting Penelope. Would she be allowed in the room? How would she even explain her relationship to the girl? If family was there, would they think that it was inappropriate for her to visit?

She pushed Taj into a trot, counting on the activity to distract her. Instead every hoofbeat pounded a reminder of where she was and why and how unfair it was that she sat in the saddle instead of Penelope. When she'd first started riding again, the familiar rhythm had filled her with memories of her carefree childhood when the biggest concern was whether Karen, one of the other barn-rats, liked her.

Now she couldn't escape her present, no matter how many times she circled the arena. The setting sun cut through the space and dust motes danced in the rays, reminding her of the way light slanted through the redwood canopy. She stopped at the gate and released the latch, heading toward the forest. Taj easily picked up the trail Kristine had showed her, but she avoided the clear-cut, trying to immerse herself in the life of the trees, listening for birds. But she still wasn't successful in keeping her brain from falling into suicidal thoughts. She had spent too long letting her mind seek out "accidents." What was the probability of being thrown and fatally injured? If she headed down the trail at a full gallop and didn't duck, would that low branch break her neck?

Depression triggered these possibilities of escaping the pain. She hung her head. Feeling guilty for being where Penelope should be plunged her right back into her self-destructive thoughts. She had to talk to Penelope. She had to apologize. She had to find a way to allow herself to embrace the joy that riding brought her and shed her guilt.

* * *

Robyn was no stranger to the sterile environment of the hospital. During her time in the coast guard, she'd watched the ceiling tiles whiz by on her way to the emergency room to be treated for such frequent and serious injuries that her colleagues teased her about having a death wish, which in retrospect, she realized was true.

At the time she'd argued that it wasn't a death wish, just an unwavering prioritization of the lives of the people, civilian and military, who counted on her. If she committed to something, she gave herself completely, holding back nothing. That mentality had spurred enough fights with Barb for Robyn to take the earliest retirement, thinking that their relationship would improve when she was home more. Now that it was over, she considered that they had only lasted as long as they did because of the demands her job offered and the truth that she'd used her "professional duty" as a coping mechanism.

The wing for extended care lacked the urgency of the ER or even standard recovery. She walked more slowly and quietly, fighting the urge to turn around and leave before she reached the room the volunteers at the front desk had directed her to. Her heart rate quickened, and she questioned her purpose and motive. She shoved her hands into her pockets and stopped two doors down from Penelope's, unable to move.

A voice startled her. "Robyn?"

She spun and found Eleanor approaching her with a look of concern and inquiry. "Is everything all right?"

She hadn't considered that her being at the hospital might be interpreted as something amiss with the horse. "Oh, Taj is fine. I'm sorry."

Eleanor looked relieved but made no move to continue to her daughter's room.

Robyn's shallow breathing started to make her feel light-headed. She backed up to the wall to steady herself. "I wondered if you would mind if I saw Penelope," she blurted out. She wished she had brought something, so her hands would have at least been occupied. Instead, she stood there feeling exposed. She watched as Eleanor's gaze shifted from her to the room down the hall and back to her.

"Kristine told me about the accident." Looking at the broken woman in front of her, she wished that she'd been on duty that day, that she could have done something for Penelope. But she also understood that it wouldn't have altered the outcome. If they had been riding together, her training might have prevented this coma, but she'd never know. She could not manipulate time to revise the past and knew there was nothing she could do to ease the future for the grieving woman.

Eleanor wore a heavy knit sweater despite the warmth of the hospital, and Robyn wondered if she had felt cold since the moment she'd answered the phone and her life had changed irrevocably.

Eleanor nodded. "I'll introduce you." She motioned Robyn to follow her to the room.

Robyn didn't question the formal introduction to a comatose patient. She hated hearing the apology to Penelope in the explanation of how Robyn had come to know the family, aware again of her gain through their loss.

Robyn's heart broke seeing the bedridden seventeen-year-old. Her long dark hair was neatly braided, someone in her family reclaiming a task that had marked her march toward independence at some point.

The pale face in extended sleep reminded Robyn of a fairy tale princess, which heightened Robyn's feeling of helplessness. The walls were plastered with pictures of Penelope's friends and Taj, filling the room with images of the life where she smiled and joked and pushed boundaries.

It was easier to keep her focus on the pictures than turn to the girl in the room, especially since her mother had settled into what had to be a familiar position in the chair at her daughter's shoulder.

Robyn's mouth went dry. She couldn't talk to Penelope with her mother sitting there, and she could feel the awkwardness intensifying the longer she stood there silently. Finally, she remembered Eleanor's reaction at seeing her and realized she could talk about Taj, as if she'd come to contribute to the reminders of the life that still waited on hold for Penelope. She told her that she'd been out on the trail with Kristine and shared with her the little things that interested or spooked the horse. She added how the horse always had her head out of the stall, watching down the aisle as if she expected Penelope at any moment.

After a few minutes, Eleanor waved her phone in Robyn's direction and ducked out of the door. Robyn sighed with relief and sat in the vacated seat. She scrubbed her face with her hands. She didn't know how to express what she had *really* come to say. She guessed it didn't matter, so she started with the thought she couldn't escape at the barn.

"I used to wish I was dead. Not so much when I was working. Doing rescues for the coast guard, your main purpose is to stay alive. I would have hated for any of my teammates to feel responsible for my death. But after I retired and figured out that it wasn't the job that made my relationship hell, it's all I could think about.

"You know that intersection in Northtown that leads right to the footbridge for HSU? I don't know if you've ever crossed there, but half the drivers have their minds on the freeway already and don't even see the pedestrians. It used to be I'd pause to make sure drivers were stopping, but then I got to thinking how much easier everything would be if one of those drivers just plowed right over me.

"I was tired all the time, and it seemed so nice to think about stopping. I got to thinking that would be so much easier than thinking about how my relationship was over. Admitting that made me feel like my whole life was over. Being dead, I wouldn't have to face anyone or feel like a failure. I wouldn't have to explain to anyone what went wrong."

Robyn rubbed her palms together slowly, feeling the friction create warmth and the catch of the calluses at the base of each finger. The sound soothed her.

"I comb the beaches all the time, and I would stare at the ocean thinking about its pull. I guess you know something about that. And I guess that's why I'm here. I wish there was some way I could give you my life. There's nothing right about my being out on the trail and you being in here. Obviously, you have more living to do, right? Look at you, holding on when I would have surrendered myself to the current and the darkness."

She looked again at the pictures around the room, at Penelope's radiant smile revealing the spirit within. "Look at this life of yours. It makes me feel ashamed to have been so cavalier about my own."

Unexpected tears ran down her face, and she quickly swiped them away. She wanted to tell her that she'd keep Taj in good shape for her and even found herself thinking about how horses are great for muscle rehabilitation. It was that easy to feel hope in the girl's room even when her medical training told her there was so very little.

Robyn stood and nodded. While she still felt the weight and responsibility that came with living, she felt buoyed by the reminder of what a precious gift life is.

CHAPTER FIFTEEN

By the time Grace paid her cover charge and made her way into The Jambalaya, the place was almost pitch black and packed, the brightest lights focused on the small stage at the back of the long, narrow space.

She'd planned it that way, so she'd be able to slip up to the bar without being seen by any of the young college lesbians who had given her the heads-up on the poetry reading. The emcee looked like most of the young people on the town plaza, with dreads and a floppy reggae-style hat, tie-dyed T-shirt covered by a flannel plaid shirt and baggy cords held up by a belt that he'd probably woven from hemp himself. From the bar, she couldn't see his feet, but she was sure he sported Birkenstocks with wool socks.

Her friends back in Houston teased her about people like this. When she'd told them about her job offer from Humboldt State, they'd immediately Googled the town, finding news about the city council proposing to ban drumming from the plaza. Looking at the pictures of panhandlers, they'd asked if it was a required dress code, and put dibs on the designer labels that filled her closet.

Despite the town's casual leaning and the constant rain, Grace still felt most like herself in her form-fitting dresses and tailored straight-lined suits. In Houston, her friends counted on her to dazzle them with her wardrobe. One had teasingly posited that Grace never bought anything unless it had metallic thread, rhinestones or faux fur. She remembered how much they loved her calf-length zebra print coat. She wondered what the crowd here would think if she'd worn that instead of the less conspicuous black skirt suit that she hoped would let her move in and out of the bar unnoticed.

The emcee stepped aside for the first poet just as the bartender delivered her frou-frou sweet drink. She'd told him to make anything he wanted as long as it included pineapple juice. Her mind was on the drink and scoping out the audience, not on the poetry. The whole drive down to San Francisco and back last weekend, she'd kept returning to Gloria's suggestion to involve herself in more local activities. So here she was.

She drank deeply from the cold glass, enjoying the immediate warmth that filled her body. She studied the space around her and compared it with the scene she'd left in Houston. There, she'd have shared a glass-topped table with her circle of friends from work instead of leaning an elbow on the bar. She missed the familiarity of the group but not the competitive spark that crackled through every conversation. When she'd taken the job writing grants for a prominent Texas museum, she accepted any invitation extended, always looking to network. Every choice was made with an eye to how it would position her for promotion or bolster her résumé.

Though they promised they'd always keep in touch and come to see her on the Northcoast, she knew it was just social politeness. They wouldn't waste their time on someone who had stopped scrambling for the next impressive chance to outdo the others' successes. She tried to picture them here at The Jambalaya, knowing very well that they would be rolling their eyes at the locals' poetry and scrunching their noses at the patchouli wafting off the bar's patrons.

She had hoped the small-town atmosphere would help her adopt a more laid-back attitude, but the voices of her friends kept inserting their critiques, overpowering the poets. Grace tried to concentrate, but after failing multiple times, she downed the rest of her drink, intending to leave.

An ancient woman made her way to the stage as Grace stood to go. She eased herself back onto the stool. Her mother had raised her better than to walk out on a crone. Remembering this picked the scab off the hurt of losing her mother long before she'd had a chance to be a crone herself.

The younger poets had adopted that self-possessed almost rap-like delivery of a poetry slam. This woman voiced her words without such posturing. Grace wished she were closer to the stage, so she could focus on the woman's lips as she read a poem about drinking her garden in a cup of tea. As she read, the text of her poem on a long scroll of paper crawled through her fingers, pouring over the music stand that served as a podium. Grace could see those weathered fingers working the soil to produce the flowers named in the poem.

The scroll draped like a fishing line waiting for a bite, and Grace realized as the poet began reading the poem from the bottom back to the top, pulling it in just as slowly as she had let it out, that she was hooked, her whole attention held through the second traipsing through the garden poem and into another called "Strawberries."

"There she was
naked to the morning
to the strawberries
and to me."

Grace reached into her briefcase and pulled out a notepad, jotting down the words before she forgot them. She sat, hand poised over the pad as the woman continued. She pictured her holding a naked woman in her arms, "her body memorized in my hands."

The last line jotted down, she joined in the applause for Ruth Mountaingrove, a favorite judging by the reaction of the crowd. A young woman stood and offered her hand as Ruth stepped away from the mike, guiding her back to their table.

Rooted now, Grace scanned the audience full of women and could feel how present they were in the room, captured by each voice that took the stage. This was the community Gloria and Kristine had talked about. Here they were, gathered in reverence for the written word, with Grace's attitude the only thing stopping her from being included herself.

From that moment, she listened intently and allowed herself to turn her face to observe the audience in between poets without worrying that the young lesbian who brought her the flyer would spot her. She found herself disappointed when the emcee returned to the stage to thank all of the evening's poets.

"But don't get up yet. I have one more request," he said. "Please welcome to the stage my good friend Buzz. He'll wrap things up here with a song."

A bearded man who looked more lumberjack than hippie took the stage in his heavy boots and jeans, scruffing at his beard with his hand to hide his reaction to the applause. He strapped a guitar around his shoulder and tipped his head to acknowledge the young woman who lit up the stage with a sparkling smile. "Jen's helping me out tonight and next Thursday when we'll do a whole set down at Café Mokka."

He met the young woman's eyes, synchronized their beat and they launched into song. Buzz knew what he was doing on his six-string guitar, but it was the woman with her violin who took Grace's breath away.

All of the brightness of the woman herself came through the strings as she pulled the bow across them, leaning into notes to give her instrument voice as she accompanied her friend's folksy tune about the ocean. The style was far from what Grace played on her cello. However, someone who could coax such a pure tone from the violin was clearly a skilled player and it was easy to imagine playing with her.

Grace was genuinely disappointed when the song ended. As they returned their instruments to the carrying cases along the wall, people lined up to talk to them. Grace longed to get in line herself to inquire about the violinist's repertoire and possible interest in playing something more classical, but spotting the young woman who had dropped off the flyer deterred her.

She briefly entertained the idea of talking to Ruth Mountaingrove, but she, too, was surrounded by a large group of admirers. Giving up, she slipped out into the night. She drove out of town out to the bottoms, a flat stretch of farmland between the town and the bay, where she rented a small two-bedroom house.

Inside, she logged onto her computer and did a quick search to see if Ruth had any poetry published. Reading through her bio, she furrowed her brow and slipped into her chair, curious about the description of Mountaingrove as a lesbian photographer. She quickly revised her search to include photography and clicked on an archive at the University of Oregon, finding more than a hundred photographs.

She clicked through the images, most of them captured in an intentional community, mesmerized by Mountaingrove's frank presentation of women working, celebrating, loving. She kicked herself for not approaching the poet after the event. Navigating away from the pictures, she searched for contact information, scanning through articles describing Mountaingrove's works and contributions.

Reading that Mountaingrove had coordinated several shows of feminist and lesbian photographs, she frowned when she heard the popping bottle cap that signaled a message on her phone. She retrieved it and pulled up the text from her sister.

You still up?

The contact, especially at the late hour surprised her. *Of course. Everything okay?*

Not working, are you?

Part of her motivation for accepting the job at Humboldt State was that she'd be closer to her sister, yet in the ten months that she'd been in Arcata, she had only been up to Oregon to see her for a handful of holidays. The chaos of following tradition left her feeling that though they had spent time together, they hadn't really visited at all.

Getting ready for bed.

Distracted by Leah, she closed her search and shut down the computer. She considered calling but changed for bed while she waited for Leah's reply.

We need to talk about Tyler.

An icy wave crashed over Grace. *What's he done now?* she typed, teeth clamped.

Nothing. But we need to talk about what's best for him.

Grace didn't want to talk to her sister. Any time they talked about Tyler, they ended up fighting, and she was too tired to fight tonight. She took a deep breath trying to remember the last time she'd spoken to her brother. The only thing she was able to recall was her heartbreak in hearing the demands and anger in his voice instead of atonement. It had taken her a long time to realize and accept that even if he was sorry, words were never going to repair the hurt he had caused. She'd cut him off completely, and when Leah had started talking about the challenges of having Tyler live with her family, Grace had begun to avoid contact with her sister as well. *I have an early meeting tomorrow*, she lied. Before Leah could reply, Grace texted *goodnight* and switched off her phone.

CHAPTER SIXTEEN

Smiling, Grace sipped her coffee and tapped the Los Bagels business card on her desk, still preoccupied with the barista's banter. It had quickly turned flirtatious and ended with the wink-delivered card with Megan's cell number scrawled on the back. Grace stared at the number, considering whether to call and ask her if she'd be interested in going to hear the violinist play at Café Mokka on Thursday.

Instead of working, she watched students descending the hill from Founder's Hall, feeling their weekend vibe, remembering the days when she could drop a book bag on the couch and vow to not touch or think about homework for the entire weekend. Oh, to be young again when it felt like the world was full of opportunity and beautiful single women. She bet herself that none of the students worried about the selection diminishing.

She itched to pick up the phone and call Megan even though she'd only left the campus extension of the bagel bakery a half hour ago. She felt foolish for how distracted she was. Slowly, she set the card down and reached into her bag, rationalizing that once she called, she'd be able to focus on work again.

"Hi, it's Grace," she said when she heard Megan's voice.

She smiled at the innuendo in Megan's drawn-out "Hello."

"Everything okay with your coffee?"

Grace turned her back to the already shut door for more privacy, easily slipping back into flirting. "If I said no, would you run some creamer over?"

"I would. If only I wasn't on my way to our shop in Eureka…"

Grace let the "if only" float for a moment, imagining Megan slipping into her office, pulling Grace into an embrace, blanketing her with toasted bagel warmth before she leaned in to find her lips…She snapped herself back to the moment. "I do have a problem."

"What's that?"

"I want to see you again, but I obviously can't ask you to coffee. I'm at a loss, and it's negatively impacting my productivity."

Megan laughed appreciatively. "So what's the same speed as coffee for a first date," she mused. "Something that can be cut short or drawn out depending on how the date is going."

"Exactly. What does that like coffee?"

"Especially mine."

"Especially yours." Grace wrapped both hands around her warm cup, enjoying their exchange.

"Got it. You can meet me at the Arcata marsh tonight. Are you free by five?"

"The marsh?"

"You haven't been? It's a bird sanctuary."

"I'm game," Grace quipped. She got directions and reluctantly ended the call, with no further excuse to ignore her work.

Luckily, the poetry reading had given her an idea about collaborating with the English department on an installation combining word and image. She picked up the phone and was happy to catch the full-time photography teacher in his office. He listened to the idea, agreed that it sounded like an interesting project but begged off, listing other commitments.

Grace sighed and prepared herself for her razzing. She used her cell for the next call. "You on campus?" she asked when Kristine picked up.

"Sure am. I've got my Portraits class out on the quad learning how to use natural light."

"But you're not instructing since you picked up the phone."

"You're a sharp one."

"Stay put. I have an idea." Taking only her office keys, she clipped across campus, heading toward the quad, part of her brain reminding her that she was headed back to the bagel shop even though Megan was no longer there. She found Kristine studying one of her students' cameras and waited for her to finish, allowing her mind to replay and comb over her morning flirtation again.

"What's up?" Kristine asked, leaning comfortably against a handrail, one booted foot resting on the other.

"Have you heard of Ruth Mountaingrove?" Grace asked.

"Of course. She was a student of mine last semester. She took my Nature Photography. Why?" One eyebrow hitched up suspiciously.

"I heard a few of her poems..."

Kristine stood to her full height a gleeful expression covering her face. "You went to the poetry reading?"

"She gave me an idea about collaborating..."

"No, no, no you don't. Let's go back to you going to the lesbian den of poetry." Kristine stepped closer and lowered her voice. "Did you go home alone?"

"I most certainly went home alone. I'm trying to pitch an idea here."

"C'mon. This is big. You finally went out here in town. Did your little baby dykes see you and hit on you again?"

"I kept my distance. I'm not trawling that crowd, I assure you. I'm not looking for anyone who furnishes their place from yard sales."

"They're not that young."

"I'm sure there are rules about not dating students," she said sharply.

"And if there aren't, you can make up something that sounds official enough to scare them all away."

Grace couldn't help it. Her eyes drifted toward the campus center where she'd bought her coffee.

"Not *all* away, then." Kristine rubbed her hands together. "You did meet someone? You said no students, but surely there aren't rules about not dating teachers. Were there cute teachers there?"

"Can we talk about my idea now?"

"Are you going out again?"

"I happen to have a date tonight. That is, I might have a date if I get my work done."

"Fine. How can I help you with that?"

"There's got to be a way for a creative writing class and one of our photography classes to collaborate on a project that we could show here on campus."

"A Thousand Words. We give them an image, they write a thousand word story, and we call it A Thousand Words."

"Did you just think of that on the spot?"

Kristine shrugged. "That's the obvious. But you could also get them to send us something, a poem or something, and then our class could try to create an image to go with it."

Grace patted her pockets, wishing she'd brought her notepad.

"You look surprised that I have ideas in my head."

"I'm just wishing that *you* were the full-time teacher. You'd be so much easier to work with."

"I used to think I wanted to be full-time, but with the kids, these hours suit me just fine. But let me know if you find anyone in English. I think it'd be fun to coordinate something."

"You're the best." Grace turned back in the direction of her office.

"This is good," Kristine called, making Grace turn back. Kristine tipped her chin to the side, studying her closely. "You're finally here."

Grace recalled the community she had felt at The Jambalaya and agreed. She'd lived in Arcata for almost a year, but she had only just now arrived. She felt it in her body.

"Welcome to Humboldt County," Kristine said, winking.

CHAPTER SEVENTEEN

"You know her?" Megan trained her eyes in the same direction across the crowded café.

Café Mokka's intimate and inviting atmosphere should have made it easy for Grace to pay more attention to Megan on their second date. She could tell that Megan had taken pains, her brown hair carefully framing her face. She'd worn make-up tonight and really did look good in her emerald green silk blouse and tight black jeans.

Instead, Grace was mesmerized by something else, or rather someone else. She couldn't see Robyn's face, but from behind recognized the cut and texture of her distinctive black hair. Guiltily, she turned to Megan, aware of how tightly she was gripping the hot apple cider. "Not really. She took over the favor at the barn that I was telling you about," she said reluctantly, hoping not to rekindle the topic that had dominated their first date.

When she'd arrived at the marsh, she'd immediately seen that she wouldn't want to walk the paths in her work heels.

Thankfully she was able to exchange them for the boots she'd worn to the barn and uncharacteristically left in her trunk.

Megan had found her there, joking that she must be a girl scout to be prepared for anything. She didn't know if she was prepared for the level of interest Megan had expressed in her friends' baby. Hoping to steer the conversation in a different direction, she said, "Do you know her? You must meet a lot of people working at a coffee shop."

"When I worked the counter, sure," Meg agreed. "I got to know a lot of people, but I've always been at the Eureka store."

"That's, what, seven miles away? I'd think that's the same population."

Megan was quick to disagree. "Not at all. Eureka's not all political, not all in-your-face demanding to be recognized like the people in Arcata are. In Eureka we just…are."

"I live in Arcata," Grace reminded her coyly.

"You just moved here. You didn't know," Megan retorted. She slipped her hand across the table to take Grace's, her eyes dark with desire. She looked like she was about to offer to teach her more about the lesbian community when the musicians they'd come to see squeezed through the line at the counter and wove their way through the tight clusters of tables to the corner of the room.

She smiled at Megan, though it was the sight of the violin that set her heart racing. She was happy to have Megan to sit with but was surprised by how distracted she felt thinking of what she would say to the young violinist after her set. The older man introduced Jen and himself and Jen briefly described their set list. She listened patiently as he sang, accompanying himself with impressive finger picking on his guitar. When Jen lifted the violin to her chin, Grace sat up taller, leaning forward into the stream of notes that floated from her fast-moving bow.

Again more fiddle than classical, the notes still carried Grace away. She shut her eyes, giving herself up to the emotion of the song, Jen's fiddle voice that sang directly to her.

When the song ended, she opened her eyes, joining the crowd in enthusiastic applause. Megan looked at her, not at the band, and Grace was self-conscious about the mistiness she felt. Blinking, her gaze fell on the woman from the barn again as she too brushed a tear from her cheek. The motion moved Grace, and she felt less conspicuous for getting so caught up in the song. Grace looked back to the musicians but saw that Megan was studying her focus on the woman sitting tables away. She smiled an apology and reached for Megan's hand.

She appreciated the warmth she found there and the way Megan ran her thumb along her skin. The small gesture made her aware of how wonderful her full hands would feel exploring more private skin. She hadn't been touched like that in a long time, not since she'd been on the Northcoast and… She traced back in her mind. Had she been single for an entire year before she left Houston? She could still hear her friends teasing her about her all work, no play attitude, getting out mostly when they insisted but never tempted by anyone she met.

Unexpectedly, she heard her father admonish her for being so picky. *You can set your standards too high, you know?* he'd told her when she'd ended one of her relationships just before the year anniversary. *You've got this list in your head, and when the woman you're dating doesn't have everything you're looking for, you give up, but you're never going to find someone who meets all your expectations. Live like that, and you'll inevitably be disappointed, especially when you discover you've let your whole life go by.*

Megan leaned across the small table, her lips brushing Grace's ear. "It's hot in here. Can we listen from the garden?"

Grace looked from the violinist to her date, knowing that the correct answer was yes. Reluctantly, she nodded. They bused their cups to the front counter and exited by the back door, losing their seat to customers who had been hovering by the front entrance. Grace missed watching the musicians but smiled genuinely when she crossed the threshold from coffeehouse to a hobbitesque wooded area.

Megan took her hand, guiding her along a lantern-illuminated path to a pond and over a tiny bridge.

"Are these all guest houses?" Grace asked about the shingled structures, each with a fenced enclosure.

"How long have you lived in Arcata?" Megan laughed. "Those are the hot tubs."

"Public hot tubs?"

Megan squeezed her hand. "You don't get out enough. They're made of redwood and are really nice." She stopped and tipped her head back. "There's nothing like the feel of the cool mist while sitting in a tub."

For a moment, Grace wondered if Megan would suggest they get a tub, and a wave of heat rushed through her at the thought of being naked together.

"We could try it sometime," she said, her eyes returning to Grace. She took both her hands and stepped closer.

Grace felt suspended in time, the trees and lanterns around her, music drifting out of the café. When Megan slipped her arms around her, pulling Grace into her warmth, the recipe for romance was complete.

Except the glaring absence of sparks when Megan's lips touched hers. Grace closed her eyes and went through the list of how right the moment was, click click clicking like the lighter on a stove's range, but minus the sparks. Instinctively, Grace took a step back, just as one would to avoid the cloud of gas that accumulates when the flame takes too long to ignite.

For all that she was thinking about how nice it would be to end her dry spell in bed, their kiss did nothing to pull her in that direction.

Megan slipped her hand into Grace's again, and it was nice. It felt comfortable, but she noticed how attuned she was to these small details rather than being lost in the moment. "Is something wrong?" Megan asked.

Feeling guilty for her distracted thoughts, Grace realized that the evening had grown quiet. Relieved that she had an excuse, she explained how she had hoped to talk to the violinist between their sets.

"Good idea, just in case we don't make it all the way through the next set," Megan said suggestively, pulling Grace in for another kiss.

But Grace's thoughts were already on her conversation about music and where that, not this kiss, would lead.

CHAPTER EIGHTEEN

Thrill

Muscles aching from a long day turning a platter on her lathe, spinning her blocks of wood while she shaped them with a variety of gouges and chisels, Robyn sat limply at the kitchen table eating cereal, too tired to throw anything else together. Low, dark clouds made it feel much later than it was, and listening to the rain, she wanted nothing more than to crawl up to her loft and into bed.

The doorbell prompted no response from anyone else in the house, so she reluctantly roused herself to open the door to the chilly evening. Her body flashed hot and excited with false recognition. The figure standing on the porch transported her back to before Barb had moved in, back to when Barb had rung the doorbell, to a time when Barb couldn't shut the door fast enough to get her hands on her.

Her body remembered this even though her brain quickly provided that Kristine's friend from the barn, not Barb, stood dripping wet on the porch. Analytically, there wasn't much this woman and her ex had in common. She puzzled over what had given her body the temporary flashback. The clothes she wore, she realized. Back when she and Barb were dating, Barb would arrive in a skirt suit. Once she'd moved in, she usually changed before finding Robyn, if she sought her out at all.

"You have another horse that needs feeding?" she asked, coming to her senses.

A series of emotions—recognition, surprise and confusion—passed over the woman's face. "No. I'm looking for Jen?" She bent to pick up a large case she'd set on the porch.

"Ah." Robyn stepped back, making room for the visitor to enter. "Up the stairs and straight back to the studio. She's already practicing. Must be why she didn't hear the door."

Grace took a few steps toward the stairs but turned before she took the first one. "Still riding?"

"Yep." She turned to shut the door, steadying herself. Even after she'd turned the lock, Grace stood there as if waiting for her to say more, but her heart pounded too much for her to think clearly.

The guest finally climbed the stairs, leaving Robyn by herself again. She returned to the kitchen, telling herself that it was the threat of soggy cereal that propelled her past the staircase when in reality she needed to sit, her head still spinning from the visceral memory of Barb's early attentions. How long had it been since anything had sent a zing like that through her body, she wondered. Her thumb instinctively traveled to her naked ring finger as if the surge of desire was something to feel guilty about.

She had spent so many years tamping down her desire for Barb that it took little to flood her system, and she sat there feeling her body reawaken. Suddenly ravenous and her cereal finished, she searched for something else in the kitchen. She scanned the contents of the refrigerator and cupboards in vain, wondering when she had let even her staples get so low. She'd have to run to the co-op.

CHAPTER NINETEEN

The narrow staircase carried Grace up to a hallway with three doors. Though the doors on either side were open, the closed door directly in front of her drew her so completely that she didn't even glance into the bedrooms she passed. Instead, she set down her cello and ran her hands over the smooth surface of the door, wondering how the woodworker had created rays that looked like Medusa's snake hair, bending and spreading out from a center of pieces of amber, a sun. Suspended above its radiance were other cut-outs for planets, some a single stone, others a collection like the sun. Dozens of stars so tiny Grace could not discern their color completed the skyscape. Finally, she turned her hand, rapping her knuckles on the masterpiece.

"Come in," Jen called from within. "Sorry to drag you out in the rain."

"Comes with the territory, doesn't it?"

Jen laughed. "Guess that's true. I'm just warming up here." she tucked her violin back under her chin and resumed her scales. Grace set down her case, surveyed the room as she pulled out her instrument, extended the endpin and tightened her bow. The polished hardwood floor would make for great acoustics. Two huge picture windows framed in fire-engine red dominated one wall. Grace's hands stilled and she sat mesmerized by what Jen must be able to see during the day.

"You wouldn't believe the view," Jen said, breaking her reverie.

"Sorry." Grace sat and accepted Jen's A to begin tuning.

"Don't be. It's such a cool space. Every day, I think about how lucky I am to be able to play in here."

"How did you ever find it?"

"I was already renting a room in the house. My landlady suggested I use this as a studio to try to build up a business."

"The one who let me in?" Grace asked.

"Older woman?" Jen asked and then quickly looked at Grace. "I'm not saying…"

Grace cut off the coming apology. "Yes, an older woman."

Jen nodded. "I moved in here after one year in the dorm. She's saved me in lots of ways. This is just the most recent example."

Her words made Grace curious about the other ways the woman downstairs had saved this vibrant young person. She spent a few minutes fine-tuning her four strings, thinking of the generosity that had been extended, more than just space since a music studio guaranteed a noise disturbance to everyone else. "Where shall I begin my audition?"

"You're kidding, right? I can already tell you're good. I don't have anything specific for a violin and cello duet, but I love this Handel Partita. I thought you could play the continuo bass."

"Usually the harpsichord part?"

"Exactly." Jen beamed.

"Let's take a look."

Jen placed the sheet music on their shared stand. "Sorry, I only have one copy."

"Not a problem." Grace scanned the bass clef and felt her pulse quicken. "You're not messing around."

The young woman raised her eyebrows encouragingly. "Doable?"

"Yes, and it looks like fun. I've been struggling with the bowing in "The Swan" from Saint-Saens' *The Carnival of Animals*." She tipped her head toward the sheet music. "This tempo and fingering looks intriguing. It's nice to have a different challenge."

"Here we go then!" Jen counted them into shared rhythm. Their instruments' voices joined, amplifying the joy Grace felt when she played. Her smile grew bigger and bigger, more so when she saw her expression mirrored by the young woman next to her. An hour passed in an instant as they played piece after piece on the stand between them until Grace's stomach added to the chorus. Embarrassed, Grace held both bow and cello in her right hand, covering her tummy with her left.

"I don't blame you," Jen said, closing her eyes and taking a deep breath. When she opened her eyes again, she beamed at Grace. "Mom's cooking again!"

"Mom?" Grace said, perplexed.

Jen shrugged as she placed her violin in its case. "Like I said, I've been here a long time. Let's see if she made enough to share."

"I don't want to intrude," Grace said, snapping her own case shut. As they approached the amazing door from the other side, a bowl perched on the top of the piano caught her eye. She set down the case, reaching out to touch the lip of the piece. "May I?"

"'Course," said Jen, pausing at the now-open door.

Grace savored the smooth surface of the bowl, the curve of the sides and flare in its base. She turned it in her hands and was not surprised to see the same Mother of Pearl signature she'd seen at Kristine's when she had joined them for dinner, suddenly recalling the soup and bread. "Is this a local artist?"

Jen laughed. "You could say she's the artist in residence. She made this door too. Come down and meet her."

As they descended the stairs, both the warmth and the aroma from the kitchen enveloped them.

"What's the occasion?" Jen asked.

Robyn, her back to them, rinsing her hands in the sink, said, "Just felt like cooking. I hope you're hungry." When she turned, her eyes immediately locked with Grace's, and she flushed red.

Something about Robyn fascinated Grace. Too rushed at the barn, self-conscious at Café Mokka when she was on a date with Megan and caught off guard at the door earlier, Grace had never fully had the chance to study Robyn. She took the opportunity now, wondering what had caused the color in her cheeks to rise, not expecting such emotion from someone who seemed so grounded. She tried to recall whether she had ever seen anyone else with Asian coloring and blue eyes.

In the warmth of the kitchen, Robyn had rolled back her long-sleeved T-shirt, revealing muscles along her forearms that rippled even with the simple task of drying her hands. She stood a head taller than Grace, even barefoot, the cuffs of her unshaped jeans loosely rolled.

"Grace, this is Robyn, landlady, woodworker and chef extraordinaire. Robyn, Grace and I are going to try to get a string quartet together." Jen reached into the salad bowl, scoring a slice of carrot before Robyn swatted her.

Robyn leaned forward to shake Grace's hand. "Nice to finally meet you."

Jen looked from one to the other with a puzzled expression on her face.

"Were you planning on running out of here as fast as you ran out of the barn when I took Bean off your hands, or would you care to join us for dinner?"

"Stay," Jen said. "She's a really good cook."

"I know," Grace said, enjoying the look of confusion on both women's faces.

"I stopped by the day you took Kristine's family dinner. They invited me to stay."

"She admired the cherry bowl upstairs too," Jen provided.

Admired more than that, Grace thought, remembering Robyn's generosity in providing Jen with such a wonderful place to practice and give music lessons. She also recalled Kristine and Gloria teasing her for not noticing Robyn's good looks

When she realized how far the gallop had carried her, she looped back around, pulling Taj back to a trot that she posted, rising out of the saddle on every other stride.

"She's such a beautiful animal." Kristine smiled when they met back up. "I'm so glad that you…" Her eyes scrunched up to pinch away more tears.

"I know. Me too. She's done a lot for me. Got me thinking about life again."

"Sorry about…"

"No. Don't apologize. Death is a part of life. I saw enough of it in the coast guard, and I thought that by retiring, I'd be able to keep my failing relationship alive. I spent too long tiptoeing around the edges of our breakup trying to delay the inevitable. My partner and I broke up a few months ago after eight years. I finally learned that even if it's harder, facing tough stuff straight on is more productive."

"That takes a lot of strength," Kristine said. "Strength I'm sure you have."

Robyn thought to argue that she was only physically strong, but something in Kristine's level gaze forced her to reconsider before she spoke. Kristine saw something more in Robyn. The affirmation made her throat constrict, but she accepted Kristine's assessment, nodding her thanks because she could not trust her voice.

CHAPTER TWENTY-ONE

"Kristine keeps giving me these looks. What's with her today?" Grace asked, joining Gloria in the kitchen. She had excused herself from the living room to get crackers and cheese, yet she stood leaning against the counter with nothing in her hands.

"What's with me?" Kristine said, following her into the kitchen. "How would you look if your wife's ex-girlfriend was in there holding your baby and looking like she's Rumpelstiltskin here to collect on some old promise." She turned to Gloria. "Tell me that you didn't promise her your first-born daughter."

Gloria stepped across the kitchen and slid her arms around Kristine. "You know I'd never do such a thing."

"Whoa, whoa, whoa," Grace said, waving her hands, catching up with the couple. "Megan's your ex? I've been seeing her for weeks. How can you not have told me!"

"I didn't put it together. Gloria always called her Meg."

"How long did you two date?"

"A couple of years," Gloria admitted sheepishly.

"Years!"

"I always knew it wasn't serious. She wasn't quite as clear on that."

"Clingon," Kristine coughed into her hand.

"Hey, what if I liked her?" Grace snapped.

Kristine's eyes widened. "Do you?"

Grace slumped onto a barstool. "She's okay company, but she's quick to jealousy."

"Very possessive," Gloria agreed.

"Is she always so bossy?" Grace asked.

"Always," Gloria said. "Everything has to be her way unless she sees it's a deal breaker. Then she'll backpedal and pretend like she doesn't care."

"What was your deal breaker?"

"I wasn't the marrying kind," Gloria answered.

"Hey," Kristine yelped. "Have you forgotten I'm right here?"

"Of course you changed my ways, honey."

"I can't believe this. You two are the ones responsible for her. Can't you do something?" Kristine looked at the two of them, guiltily rooted where they stood.

"We really shouldn't leave her out there alone," Gloria said, still not moving.

"I'm not going out there," Kristine said firmly. "She still looks at me like I'm a thief. You go. You're the one with the most experience."

"You say that like she's a rabid bear," Gloria said.

"Precisely! Here's your chance to save the day again."

"You so owe me," Gloria huffed, ignoring her wife's radiant smile as she trudged toward the living room.

"Happy to make it up to you," Kristine said, running her hand over Gloria's ass as she passed, earning her a smack.

"You're not scared to send her back out there alone? The way she looked at me once she got her hands on Eliza..." Grace said, shivering.

"She'll be okay. What about you?"

"Time to be upfront about how I don't see a U-Haul in our future."

"Blame it on me if you like. She already hates me."

"Aren't you coming back?" Grace asked, paused at the doorway.

"Are you kidding? Somebody's got to get the snacks and food."

"Coward." Grace returned to the living room, relieved to see the baby back in Gloria's arms.

"Think we've got a stinky," Gloria said, standing to leave the room as soon as Grace entered.

Grace wished she could follow, her thoughts on how painful the rest of the evening was bound to be now that she knew Gloria and Megan's history.

Megan took Grace's hand as she sat down, threading their fingers together.

"I'm sorry," Grace offered, aware that Megan had to be feeling awkward too.

She shrugged. "Small town. You didn't know." She looked away from Grace. "Do you…Would it be too terribly strange to bail? I thought it would be okay, but I don't think I can sit through a whole dinner."

Relief washed over Grace. She squeezed Megan's hand. "I'm sure they'll understand."

"I'll just wait in the car."

Megan ducked out the door without waiting for an answer. Grace turned to see Kristine standing with a bowl in each hand. "Chips and salsa?"

"We're going to go. The baby's still here. Gloria's either changing her diaper or hiding out in the bedroom. Tell her I'm sorry?"

"Forget about it. You just have to promise to come back soon with a report."

"PowerPoint?" Grace jested, delaying her departure.

"Gloria insists on it." Kristine set down her snacks and crossed the room to give Grace a quick hug. "Good luck."

"Thanks. Hope your evening isn't ruined."

"On the contrary. I see an early bedtime and some penance sex on the menu now."

"So didn't need to hear that," Grace called as she shut the door and jogged to her car.

She slipped into the driver's side and found Megan sobbing in the passenger seat. She glanced back at the house feeling stuck. Tentatively, she reached across the console and rubbed Megan's shoulders.

"I'm so sorry," Megan sobbed, her face buried in her hands. "I just couldn't sit through a whole night seeing the two of them and their family. It's all I ever wanted. *She's* all I ever wanted."

She sobbed again, sending Grace looking for a tissue. All she could find were crumpled napkins. She offered these to Megan who took them and blew her nose and mopped her face. "She's my white whale, you know?"

"White whale?"

"The one that gets away and keeps messing with your head."

"Never was a big fan of *Moby Dick*," Grace said, emphasizing dick in an attempt at humor. The look Megan flashed sobered her. "Sorry. That was uncalled for."

"No. I'm sorry. I thought…You're so beautiful, so successful. I really thought that we had a chance, but I can see that I have a lot more work to do with my therapist."

Grace bit her lip, trying to absorb the quick shift the evening had taken. Of course she was relieved to be off the hook when it came to the breakup. But she hardly thought it was appropriate to simply drive Megan home and leave her in such a state, even if she was slightly stung by being dumped when Megan didn't even know her well enough to realize what she'd be missing. "Do you need anything? Ice cream?"

Megan wiped her face again, sniffing. Finally, she nodded. "That would be nice."

Grace stopped at the store, leaving Megan to a new round of tears. She went inside to find Megan's request: mint chip. For a moment, she thought about grabbing two tubs but realized that was excessive.

She walked Megan to the door, holding her while she continued to cry, thankful that she accepted only the ice cream and not the offer to sit with her for a while. Back in her car,

Grace rested her head on the steering wheel. With nowhere to go but her own empty house, she realized how missing dinner disappointed her even more than Meg's dumping her did. She found herself thinking about the meal Robyn had made for them and the dinner invitation she had declined the other night. If not for Robyn's stubbornness, she would very much have liked to spend an evening in her company.

CHAPTER TWENTY-TWO

Gloria and Kristine had been right, Grace decided, strolling along the road at Patrick's Point State Park. She needed to get out and explore the Northcoast instead of running off to San Francisco every weekend. After finding such a treasure at the poetry read, she had bought a book of local hikes and selected one to try each weekend.

The dark forested area opened to a small meadow that afforded a view of cliffs to the north and the pounding ocean below. She stood at a fork. In addition to the road splitting for drivers, walking trails twisted off in multiple directions. With no particular destination in mind, she turned left, thinking it looked like the most direct way to view the ocean. The hair on the back of her neck prickled, so she turned. It wasn't a sound that put her on guard but a feeling, like she was being watched. Her eyes traveled up and found Robyn standing atop a rock formation adjacent to the meadow, her hands buried in the pockets of a peacoat. Her stance and expression made her look like the captain of a ship. Nothing but trouble could come from being interested in someone so aloof and cold, Grace mused.

She'd taken to thinking of Robyn as The Sourpuss after she had been so easily dismissed following that first music session with Jen. Robyn had been nowhere in sight the other times she'd been to the studio. At first it was just her cello and Jen's violin, but quickly two more, a violin teacher from the school in Blue Lake and a violist Jen played with in the Community Orchestra. Think about that, she told herself. Focus on the good energy to be found instead of the sour landlady.

Turning on her heel, she continued out to the Rim Trail, enjoying the way it ducked deep into the dark coverage of the trees and then wove out to the very edge of the cliff where she could watch the waves crash against the rocky shore far below. On the coast, the sun quickly warmed her, but as soon as the path dipped back into the forest, she shivered, the temperature shift as notable as the frostiness she felt whenever she'd encountered Robyn. Arcata was small enough that their paths crossed a few times a week. She recalled passing Robyn on the footbridge to campus just the other day. She didn't expect Robyn to stop and talk to her but the pursed lips and curt nod surprisingly dampened her spirits.

The next time she emerged from the trees, she saw a massive rock off the coast to the north. A trail snaked from the cliff down to water level and back up again to the almost island. She could continue along the path, but she had no idea whether the trail was going to take her back to the road and main gate. She'd learned that she needed to turn around before she felt tired. More than once, she'd walked much further than where her halfway point should have been. The rock face intrigued her, so she decided to retrace her steps on the Rim Trail and make the interesting outcropping her last destination before heading back to her car.

By the time she made it back to the trail that stair-cased down the cliff, another figure was out on the rock itself. Grace frowned, recognizing Robyn once again. She almost turned to the road but steeled herself instead. There was no reason for Robyn to make her feel unwelcome. Even in the full sun, hiking down to water level and then out over the ocean, the salty air had more of a bite. Grace zipped her coat and shoved her hands deep in the pockets.

She stood on a patio of flat stones catching her breath, marveling at someone's handiwork that made her feel like she was standing on a castle turret. Though there was only one trail out to the rock, and she had not passed Robyn, she didn't find her immediately. Once Grace reached the rock wall, she spotted her on a plateau further up the rock. She faced the ocean, still and alone. For an instant, Grace welcomed the opportunity to study her before she became aware of Grace's presence. Grace wondered what she was thinking, face turned to the sea with her eyes tightly closed. But then Robyn must have felt her presence because she turned her head and found Grace.

The faraway look vanished, replaced by the familiar guardedness. Despite the prickly shift in Robyn's demeanor, Grace felt Robyn's eyes quickly skim over her. She felt betrayed by her body as it warmed at the attention. Everything about Robyn's stance told Grace to keep her distance, yet her body declared how very much it would like to step into the obvious strength of those arms. Instinctively, she knew how her smaller frame would mesh with Robyn's. She pulled her hands from her pockets and crossed them over her chest, feeling the need to protect herself.

Robyn's gaze fell away, and it struck Grace that the expression she was having trouble defining was one of loss and sadness. She'd never seen Robyn as anything but capable and composed—not vulnerable. It frustrated her that the woman took up any of her brain space, that she could not simply accept that Robyn didn't want anything to do with her. The remoteness made her more interested, not less.

People usually like me, Grace insisted internally. It made her good at her job. She could pull people out and make them feel comfortable. Why that didn't work on Robyn stymied her. She was dogged though, another quality that suited her for the workplace and made her decide to stand at the rock wall until Robyn descended. Minutes passed, and though she kept her eyes on the ocean, she could feel Robyn's gaze shift to her every so often when she checked to see if her escape route had cleared.

Grace's feet started to get cold, and she zipped her coat up to her chin to ward off the biting wind coming off the ocean. She didn't care if she froze. Robyn was going to have to walk by her.

CHAPTER TWENTY-THREE

Kiss

Grace wasn't budging. Robyn wasn't dressed to stand out on Wedding Rock for the entire afternoon, and the longer she stayed exposed to the relentless wind, the more obvious it became that she did not want to walk by Grace who seemed to be strong-arming her into a social encounter. She pushed her hands deeper in her pockets, wishing she'd never set foot on the rock.

It was foolish to have returned, searching for some sort of validation that her relationship with Barb had meant something. She didn't want the relationship anymore, but the fact that Barb had moved on so completely wounded her. Robyn wanted an answer to what those years had meant to Barb. Anything? Did she think about the vows they had exchanged on this rock, in private, five years ago?

Just as she had fingered the stone with *Kiss* on it that morning, remembering the kiss that had sealed their commitment, she fingered the now-pocketed ring she had worn for so many years. She had closed her eyes, trying to remember Barb's lips on her own. When she opened them, she was startled to find that Grace had joined her on the rock. Before she'd appeared, Robyn had been thinking of tossing the ring into the ocean, but now she'd have to explain such a gesture. Her fingers moving over it, she remembered the feeling of Barb's hands on hers, slipping the ring on, claiming her.

Those words they had spoken to each other on this rock had felt like forever, but those promises had blown away, leaving her bereft. What did it mean when you gave your all to a relationship for years and then were left with nothing? What did the ring mean anymore, loose in her pocket?

She frowned at where nostalgia had gotten her, trapped on the exposed point of the rock without any warmth of the past to comfort her. No answers, only the annoyance of Grace parked in her path. She willed herself not to look at the way Grace's stretchy hiking pants hugged her curves. Standing there with the wind doing its best to free her wavy red hair from its ponytail, Grace could have been a model for the catalog of expensive athletic clothes from which she'd no doubt purchased the pants. She eyed her watch, annoyed by the turn of her thoughts. She had to leave if she hoped to get to the barn and feed Taj in the window of time the mare expected.

If not for the horse and her sense of responsibility, she would have stood there until it grew dark, but thinking about Taj waiting for her forced her into action. She took a deep breath and descended the stairs.

"Hi again," Grace said.

"Hey," Robyn answered, avoiding eye contact. She held her breath as she passed, her senses alerted by Grace's stiff posture, so she wasn't surprised when Grace turned and followed her.

"What's your deal?"

"Excuse me?" Robyn said, though she'd heard Grace's words.

"Even without the friends we have in common, this is a small town. We keep seeing each other, and whenever we do, I can't help but feel like I'm invading your space."

Robyn hadn't expected this and took another step away. She didn't owe Grace an explanation, did she? So they had friends in common. It didn't mean they had to like each other. She forced herself not to look at Grace, already feeling the effect of her presence like standing dangerously close to a fire.

"I'm a private person," she offered, taking another step back.

"People *like* me," Grace pushed.

"I'm sure you're a very nice person," Robyn replied, flummoxed by her statement. She tried to look away but couldn't. Before her, Grace stood taller and squared her shoulders. Robyn could see that her trying to slide away from the issue ignited a fury in Grace that heightened her beauty. Grace's keen hazel eyes bored into her and wisps of her hair floated on the breeze, making her look like a sea seductress about to cast a spell.

"You're attracted to me," Grace said with utter certainty.

Robyn knew she gave Grace her answer when she quickly averted her gaze because Grace's posture immediately relaxed. She cocked her hip, studying Robyn, a smile playing at her lips, not smug, but somehow satisfied. Robyn had nowhere to hide.

"That's why I scare you?"

"You don't scare me," Robyn fired back too quickly. That wasn't true. Her attraction, so raw, did scare her. She was so used to feeling nothing that she was easily overwhelmed by her response to Grace.

"Then what?"

She couldn't help but flash back to Barb standing with her on the same rock all those years ago. Their petite build was the only thing they really had in common physically, but the challenge Grace so easily hurled back at Robyn reminded her of Barb's unbending nature, her insistence that their commitment be private, not one shared with family or friends. Robyn had deferred without the foresight of what she would ultimately lose by capitulating.

Barb had sold it as a compromise, saying she didn't think they needed to formalize their relationship at all. Robyn had wanted a wedding. Thus, a private exchange of their vows was meeting her halfway. Robyn realized with a shock how little

Barb had actually offered and how much ground she had given up by agreeing. She was embarrassed by how grateful she had felt to Barbara for giving her what she did. Resentment boiled up in her, and she turned it full force on Grace. "I've dated you before."

Grace's eyes grew wide with surprise. "How's that?" she snapped.

"I'm drawn to this..." Robyn waved her hands at Grace's force that crackled in front of her, trying to put into words what she felt, "...energy, but it doesn't work."

Grace seemed to be waiting for more, but Robyn sensed that the more she said, the more Grace had to use against her. She felt it safer to say as little as possible.

"Why?" Grace demanded.

"I know who I am. I'm a rock. I'm grounded. Stable. You're this force that comes in and demands I move. I'm the one forced to change. I'm the one who gets hurt trying to bend. I'm not going to do it again." She felt the way the landscape of herself had been weathered by the relationship with Barb. Having put the effect her commitment to Barbara had had on her into words settled her visibly. She couldn't wait to get Isabel on the phone and share her revelation.

Distracted, she dropped her guard. She didn't sense Grace moving into her space until she was already there, one arm snaked around her waist and the other curled around her neck, pulling her into a kiss.

Her body reacted on instinct alone.

How could her lips be so warm when everything, everything was so cold? Her whole body lit up when Grace's lips touched down. She gasped in surprise and Grace quickly took advantage, engaging Robyn's tongue in a dance she thought she had forgotten. Grace's hands left Robyn's body, weaving through her hair to pull Robyn closer. Her arms blocked out the dimming afternoon light and Robyn was lost, bending to press her body to Grace's.

Her own hands betrayed her as they navigated from Grace's shoulders to her hips, urging her to mold her body against

Robyn's own curves. Grace sighed into the kiss and slowly rocked her hips in response. Robyn wanted to unzip Grace's jacket and slip her hands inside and feel her figure without the bulky coat.

That thought snapped her out of action and back to reality. She did not know this woman but she knew very well the burn of stepping into the fire. She broke away, her chest heaving.

Grace licked her lips. She placed a hand on Robyn's chest as if to confirm how very much her kiss had affected Robyn. A sexy smile crept across her face highlighting dimples Robyn hadn't noticed before. "Too bad you've dated me." Her hand dropped slowly away. "I wouldn't say no to a second serving of that."

Robyn watched helplessly as Grace climbed a few stairs before quickly disappearing on the trail. She wished that she'd been the one to take the first step. Now she was stuck waiting for Grace to get enough of a head start that she wouldn't be tempted to watch her ass the whole way out of the park.

CHAPTER TWENTY-FOUR

Humble

Robyn much preferred the quiet atmosphere of area coffee shops to the bustle of the Lost Coast Brewery, but Jen had been so excited about getting to play fiddle for the local Cajun Zydeco band that she would at least sit through the first set.

The citrusy Great White beer in her mug went down easily, and she found herself considering a second drink as she tapped her toe to the rowdy music. Unexpectedly, she recognized the opening drum intro to the next song. Her eyes found her tenant's. Tight blue jeans and a bright purple vest made her almost fit in with the rest of the country-clad musicians. Jen smiled at Robyn and dug into the lively fiddling of Mary Chapin Carpenter's "Down at the Twist and Shout."

The song flooded the already crowded dance floor. Robyn had no desire to join in, happy to sit watching. She was surprised to see Kristine take the floor with a beautiful blond woman. From the way they moved together and a bigger version of Caemon's smile lighting her face, Robyn knew that her friend was out with her wife. When Kristine's eyes found her, she felt guilty for staring so long, pulled by the obvious energy between them. She tried to watch other couples but constantly slipped back to the pair who out-sparkled everyone.

"Robyn!" Kristine shouted as the song closed. She steered her wife over to Robyn's table. "I'm surprised to see you here!"

"One of my tenants is fiddling tonight," Robyn explained.

"She's wonderful!" the blonde said. She extended her hand. "Gloria. So lovely to finally meet you. Caemon talks about you all the time."

"He's a charmer," Robyn said. "You two are kid-free tonight?"

"Thank goodness for grandparents," Kristine said. "Come upstairs and join us!"

"Yes do," encouraged Gloria. "We're in the back where it's not so loud."

Robyn hesitated but remembered Isabel encouraging her to be more social. "I'll join you after I grab another beer. Anything for either of you?"

They waved off her offer and eeled their way through the crowd to the stairs. She hovered at the bottom of the stairs until she caught Jen's eye, letting her know she was heading up, so she'd be able to find her in between sets. That done, she climbed the stairs and looked for Kristine and Gloria.

She was not expecting to see Grace. She kicked herself for hesitating when their eyes met, sure that Grace was replaying the kiss on Wedding Rock. That same sexy smile played on her lips, and she cocked her head to the side, her loose hair swinging off her shoulder and exposing her neck.

Robyn gulped. Just as she was hoping she could sneak back down the stairs, Gloria saw her and motioned Robyn in their direction. Robyn's feet obeyed, carrying her to the table and closer to the skin exposed by Grace's very low-cut blouse.

"How nice to see you again," Grace said sweetly when Robyn sat down next to Kristine. The way the three had clustered around a corner of the table to face the band, Robyn ended up sitting almost across from Grace.

"Again?" Gloria asked.

"I didn't know you knew each other," Kristine said.

"We went hiking together last weekend," Grace explained.

"Not together," Robyn clarified.

"We were both at Patrick's Point and kept bumping into each other."

Did she have to put so much sauciness in her voice, Robyn wondered. "Just once," she argued. She set down her drink and rubbed her shaky hands along her thighs.

"But it was the highlight of my hike. Wasn't it yours?"

There was that smile again, lighting up Robyn's pleasure sensors and freezing her mouth.

Kristine and Gloria followed the back and forth like a tennis match, shared confusion on their faces. Obviously Grace had not told them about the kiss.

"There's no recapturing the thrill of your first time out on Wedding Rock," Robyn finally answered.

"We'll see about that," Grace responded quickly, holding Robyn in her gaze long enough to make Robyn regret again that she'd allowed Grace to leave first, thus putting her in a position of power. Having made her point, Grace shifted her attention to Kristine. "Before you left, you were saying something about the gallery in Houston."

"Yes. They loved that rodeo series I did. I'm sending them several prints and they said to let them know when the website is live, so they have it as reference."

"Oh, that's wonderful news. Sorry I haven't put more time into the website."

"I know you've been busy at school. Please don't feel bad if you need to refer me to someone else to finish it up."

"Are you kidding," Grace laughed. "And lose my excuse to come visit that yummy baby? How is my little Eliza?"

"Settling into a more doable schedule now," Gloria answered. "We take turns getting up for the night feeding. It's amazing what an uninterrupted night of sleep does for a person."

"How do you manage that?" Grace asked, pointedly staring at Kristine's chest.

Robyn looked away, flustered by Grace's bold behavior. Even more than on the hike, Grace seemed like a storm to be avoided.

"She pumps the goods before she turns in."

The three women continued talking about the new baby's nursing habits, leaving Robyn wishing that she'd stayed downstairs where she could see the band. She could still enjoy the music, but she missed being able to watch Jen bow. She noticed the lull in the conversation but didn't realize they were waiting on an answer from her until Kristine said, "I told her we've never talked about jobs."

"Oh," she said, realizing she'd missed a question directed at her.

Gloria looked apologetic. "Baby details aren't for everyone."

"I don't mind," Robyn said honestly. "I'm retired coast guard."

"Were you posted here?" Gloria asked.

"For the last part of my career. I served at the Motor Lifeboat Station on the north end of the bay, but I spent my summers with my grandparents in Arcata when I was young and always had my eye on settling down here permanently."

"That's why we're here," Kristine said. "Gloria feels the same way about Eureka since this is where her family is."

"Was the place you live in now your grandparents'?" Grace asked.

"Yes," Robyn said.

"Wait, you've been to her place?" Kristine asked Grace.

"That's where my quartet rehearses."

Kristine smacked her forehead with the palm of her hand, and turned toward Robyn. "Your tenant the fiddler."

"She's leaving out how she's an artist as well," Grace said. "Robyn made that bowl I admired in your kitchen, Gloria."

"Did you really? I keep telling Kristine to take it to the barn to give back to you," Gloria confessed.

"I would but you keep using it," Kristine teased.

"Please forgive us for keeping it so long."

"No, no," Robyn said, embarrassed by the attention. "I meant it as a gift. Not the most appropriate baby-welcoming gift..."

"Perfectly appropriate," Gloria corrected. "I'm sure we'll have it long after we've moved along all of the baby clothes and accessories. Thank you. I'm so glad we don't have to resort to stealing it."

"I'm glad you like it." Robyn rotated her glass between her palms, wanting the conversation to shift but unsure of how to make it happen. She had always hated to have the attention focused on her, preferring to keep a low profile. In her mind, expectations followed acknowledgments, and she had spent her time in the coast guard trying to avoid both, much more content to fade into the background and get on with her duties quietly. Facing reporters after a dramatic rescue always took more effort for Robyn than the rescue itself. Here with her friends, she worried that Grace would use the opportunity of Gloria's praise to pressure her to make more than a hobby out of her craft. Thankfully, the band saved her by taking their first break of the night. She excused herself to find Jen and say goodnight so she could retreat from the social gathering that made her feel like she had to be on ready alert.

CHAPTER TWENTY-FIVE

Standing in front of the carvings on Robyn's front door, she heard its creator yelling up the stairs for Jen. Grace couldn't hear Jen's reply but waited patiently knowing full well that it was her presence on the front porch that caused Robyn such angst. She smiled as she pictured the strong woman debating with herself about how to deal with the situation.

The door handle turned quickly but only just enough to disengage the tongue from the jamb. Grace tentatively pushed the door inward and almost laughed out loud to see Robyn scuttling to the kitchen.

"It doesn't smell like anything is burning," Grace said, humor in her voice.

Her words stopped Robyn in the doorway. While Grace's blood thrummed at the memory of the kiss they had shared out at the state park, she realized that it was mean to tease. She turned to mount the stairs. Wanting to know more about Robyn, she risked a peek into the dim living room. In the wide doorway to the left of the staircase hung a string with upside down metal nesting bowls spaced in four-inch increments with a small brass stick hanging at the very bottom of the string.

Intrigued, Grace laid down her cello and grasped the stick, striking each of the bowls, the tones deepening as she pinged from the smallest on the bottom to the largest, the size of a small cereal bowl, at the top. The precise pentatonic scale of the bowls rang out and reverberated inside of her. Unable to resist, she tapped out a short melody before she gently released the striker.

"My grandfather brought it back from Japan, along with his bride." Robyn said from the kitchen doorway, not chancing closer proximity to Grace. "Some people mark their growth with pencil on a doorframe. Each summer I visited, the first thing I did was see if I could reach the next one up."

Grace waited, sensing there was something more. Robyn's eyes found hers, and she seemed surprised to find her there listening. Without another word, she turned and disappeared out the back door. Puzzled, Grace climbed the stairs and entered the studio without pausing as she usually did to study the door with its glass inlays. "Lay it on me," Grace said, plunking down her cello in Jen's studio and waiting, hands on her hips.

"What?" Jen said unconvincingly.

"What you know about Robyn. Last time when I asked about her, you hedged. You know things."

"I do?"

Grace folded her arms and eyed the clock. "Patty and Kim will be here in five minutes. Spill."

"It doesn't feel right to divulge Mom's heartbreak. Why don't you ask her?" Jen suggested, busying herself in the file cabinet that held her sheet music.

"Because she won't talk to me. You know as well as I do that she didn't even want to answer the front door just now."

Jen handed her a copy of the Ravel she'd tracked down, squinting her eyes as she considered Grace's request. "The relationship she was in for a long time didn't end nicely," she said vaguely.

"What's her name?"

"I'm so not telling you," Jen said emphatically.

Grace shook her head, remembering how awful it was to find out she'd dated Gloria's ex. "This is a small town. I don't want to inadvertently end up with Robyn's ex."

"Oh, that won't happen," Jen said, busying herself with music stands that didn't need adjustment.

"What makes you so sure?"

"Nothing."

"I won't tell her you told me," Grace assured her.

Jen held her temples, clearly distressed. "It's just that...I bet you know her because she works at the university."

Grace motioned with her fingers for Jen to continue.

"She books all the shows at the Van Duzer."

"Barbara?" Grace said, sounding doubtful. "Barbara Rivers? That can't be."

"It is."

"No. She just announced that she got married." She raised her eyebrows, gauging Jen's response. "To a *man*."

Jen sat, stunned. "She married him? Are you sure?"

"You don't seem surprised about the *him* part." Grace still couldn't match Robyn to the woman she knew from coordinating some projects for the gallery space in the foyer of the theater. She'd never had the impression that Barbara was gay.

"Robyn already dropped that bomb, but I didn't think...oh, no. I bet she doesn't know yet." She took in and slowly let out a big breath.

"How long have they been broken up?"

"Only a few months."

"Ouch," Grace said, understanding a lot more of Robyn's guardedness. She almost wished that she hadn't asked. The doorbell rang, pulling Jen from the room. What had always felt like Jen's studio suddenly felt like Robyn and Barbara's home. She wondered what energy Barbara had contributed to the space and how she could have walked away from it.

Then it occurred to her that Robyn had compared her to Barbara out on Wedding Rock. *I've dated you before.* How exactly was she like Barbara? They looked nothing alike. Though maybe the same height, Barbara was willowy in comparison to Grace's trim yet curvaceous form. She conceded that they both looked professional, but Barbara accomplished that with a natural sleek elegance, her glossy black hair always swept up in a way that accented her suits whereas Grace felt like the work she put into coordinating her wardrobe and taming her hair seemed more contrived.

She frowned, uncomfortable with the effort expended on comparing herself to someone she barely knew. That in turn reminded her that Robyn barely knew her, which added to the puzzle. At a loss, she decided that she didn't want to be involved with someone who made such snap decisions anyway. Immediately, she heard her mother's voice admonishing, *sour grapes*. Yes, she knew she would certainly grab Robyn if she could, but now she finally understood why she'd put herself out of reach.

CHAPTER TWENTY-SIX

"Happy birthday," Grace said, placing a kiss on Kristine's cheek as she slid a box of cookies onto the counter.

Kristine recognized the box and smiled. "Tell me there are some of those chocolate-dipped peanut butter cookies in there."

"Of course," she answered, slipping the knockoff Peekaboo bag from her shoulder and hanging it on the back of a chair.

"Unless you want Caemon digging through that, I'd hang it on one of the high hooks by the back door."

Grace followed Kristine's instructions. "Where is Mr. Mischief?"

"He's doing puzzles with Granddad."

"What can I do to help?" she asked, pushing up the sleeves of her black turtleneck.

"Steal Eliza from Gloria. I could put you to work chopping fruit, but I know holding a baby is more your speed."

"Everyone is here to celebrate your birthday. Tell me what needs doing and go join the party."

"Honestly, I don't even know what I'm doing. Robyn told me to slice tomato and mozzarella."

"Sounds like she wants bruschetta. Got it. She's on her way?" Grace tried to ask casually.

Kristine leaned into Grace. "With a lasagna she made me for my birthday."

"It really is too bad that woman doesn't like me when I could so get used to her cooking." And kissing, she thought to herself.

"There's a filly you wouldn't mind having in your barn?" Kristine asked, resting the backs of her elbows against the counter instead of leaving to join the party.

"Are you for real?"

"She is," Gloria said, breezing through to grab a bottle of wine and a few glasses.

Kristine wiggled her eyebrows in response. "And taken," she added as Gloria passed through the kitchen, planting a kiss on her and attempting to catch her in an embrace.

"Hands off! I've been sent in for drinks. I've got wine for my dad, but I told your brother and Dani you'd be out with their beers."

"You bet." After she pulled the drinks from the fridge, she returned to her original question. "Is it just her cooking, or could you really be interested in her?"

"I realize I don't know her well," Grace said, slicing the Roma tomatoes precisely. "But I would very much like to."

"Why not ask her out?" Kristine asked. Bottle tops off, she held three beers, poised to join the party.

"Her tenant divulged that she's only recently out of a long relationship. She's not ready for me."

Kristine laughed. "Would anyone ever be ready for you?"

Grace joined in the laughter. "Of course not! No one is ever ready for a fiery redhead."

A cheer rose from the living room. "They're not supposed to be having fun without me," Kristine said. "I'm off to investigate."

Moments later, Grace felt Robyn's presence in the kitchen. The flit of butterflies in her stomach made her want to say something saucy, but she checked herself. "Would it be easier if I left the kitchen to you?" she asked, wanting to make Robyn's life less complicated.

"No," Robyn answered simply. "Kristine said you volunteered to help?"

"Happy to," Grace answered cautiously, wondering if Kristine was working some mischief of her own.

The kitchen felt smaller than it had when she'd shared it with Kristine. Robyn wasn't a lot taller or more muscular, but she carried none of Kristine's zany energy. Robyn's posture brought a cool formality that made Grace feel like she needed to take care. As they worked side by side, Grace was tempted to talk, her mind spinning on the information she had about Robyn's breakup and her ex. She imagined sharing the dating fiasco she'd experienced with Meg. She ran several conversations in her head at the same time wondering if Robyn's mind was equally busy.

For all of the caution she felt initially, the longer they stood without talking, the more Grace relaxed. She began to carry the sides out to the table, ignoring Kristine's attempt to excuse her from the kitchen.

She'd assured Kristine that she was having a fine time, pleased to be able to free her from the party details. Returning to the kitchen, she said, "That lasagna smells divine. And you made that bread, didn't you?" she asked.

"Kristine said they enjoyed the bread I brought when Eliza was first born."

"Yes, I remember." Grace saw Robyn's hands pause at the task of slicing olives for the salad. She wanted to place her hand between those still shoulder blades. Touching people came naturally to her, yet while Robyn's body called to her, she sensed the action would push her further into retreat.

She felt a ridiculous desire to protect Robyn from the praise she would obviously receive when they sat down to eat. "Surely you know that people love everything you make."

Robyn's light blue eyes flicked to her, and Grace could see that she didn't know. She might hear the kind words people said, but she didn't believe them in her heart. "Salad's finished," she said, carrying it out to the table.

Tucking away her newfound knowledge of Robyn's modesty, Grace joined her at the decked out table, surprised when she sat next to her. Robyn chatted easily about her grandmother's recipes and how she remembered working the same garden plots in her backyard with her grandparents during the summer. The guests at the table echoed her reverence for family, and Grace felt envious of how lucky Kristine was to be surrounded by such loving people, both relatives and friends. Caemon clearly adored his grandparents and was over-the-moon excited to see his Uncle Gabe. Kristine's brother had driven from Quincy with his friends Hope and Dani.

Ironically, it was Robyn who engaged the couple, who had used Kristine's birthday as an excuse to visit Eureka with their one-year-old daughter, Joy. Robyn and Hope talked gardening, Hope earning Caemon's immediate respect when she admitted that she prepared her garden with a small tractor. Although Kristine had introduced Dani as the subject of the rodeo series she'd sent to the gallery in Houston, Grace had failed to use that tidbit to generate a conversation. Normally, it would have given her all she needed, yet she found herself drawing back from the group, observing rather than participating.

How many of her birthdays had she celebrated without her parents when they were still alive, believing that it didn't matter since she'd see them the next holiday? Four birthdays had passed. She and Leah didn't even call each other anymore, largely because of Grace's refusal to give their brother another chance.

Eliza began to fuss in Gloria's lap prompting her to push back from the table. Grace intercepted her. "I'll change her. You enjoy your food hot."

Gloria accepted, and Grace cradled the baby against her chest, carrying her back to the room the children shared. "I hope your brother is like your uncle Gabe," she whispered as she changed Eliza's diaper. "I'm guessing he's why you and Caemon look so much like your mama, isn't he?" She blinked back tears to finish her task, swooping the baby into her arms, applying her like a balm to the heartache that burned in her chest.

Even if she'd wanted children, she couldn't ask her brother whose troubled past had shattered her trust in him. She dabbed at her tears. Another thing he had taken from her, whether she wanted it or not. Again, his choices affected others, and she knew he would never admit to it, would never own that if not for his needing to be bailed out yet again, their parents would still be alive.

CHAPTER TWENTY-SEVEN

Grace sat in the dark in her Mini Cooper, watching the rain fall quietly, knowing she should join the other three players inside. She glanced at her cell on the seat beside her where she'd thrown it after ending the latest call from her sister. Why hadn't she let it roll to voice mail? Her anger kept her from crying, but the enormity of the call kept her from moving.

She could pick up her phone and call Jen and tell her that she was sick. Truthfully, her sister's call had made her feel ill, but she couldn't make herself reach for the phone. They had already begun practicing. Robyn's house sat on a one-way street, and she'd parked right in front where she could hear the sweet harmonies of the Mendelssohn scherzo, minus her cello's rich voice.

Movement on the porch caught her eye, and she saw Robyn walk to her truck parked in the drive parallel to Grace's car. Only the sidewalk separated their vehicles. Despite the rain Robyn's movements were unhurried as she folded her frame behind the wheel. About to crank the ignition, she looked out at the street, her eyes instantly finding Grace.

Grace bowed her head toward her lap, willing Robyn to leave. She closed her eyes and mentally put herself back on her porch playing "The Swan," a soothing piece which she turned to when the chaos of her mind threatened to overwhelm her. The score had the power to force everything else in her life to drop away. Frustrations and demands created hard angles, points and sharp edges inside her. She knew some musicians who turned to pieces that demanded an attack that mirrored their feelings inside. Instead, she turned to Saint-Saëns' gentle melody which smoothed her jagged emotions into an arc-shaped serenity. Suspended in time by the music, she could find calm.

Any other day, she would have leapt from the car and dragged her cello inside. Any other day, she wouldn't have even been in her car to see Robyn leaving, but she was immobilized. "The Swan" wasn't working.

Wondering why it was taking Robyn so long to leave, Grace chanced another look in the truck. Robyn sat with her hand poised on the key in the ignition, but she was still looking Grace's way. When their eyes met again, she pulled the key from the ignition and, to Grace's dismay, got out of her truck and walked to the Mini.

Grace rolled down the window.

"Everything okay?" Robyn asked. She kept her distance from the car and pulled the hood of her coat up. "Do you need an umbrella to carry in your instrument?"

"That's nice of you to offer," Grace said. "But..." Robyn's generosity spun Grace's mind back to her sister's angry voice demanding to know when she'd become so selfish. Growing up, the two of them had been so close, but their parents' deaths had highlighted the differences between them, differences that were increasingly difficult to ignore. The tears that anger had held at bay slipped.

"You're not okay," Robyn stated, concern in her voice. "You're shaking. Come inside?"

"No, no. I'm okay," she said, crying harder because of Robyn's kindness. "You were leaving. I don't want to keep you."

"It's nothing. Come inside."

The statement engaged her rational mind. She needed to unload her sister's demand and see if she was crazy to think it so unreasonable. If Kristine weren't so busy with kids and work, she would have called her, but Kristine trusted Robyn, so by extension, Grace did too.

Inside, she shrugged out of her wet coat and let Robyn take it from her. "Tea to warm you up?"

Grace paused. "If you've got something to spike it with."

"Hot toddy?"

"That would be so lovely." She glanced at the staircase. "I need to tell Jen I'm not up for practice."

"I'll tell her. There's a throw on the couch. Sit tight."

The large living room was dark with only one floor lamp against the far wall between the couch and bookcase. Grace remembered that huge hydrangeas surrounded the house, blocking the streetlights. The corner formed by the outside walls was taken up with two worn couches. The tips of the armrests touched, and a table with a towering philodendron sat between them. An old roll top desk occupied the space closest to the door and a floor-to-ceiling bookcase ran the entire length of the inner wall. A tiny TV sat surrounded by stacks of books. Arms wrapped around herself, Grace browsed the titles.

Robyn sat on the couch facing the bookshelves and set two mismatched mugs of amber liquid on the large burl table in front of the couch. Grace sat on the other and reached for one of the mugs.

Grace studied Robyn's completely unmasked face. The beginnings of crow's feet revealed her concern, and she realized that Robyn was completely at ease. In every encounter they had shared, Robyn had proven unflappable. While that quality bothered her in the sense that Grace had done her best to rattle her with the kiss on Wedding Rock, she realized it would make Robyn the perfect sounding board.

"Tell me about forgiveness," she began. "Say a person's bad choices rob you of everything you love in life. Do you owe that person another chance? Do you owe them a place to live?"

Robyn sipped her toddy and leaned against the side of the couch and rested her temple on her thumb. "Depends on how much it costs you either way. A girlfriend burns you, I say no. She doesn't deserve another chance to break your heart."

When their eyes met, Grace wondered if Robyn had heard about Barbara's marriage yet. Would Jen have told her?

Robyn pulled her bottom lip between her teeth and looked away. "Family's different. You always forgive family. To withhold ends up harming you as much as it does them."

Grace sipped her drink, absorbing Robyn's words. She took a deep breath. "My brother's been living with my sister and her family since he was released from prison." She avoided Robyn's eyes, staring into the liquid that warmed her hands and insides. "Tonight she dropped the bomb that it's not working for her and she'd like him to come live with me."

The few times she'd listened to updates about Tyler, Grace had ignored Leah's not so subtle suggestions that a change in scenery would be good for him to make a new start. As long as he wasn't getting into trouble again, Grace didn't see why they were talking about it at all. Drinking deeply from her mug, she tried to stop the shaking inside that had started the second she pictured seeing her brother again.

"You're not close?" Robyn asked.

"You could say that. How could we be with a seventeen-year-age difference?"

"Ooops?"

"A big one. I was a junior in high school, and my sister was twelve. For the longest time, the family joke was how their accident was hugely effective as birth control for us. After we saw firsthand what looking after a baby actually meant, there were no unintended pregnancies for me or my sister!

"I barely knew him. My sister babied him, but I went away to college. I felt like an aunt more than anything, not really knowing quite how to act with him when I went home. As a teen, he started defying my parents, and my mom would call asking me for advice. Like I had any insight at all about how to control him. I graduated at the top of my class, and he dropped out of high school. I got a job right out of grad school and have been financially independent ever since. He got his GED when my parents threatened to stop supporting him. My mom took over my room as her craft space since I only went home to visit. Tyler never moved out, but he hardly lived there. He always treated our parents' home like a place to crash and grab an occasional meal."

"Sounds like they were preoccupied. Did your sister feel sidelined as well?"

"She met her husband, Craig. My mom didn't want to bother them. Who wants to ruin the mood for the new couple?" Grace's tone was sharper than she intended.

"You weren't with anyone?"

"I was."

"But your mom didn't consider your relationship?"

"No. If I wasn't there to hear her gripe about Tyler, she'd lay it all on my girlfriend Steph. Anyone was fair game."

Robyn sipped her drink patiently while Grace thought about how upset her father had been when she and Stephanie split. He couldn't understand how she could walk away from someone so perfect. Stephanie's involvement in the drama about Tyler made her seem part of their family. But despite that, Grace had never felt that deeply for her.

"She couldn't handle it?" Robyn asked.

"Oh, she loved it. Ate it up, insisted that I couldn't cope with any of it on my own, especially when…" Grace swallowed and considered taking another sip of her toddy but set it down, aware of how her hands shook. She folded them on her lap in front of her. "Especially after my parents died."

"Oh, Grace." Robyn set down her mug and reached across the space to squeeze Grace's hand.

If the tears came, Grace knew Robyn would move to hold her, and she didn't want that, didn't want to break down and relive that grief tonight. She was too angry. She wanted to be able to see Robyn's reaction and ask again about forgiveness and see in her eyes if she still felt the same. She pushed back the tears, cleared her throat and poured out the details.

"My parents refused to give him any money unless he continued his education. Instead of enrolling at the local community college, he funded his pot and gaming with petty crime. That eventually escalated to burglary, and he was arrested climbing out of the window of a neighbor's home. As always, he called our parents to bail him out, with his usual promises to clean up his act. My parents were on their way to the police station when a truck crossed the center divider."

She still had trouble with the next part. Saying they had died still sucked her breath away.

Robyn scooted forward until her knees touched Grace's. "Were they killed instantly?"

Grace nodded, thankful that Robyn supplied the words.

"How many years ago?"

"Four. He was sentenced to four years for burglary of an occupied residence, but he only served two. He was the model prisoner and sailed through his parole," Grace said bitterly. "So...Tell me about forgiveness."

She regretted her bitter tone when Robyn scooted back on the couch. "Your sister forgave him? You said he's been living with her family."

"Yes, and I thought it was fine. She's been so enthusiastic about some projects of his. I thought that she was just trying to nudge my professional side into acknowledging him. Then she made the ridiculous suggestion about him living with me, so I could help him be seen...But then tonight she came clean and told me that Craig had never wanted Tyler living with them. Now I learn that he's not thrilled an ex-con is living with his kids and that no one in town sees him as anything but the loser responsible for his parents' death."

Robyn didn't say anything.

Grace leaned back into the couch. "I know. I recognize the irony. But he robbed me of my mother and father. He took away their future, my future with them. Why would I want to help him start over?"

She ran a hand through her short hair, leaving it tousled. "Because in hurting him, you hurt yourself. "I don't know the hurt of losing a parent—mine weren't around enough for me to feel abandoned when they chose to live with my brother in Japan. But I know what it feels like to lose something you treasured. My ex made me feel like that, and I spent a lot of time holding on to my anger toward her, but that only made me unhappy. My friend wanted me to punish her, sell off all the stuff she left here. I didn't because I knew that it wouldn't make me feel better. If I feed the bitterness, I'm the one who suffers."

"I don't understand how you can let go so easily I'd be spitting fire over her getting married." Grace clapped her hand over her mouth when she realized she'd spoken the words out loud. They didn't have any effect on Robyn's expression. She revealed neither surprise nor hurt.

"You don't know how long it was over before she left, how much time I spent being angry and hurt and confused. But I got to the place where I could let it go or let it sink me."

Grace wondered how long it had been and why Robyn had never chosen to leave. Given how uncomfortable Robyn seemed sharing personal information, Grace wasn't surprised when after a long silence, Robyn changed the subject.

"Why does your brother have to live with you? He's an adult, isn't he?"

Grace nodded, eyeing Robyn's drink and seriously thinking about taking it. "Yes, he's twenty-three. But he doesn't have the money to get a place on his own. He doesn't have a trade and never finished high school. Nobody in Bend wants to employ him. I don't know what he's going to do here, how he's ever going to become independent. He says I owe him since I'm the executor of our parents' will. My sister agrees with him. She thinks it's in our best interest to get him on the right track before he comes into his money when he turns twenty-five." She massaged her forehead, wishing she could expunge the constant churning of painful memories and pressure.

"Do you have the room?"

"I have a two-bedroom place," Grace answered. She had the physical space but did not know if she could share it with him. She flashed hot when she heard footsteps on the stairs. She'd intended to leave before the rehearsal was over and hadn't realized how long she and Robyn had been talking. She stood up apologetically and hesitated, knowing she couldn't simply slip out unseen. The trio of players reached the hallway at the same time Grace did. They looked startled to see her.

"I'm so sorry I missed tonight. Family emergency."

Patty and Kim assured her that it had still been good and quickly took their leave. Jen stayed, looking curiously from Grace to Robyn who had approached with the two cups in her hands.

Steeling herself, Grace spoke again. "I know it's terrible timing, but I'm going to have to go out of town for a while. I'll have to miss a few more sessions."

"Don't stress," Jen said, giving her a quick hug. "It isn't like I've booked us anything yet."

"But I don't want to hold the group back."

"Family first, right Mom?"

Robyn smiled at Jen's comment, but her eyes stayed on Grace.

"Thank you for talking," Grace said, wishing she could slip her arms around Robyn as easily as she could Jen, but knowing that the level of emotion she had shared with Robyn would make it a very different gesture.

"Glad to help. Are you okay to drive?" She held up the empty mug with the same look of concern that had prompted Grace to follow her inside in the first place.

"I'm sure. Thank you...again." She'd almost said for saving me. She stepped out into the rain, and instead of running to the car as she always did, she let the rain fall on her as Robyn had, feeling the cool water on her face.

CHAPTER TWENTY-EIGHT

Grace woke in her childhood home. Down the hall, she heard Leah bustling from room to room helping Zach and Alison pick out their clothes for the day. She covered her head with her pillow, wondering if they were purposely making so much noise to rouse her from bed. Leah had been shuttling them away from her doorway all morning trying to keep them quiet.

When they descended the stairs, Grace thought she'd go back to sleep, but she couldn't quiet her brain. She pushed the pillow off her head and studied her sister's sewing projects. She was ten again, perched on a stool, willing her mother to put the finishing touches on her Holly Hobby quilt. She tossed off her covers and dressed in flannel-lined jeans and a heavy wool sweater to ward off the winter chill.

She stood at one of the dormer windows with her arms wrapped around herself, staring out at the land, remembering the plans her father had for building a riding arena next to his barn. The only one in the family to ride, the barn was his domain. Leah's husband, Craig, wanted to sell the place. It really was too big for them, but Leah had argued that they could not sell the house with their brother in prison. She had insisted that he deserved the right to say goodbye to their childhood home. Robyn wondered if Craig was pressuring her to sell and whether that discussion was also on this trip's agenda.

Closing her eyes, she imagined her parents alive and everyone gathered at the house for the Christmas holiday. What would it be like if they were visiting the house instead of living in it? Would Leah's kids be out in the barn watching Granddad feed the horses, chatting excitedly about wanting a ride? She and Leah would be in the kitchen perched at the bar, warm cups of tea in hand, watching their mother flip her perfect pancakes, letting her take care of them. She leaned into that warm fantasy wanting it to be real instead of this ordinary weekday. Her sister did live here and was downstairs throwing breakfast together for the kids before she took Zach to preschool.

When she opened her eyes she saw her father sweeping the barn door closed. She gasped at the sight, her heart squeezed tight with the desire for what she saw to be true, the tall figure in the forest-green barn coat and brown Carhartt work pants to be her father. Too much hair, her rational brain said, the jacket too short at the waist and cuffs. Tyler turned toward the house and his footsteps pounded in her ears. Her brother alive in their dead father's clothes and in his space.

She couldn't go downstairs, but her stomach growled in protest. In an attempt to distract both, she pulled out her laptop to check her email, justifying her actions with the promise she had made to Aaron to check in frequently. She easily fielded questions she should have forwarded to Aaron, quickly losing track of time.

Leah rapped at the door before pushing it open. Dressed in old jeans, the T-shirt she'd worn yesterday that now had oatmeal handprints on the hem and one of Craig's fleece pullovers, Leah looked every bit the frazzled mom. Grace knew she wouldn't be raiding her sister's closet again anytime soon. Grace glanced at the clock and saw that forty minutes had passed. The house was eerily quiet, she realized. "Where are the kids?"

"Tyler took Zach to school, and he and Alison are hitting the hardware store on the way home."

"What was he doing in the barn this morning?"

"If you'd come down to breakfast, you could have asked him yourself." She folded her arms across her body. Pregnancy had widened her hips and shrunk her chest, but she'd worked hard beyond chasing her two active children to keep her figure. She had no hint of the belly bulge Grace remembered their mother having.

Grace went back to her emails. Leah sighed dramatically, threw her arms up in the air and left the room, tossing "There's cold lumpy oatmeal on the stove," over her shoulder.

Guiltily, Grace set the computer aside and followed Leah downstairs. "I'm sorry," she said. She served herself oatmeal and topped it with raisins and sliced almonds.

"I know it's not easy for you to be here or see Tyler, but sometimes I need your help. And I need your help now."

"I'm here," Grace said.

"You could at least pretend to be enthusiastic."

"I don't know how you stay here, how it doesn't get to you. I see him, and I feel like he's ripping tape off my heart."

Leah sat down with a steaming cup of tea and stirred in a heaping teaspoon of sugar. "We're not staying here. Craig and I are ready to sell."

Grace nodded. "And the place you get isn't going to be big enough for Tyler."

"We have our own family to raise, Grace. It makes more sense for him to live with you. We did two years, and he'll get his inheritance soon. If you've had it, you can wash your hands of him. But I think you should give him a chance. He's really trying. It's not like before."

"What's he been doing?"

"He's been building furniture, mostly tables he fashions out of stuff he finds. He's been trying to sell it on the Internet since nobody in town would ever hire him. We've been trying to put together a website, but I know he'd do better with your expertise," she said, looking pointedly at Grace.

Grace felt nauseous, anger turning the oatmeal to stone, but she kept eating. She recalled Robyn's saying that withholding forgiveness was hurting her as much as it hurt her family. Sitting across from Leah, she could see what she meant. Her attitude spilled over and affected everyone.

She set down the suitcase of pain and hurt she'd been lugging around and stepped away from it. Until she visualized it, she hadn't realized how much effort she expended keeping it close to her at all times and how very exhausted she was. If she could be free of it, she could move through her world more easily. "So let's go take a look," she said, testing what it would be like to start fresh.

They shrugged into coats and walked to the barn. Grace forced her hands open in her pockets so she would carry nothing into the barn, no anger or expectations. Stepping into the barn, she kept her mind on artistry, divorcing the glimpse of her brother's future from the past.

What she saw stopped her in her tracks. Stalls that once held horses now held a dinner table made from a discarded door, a sheet of glass giving it an even surface above the weathered, detailed surface. Another door he'd turned into a matched head and footboard for a twin bed. These pieces she understood, but the dozen old ladders that hung from the ceiling didn't make any sense. Grace turned to her sister, confused.

"I didn't get what he was doing, either, so he hung them to show me how these big hooks can hold pans in a kitchen or baskets in a storage room. Or you can pile towels on top. This one can hang in a corner and be used as a bookshelf. He has a bunch of other ideas for ladders once he gets his hands on them."

Grace's eyes stopped on a bench. "Is that…?"

Leah nodded. "You never answered the text I sent about whether you cared if I sent on our old cribs. That's actually what got him started. We were just moving Alison into her big girl bed, and our old cribs don't convert. When I explained how the newer cribs turn into toddler beds, he started thinking about what else an old crib could be."

Tyler had used the longer sides of the crib as the backrest for two Shaker-style benches. Grace ran her hand along the smooth polished surface.

"Are you mad?"

Tyler's voice startled her, and she turned to see him holding their wide-eyed niece.

"Say hi to Aunt Grace," Leah said, holding out her arms. From her mother's arms, Alison waved shyly. She looked as much like Craig with her dark straight hair and brooding expression as Zach looked like his mother and aunt with his wavy, ruddy hair and pale complexion. "Let's go get a snack and let Uncle Tyler and Aunt Grace talk by themselves," Leah said.

When mother and daughter left, Grace sat and ran her hand along the solid bench. "It's stunning."

Tyler tentatively sat down next to her and Grace studied his profile. She hadn't seen him since their parents' funeral, and his expression held none of the youthful defiance she remembered. His cheeks had lost their smoothness and seemed gaunt under the stubble of a few days' growth. The regret she had never heard him express was clearly evident in his gray eyes now that she finally allowed herself to look into them.

When their mother had spoken about reaching her own limit with Tyler, her gray eyes had looked the same—lost. Grace realized her own part in the chain of events. Her parents hadn't been equipped to help Tyler even though she had always believed they had all the resources they needed. She had thought they could handle anything. But now she understood that they hadn't a clue what to do and how that had cost everyone.

Now she and Tyler had a second chance, one that frightened Grace. They no longer had their parents to fall back on, and it wasn't like she'd learned anything about how to help Tyler begin a new life. All she had was control of his portion of the inheritance. Somehow her parents had believed she would know what to do in their place.

She hesitantly slipped her hand into his, feeling how calloused and rough it was. "There's a place on the plaza in Arcata that would sell stuff like this in a heartbeat."

"Maybe you could tell them about what I have?" He did not look at her when he spoke.

"I can get you an appointment with them, but I thought the plan was that you'd be there to sell it yourself."

"Really?" he asked, his voice cracking with emotion.

"It's not going to be easy. Don't think that a few pieces is a career. You're either in school or working a job with a payroll at least twenty hours a week."

"Done. This is…" His Adam's apple bobbed as he struggled not to cry.

"I have a lot of rules," she added. She really hoped that structure would give them a new start.

"I won't…I'll try really hard not to let you down, sis."

Grace cupped the back of his head, his shorn brown hair bristly underneath her palm. She tipped her own head, pressing her temple to his. She prayed she'd be able to do the same.

CHAPTER TWENTY-NINE

Worrier

"Why you ignoring me, *chica*? You call me and say you need to talk but then do not pick up your phone when I try to call back. You are not nice. I worry about you all day."

Robyn rested her head against her palm and stared at the reason she was tardy in returning Isabel's calls. "I've had Caemon today because he's too much of a handful for his grandparents. They could only handle Eliza while Kristine and Gloria went to Penelope's service."

"*Lo siento*. That's terrible news."

"So that's why I called you." Robyn reached across the table and married the peanut butter side of the bread to the jam side. Caemon blinked at her before dismantling it again, so he could run his thumb through the peanut butter and lick it. Too exhausted to fight him, she gave up and studied his method instead.

"Because you can't handle one three-year-old on your own?"

"Have a little faith…"

"Yakkum?" Caemon said.

"Yakkum?" Robyn repeated.

"Napkin," Isabel easily translated. "You sure…"

"I've got this," Robyn said, handing Caemon a cloth napkin. He furrowed his brow. "Wet."

Robyn sighed heavily and got up to wet the napkin. "Okay, maybe this is harder than I thought it would be."

Her friend laughed. "Do they want to know if you will buy the horse?"

"No. I haven't heard from them. I'm betting the horse isn't something they want to think about right now."

"Then I am confused."

Robyn didn't know where to start. Kristine had also tried Grace who was unexpectedly out of town. Robyn was surprised that Kristine didn't know about Grace's brother. If Grace was out of town, that meant she had decided to give her brother a chance. Robyn wondered if she had come to that conclusion because of their conversation about forgiveness, and she was surprised that Grace had confided in her and not Kristine. That, Robyn realized, was why she'd called Isabel. Isabel would know how to translate Grace's actions.

"Someone kissed me," Robyn stammered.

"A female someone? Not this little boy, no?" Isabel replied.

"A very attractive, successful female someone."

"When?"

"Three weeks ago."

"How am I just now hearing about this?"

"I'd just told her that I didn't want to date another white knuckler, and she planted a kiss on me." Isabel had coined the term to capture Barbara's desire to control every single thing in her life.

"For this she kisses you?"

Robyn helped Caemon wipe peanut butter from his hands before offering him a banana. "She wanted me to know what I was missing."

"And is it something?"

Remembering the kiss sent a surge of electricity through her body again. "I'd forgotten what it was like to feel like that."

"What does the horse girl have to do with this?"

"Hang on," Robyn said, wanting to tell her about how Grace had trusted her. She steered Caemon to the living room and offered him the coloring book and crayons Kristine had packed.

"Plea you draw wi' me?"

"In a minute, kiddo." She returned to the kitchen to clean up lunch and attempt to explain why she'd called Isabel. She ran through the truce-like birthday dinner at Kristine's a week after the kiss and how Grace's backing off since then had made her feel unbalanced.

"You cannot need me to explain this to you," Isabel laughed.

Caemon returned to the kitchen hands pinching his parts with a panicked look on his face. "Hang on," she said to Isabel. "You need to go potty?" she asked Caemon.

Caemon nodded, so Robyn showed him where the bathroom was, stepping outside to give him privacy. "Obviously, I do need you to explain," Robyn sulked.

"You took her bait. Now all she has to do is reel you in. One kiss. That is impressive!"

"I'm done!" Caemon sang from the room. Robyn waited, but he didn't emerge.

She listened to Isabel go on about the kiss but had to interrupt her. "Caemon just keeps saying he's done going potty. Am I supposed to do something?"

"You left him alone in there?"

"He seemed like he knew what he was doing." She peeked in and saw him perched on the edge of the potty. "He's just sitting there."

"Give him a wipe."

"Three-year-olds don't wipe themselves?"

Isabel's laughter prompted her to go in and assess on her own. She pulled a few pieces of toilet paper in preparation and was surprised when Caemon flung himself forward to hang onto her legs. Trying to maintain her posture, she dropped the phone into the garbage. "I dropped you, Isabel. Hold on a sec."

Wiping out of the way, she and Caemon washed hands, and she directed him back to the living room.

"Stop laughing," she said, retrieving her phone.

"I wish I was there to witness all of this myself," Isabel responded.

"Then you'd be the one doing all of this stuff. It comes naturally to you. What were we talking about?"

"About how the hot lady is reeling you in," Isabel reminded her.

"This isn't about romance," Robyn insisted.

"Oh?"

"She stopped hitting on me, and now she trusts me with these details of her life."

"Details?"

"Family stuff she's dealing with. I want to know what that is."

"It is called trust. If she trusts you to talk about this pain, then it follows that she trusts you with her heart."

"She barely knows me."

"Since when has that stopped anyone from falling in love?"

To give her hands something to do Robyn went ahead and dried the dishes with a dishtowel and put them in the rough open-faced cupboard.

"It's too quiet there. Where is your little friend?"

"Oh, shit." The curse left her lips when she realized how distracted she'd become. She jogged across the kitchen through the hall to the living room which she found empty. "Caemon!"

"You lost him, no?"

"He was coloring."

"Can he open the front door?"

Robyn flung open the door, ran out to the drive and looked up and down the street. No sight of Caemon. She ran her free hand through her hair, tugging it with worry. "Nothing."

"I bet a hundred dollars he is in your loft."

Immediately, Robyn pictured the steep set of stairs in her room that led to the loft. The steps had no railing, and there was just the bed and a gaping hole back to the floor eight feet below. Taking the steps two at a time, she rushed upstairs calling his name. Sure enough, when she ran into her room, she looked up to the loft and found worried blue eyes staring back at her. "Caemon! You scared me."

"You angy?"

Robyn thanked Isabel for her help and tucked her phone in her pocket. "Not angry. I just need you to answer when I call you. Come on down."

Instead of complying, his eyes left hers guiltily.

"What do you have up there?" She climbed up and turned to sit with her feet resting on the top step. Caemon sat on her mattress, her collection of agate rocks lined up carefully on her blue bedspread.

His tiny hand reached out to straighten a few that had been knocked out of line by his crawling to the opening. He began to pick up the rocks, but Robyn reached out and stilled his hand. "It's okay if you play with the rocks. I was just worried about you. I wouldn't want you to fall down the stairs."

"Baby Eliza can't climb the stairs."

"No, she can't. She's not a big kid like you are."

"She's not allowed of choking hazards."

Robyn laughed in surprise. "Your moms told you that?"

He nodded solemnly.

"Are you going to put the rocks in your mouth?"

"No! Them is not for eating."

"Then we're okay. Let's take them downstairs. I'll tell you about why they're so special."

He scooped up the rocks, and let her lift him down from the loft space. She shut the door and followed his careful progress on the stairs, chastising herself for letting him out of her sight, relieved by the easy resolution.

* * *

When she picked up Caemon, Kristine shrugged off Robyn's apology for losing him briefly, assuring her that he had a knack for slipping off quietly. Caemon had enjoyed the agates so much that he'd wanted to take one with him. Robyn would have been happy to have him keep one, but Kristine gently reminded him of his baby sister and pointed out that he could come back to play with the rocks at Robyn's house another time.

After they drove away, Robyn sat on the porch as the fog rolled in off the bay, thinking about the boundaries that kids naturally tested. At what point did Grace's brother step over the line of what his parents could cope with? Robyn wondered how Grace had come to peace with the idea of taking Tyler in and whether she'd be able to establish the boundaries that he needed.

She wanted to help Grace but could see how little she knew about parenting a three-year-old, let alone a troubled adult. Strangely, it was not the spontaneous kiss that made Robyn realize that Grace had snuck past her own boundaries. Fretting about whether Grace would be able to deal with her brother living in Arcata made Robyn want to wrap Grace in her arms. Suddenly she found herself worried that she had blown an unrecognized opportunity when Grace had kissed her on Wedding Rock.

She could hear Isabel's *I told you so* without even reaching for her phone.

CHAPTER THIRTY

Had to run an errand. Robyn's in back and can let you in. Be back soon, promise. Jen.

Grace carried her cello to the front corner of the house. A hothouse ran the length of the south side, ending in an arched doorway with a purple door topped by glass panes. It opened to a yard with tidy raised-bed garden boxes and fruit trees. She followed the cement path that curved around to the back door. A grating racket came from somewhere nearby and she puzzled at the two sets of porch stairs, one to her left and one directly in front of her. She chose the set of stairs on the left, figuring they led to the kitchen, thankful for the quiet of the small house she rented.

Her rap at the door produced no results, so she leaned her cello against the porch railing and descended the stairs. She briefly entertained the idea of knocking on the second door but noticed a path in the grass that led in the direction of all the noise. Tentatively, she followed it, pausing at what she thought would be the property line. There she found an answer to the horrible noise. Inside a garage with doors open wide was Robyn pressing a metal tool to a spinning hunk of wood. A thin line of the wood curled in long ringlets, crawling up Robyn's left arm before falling to the pile on the ground.

Grace stood mesmerized by the slow arc Robyn made as she whittled the outer edge to a curve. Soon she clicked off the machine and pushed her protective glasses back on her head. Rather than brushing the sawdust that covered her head, shoulders and chest, Robyn's hands caressed what would eventually be a huge bowl.

Before Grace had kissed Robyn, she would have let herself imagine what Robyn's hands would feel like on her skin. Now she felt foolish watching someone who had made it clear she wasn't the least bit interested. Had she not just brought her brother back home with her, she might have pushed a little harder, but Tyler's living with her dropped her love life significantly lower on her list of priorities. Not wanting to stand there pining about how many things had shifted, she broke the silence. "I had no idea your shop was right here."

Robyn's hand flew to her chest. "You startled me!"

"I didn't want to interrupt you."

"I was just thinking I'd call it a day." She tucked the tool she'd been using into a box hanging on the wall and brushed her hands on her thighs.

"How long will it take to finish this piece?"

"It'll be pieces, actually. Tomorrow, I'll cut out the middle in stages. I'll probably be able to cut three stacking bowls. They'll get coated in wax and hang out in the shop until they're dry enough to do a more finished turn." She pointed to shelves deeper in the garage filled with all different sizes of bowls as well as hunks of wood that had yet to be touched.

Grace stepped carefully across the carpet of sawdust and picked up a bowl. She puzzled at a notation in pencil.

Robyn stood so close their shoulders touched, and she did nothing to avoid Grace's hands when she took the bowl. The brush of her fingers sent a zing through Grace. So much for her priorities shifting.

"I mark them to remember where I found them, what kind of wood it is and how long it's been curing. This is madrone I found on the Oregon coast. I did the rough turn in June. See how it's elongated in the last six months?" She tipped it to look at it in profile, showing Grace how the sides had also curved up in the middle, giving it the shape of a football, not a bowl.

"Why the Oregon coast?"

"I find different wood to work with, and there aren't many places you can actually take driftwood off the beach."

"I was just in Oregon. I could have combed the beach for you."

"Kristine said you were away. So you have a roommate now?" Robyn asked, putting the bowl back on the shelf.

"Yes, I brought Tyler home with me."

Robyn's eyebrows popped up.

"What?"

"I'm just surprised."

"You're the one who said I'm only hurting myself if I don't let go of my anger."

"I know what I said. But there's a big difference between hearing something and listening. You listened. I'm impressed."

Grace wasn't sure what would have made Robyn think that she had trouble listening, and bristled at the suggestion. She gestured at the walls lined with neatly organized tools. "He'd love this. He'd made a shop in my sister's barn, changing my sister's junk into things he's trying to sell. Upcycling he calls it."

"Did he bring anything with him?"

"We only had room for the bench I bought from him and a few of his smaller projects. I'm making a website for him, and we'll put pictures of the other things he's made on it. He'd like to jump into that a hundred percent, but I've got him looking for work that offers a steady paycheck. Either that or enroll at the community college."

"I'd like to see what he's doing to recommission old things," Robyn said, genuine interest sparkling in her eyes.

Grace hesitated. She was proud of what Tyler had made but didn't want him to get distracted from the goal they had set.

Robyn seemed to sense Grace's discomfort and asked, "How's it going with him?"

"It's only been a few days…" Grace appreciated that Robyn didn't push about Tyler's projects and that she seemed interested in the shift in her life. "He's doing fine. We're finding a rhythm. I want to support him, but I feel a lot of pressure to make sure he finds the right path."

Silence hung between them momentarily. Robyn opened her mouth to speak but turned her head and let out a long breath. When she glanced back at Grace, Robyn brushed sawdust off her forearms and said, "I'm glad you're helping him."

Grace could see clearly that Robyn had been about to say something else, but whatever it was, she took it with her out of the shop, waiting for Grace to follow before she swung the doors shut. "What were you going to say?" she pressed.

"Nothing," Robyn said without meeting Grace's eyes.

Grace crossed her arms and stood her ground.

Robyn relented. "I thought I got you. You had your big speech about how I could do something bigger with my bowls, yet you don't want to encourage your brother's craft. That's a puzzle."

Grace took a breath to argue that Robyn had artistic talent that deserved more attention than she got, and then realized that Robyn was suggesting that what Tyler did was art. "Wait. His stuff could be terrible. What do you know until you've seen it?"

"The look on your face when you said you bought one of his benches. It means something to you."

"He made it out of our childhood crib. It holds great sentimental value."

The smile Robyn attempted to hide betrayed how little she believed Grace. "Somehow I doubt that you would buy something solely for the memory. I'd put money on it having more value than that. Upcycling is hot right now. If he's got a knack, he could be successful…" She paused, searching Grace's eyes with an intensity that made Grace feel utterly exposed. "But I guess it depends on what your idea of success is. Barb called stuff like that junk." She bowed slightly before she walked away from Grace.

Grace refused to follow immediately, stung by Robyn comparing her to Barb. And she didn't appreciate Robyn's insinuating that she was a snob. Digging her phone from her pocket, she marched after Robyn. "He doesn't make junk," she insisted, pulling up some pictures of the table she had liked so much.

"I never said he did," Robyn said, accepting Grace's phone. She nodded appreciatively as she scrolled through a dozen pictures. "That's really something." Her words were heavy with meaning. "You have a chance here to encourage beauty. Isn't that sometimes what's most important?"

Despite the chill in the evening air, Robyn's hands were warm against Grace's when she pressed the phone back into her hands. For a moment, Grace forgot they were talking about her brother. She'd never seen such an open expression on Robyn's face. She felt the urge to step closer and find Robyn's warm lips again but resisted. Robyn must know how she felt. Her skin still tingled with the memory of their one kiss. However, knowing the details of Robyn's recent breakup, she wouldn't push again. Whether more developed between them was up to Robyn.

"I'm hitting an estate auction tomorrow. I'm sure he'd find stuff to work with if you want me to take him along," Robyn offered.

"How about you text me the info and we'll join you if we can." Grace somehow felt jealous of the invitation extended to her brother, but not to her.

Robyn held out her hand again and raised her eyebrows expectantly.

"What?" Grace finally asked.

"Won't you need my number in your phone?"

"Of course," Grace said, flustered by the decidedly flirtatious way Robyn had delivered the line. Robyn had said earlier that she thought she "got" Grace. As she pulled up her contacts and handed the phone to Robyn for her to punch in the number, she realized that the tables had turned, she didn't know Robyn as well as she thought.

CHAPTER THIRTY-ONE

Hope

Robyn studied the battered legs of a small desk. The dings and scratches would work in her favor, keeping the sale price low. With an afternoon of sanding and a fresh coat of varnish, she could easily quadruple the price in the fall when students flooded her yard sale eager to furnish their apartments. She'd also bid on many of the pots and other kitchen utensils, all well-used and mismatched, which would keep most people from giving them a second thought but give her a great selection.

She wandered from the packed room, not having seen what she was really looking for all morning. Though Grace had texted for the address, Robyn had yet to see her or her brother. Her level of disappointment surprised her. It wasn't as if they'd made a firm plan. She tried to tell herself that what she felt was tied to whether Grace would support her brother's talent, trying to nudge out of her brain the hope that Grace would want an excuse to see her.

With a half hour to kill before the auction started, she walked out to the garage on the off chance that they'd have any old tools that would interest her. Hands tucked in the pockets of her Windbreaker, she heard Grace before she saw her.

"We don't have the room," Grace's voice had a hard edge with no room for bargaining.

A deep male voice answered calmly, "You've got that carport. I could throw a tarp over them."

"The ladder I get. I've seen what you can do with ladders, but building a greenhouse out of windows...And you said there aren't enough here, anyway."

"That's why we store them for now. No one is even looking at them. I'm sure I can pick them up for next to nothing. Then I'll find more."

"To build a greenhouse."

"Yes."

Robyn took a few more steps and found Grace standing tall in defense, her hands crossed over her chest.

Coatless, Tyler's T-shirt stretched tight over his muscular chest and arms. The sleeve hid half of a tribal pattern tattoo. His posture held none of his sister's erectness of carriage. Her stance struggled to gain power, yet he stood relaxed and impassive. Though fascinated by their standoff, Robyn couldn't resist introducing herself.

"I'm happy to see you made it," she said, entering the garage. Grace's eyes widened for an instant, either in surprise or pleasure to see Robyn. Robyn hoped it was the latter.

"Tyler, this is my friend Robyn," Grace said, her voice clipped and annoyed.

Robyn smiled, figuring that Grace held her responsible for the situation.

"A greenhouse, huh? What are you thinking as far as framing goes?" Robyn asked.

Tyler lit up as he explained the design he had in mind, quickly brainstorming the materials he would need to pull off the project. The more he talked, the more Grace scowled.

"And who is going to pay you to construct this thing on site?" Grace asked.

"I know you think everyone in Humboldt County grows pot, but I could sell this legit," Tyler said, volleying back Grace's objection.

Robyn agreed. "There's a huge community of organic gardeners. You could pitch the idea at the farmers market once it gets going in the spring, see if anyone has been thinking about expanding with a greenhouse."

"And that gives me time to collect the rest of my materials," Tyler said excitedly.

Ignoring the way Grace's eyes were glinting, Robyn added, "You could check the recycling center in town. They have a great selection of recommissioned building materials."

Tyler turned to his sister for approval.

"Where do I start? I already said you weren't storing a bunch of windows in my carport, and even if I had changed my mind about that, how were you thinking you'd get them home? There's no room in the Mini." Grace stood hands on hips, her hazel eyes blazing.

Tyler turned pleading gray eyes to Robyn. She didn't need a secret hand signal to know that the correct response was to back up Grace, but she instantly liked Tyler and wanted to help him. The way Robyn saw it, pursuing his own projects might just keep him from becoming bored and getting himself into trouble. She willed Grace to intuit her motives when she said, "I've got plenty of room in my truck and in my shop. You're welcome to use the space for storage and planning the design, so you're ready for your buyer."

"Yes! Yes!" Arm curled, Tyler pulled his fist to his waist punctuating his victory. "Aww, this is going to be great. You'll see, Grace. Thanks Robyn."

Surprisingly, Grace's posture relaxed. "You really think he can make a profit from this?"

Robyn glanced at the price tag on the windows. "I do. Plenty of people are replacing their windows with double-paned, so it shouldn't be hard to grab up the glass. What he's really investing is time."

"Right," Tyler said, clapping his hands once before throwing his arms around his sister.

Robyn didn't want to intrude, but Grace made eye contact over her brother's shoulder. "It's okay?" she mouthed.

Grace gave her a subtle nod before releasing her brother. "Time for the auction?"

Robyn consulted her watch. "Looks like it. You have your number?"

"And a budget," she reminded Tyler as they headed to the house.

* * *

Hours later Robyn and Tyler slid the last of the windows into place in her shop.

"This is sweet," he said, taking in her workspace.

"I'll get you a key, so you can work on this whenever you want. The side gate's always open."

"I don't know what to say," Grace said, eyes on her brother, not Robyn.

"Yeah. Thanks for all of this," Tyler added.

"I'm happy to help. Feel free to take a look around the shop," she said to Tyler. "Grace, you want to give me a hand with the stuff I picked up?"

"Definitely."

Once they were out of earshot of the shop, Robyn spoke. "Thank you for agreeing to the glass. I know how you feel about him getting a stable job, but it seemed right to fan his enthusiasm for this project."

"For a minute, I felt like punching you, I'll admit that. But I've been worried about him when I'm at work. I can't be with him all day, and I can't force him to go to school. When you said he could keep all of his stuff here, I felt so relieved. If he's here..." They stopped by the gate. She searched Robyn's eyes.

"That's what I was thinking."

"I don't know what's in it for you."

"Don't you?"

Robyn remembered the kiss Grace had surprised her with and wished she could be as impulsive, but she couldn't read Grace well enough to risk it. Instead she offered a hug, trusting that if Grace had been able to follow the logic of offering her workspace to Tyler, she would also pick up on the connection Robyn hoped to convey.

The way Grace's arms wrapped snugly around her back, Robyn was sure she understood. Robyn's arms offered sanctuary and protection. She poured her strength into the embrace, offering all she had to Grace, and Grace accepted it with the press of her body. If Robyn held her any longer, she would have to kiss her, and if she kissed her, she knew she would not be able to stop. Though she thought the shop would occupy Tyler for a while, she would not risk him stumbling on such a moment.

Reluctantly, she stepped back from Grace. "You said you'd help unload the truck."

Grace's answering smile gave Robyn hope that she understood Robyn's real motive in helping Tyler.

CHAPTER THIRTY-TWO

"Oh, baby girl, what do you want?" Grace cooed to the infant as she gently bounced her. "Your mama promised you'd be asleep for hours."

She held the baby close, trying to figure out whether to offer the bottle in the fridge. Kristine had explained how to heat it if she hadn't made it home by the time Eliza woke for her nighttime feeding. But Grace couldn't imagine she was hungry already. She'd ruled out uncomfortable by changing her diaper. On the possibility that she'd just angered Eliza by exposing her to the chilly evening air, she held her tight and kept walking.

"Please please please please please don't wake up your big brother," she whispered. Even Kristine had showed some worry, crossing her fingers when she said Caemon usually slept through the night.

"Mooooooooommmmmmy," a groggy voice joined Eliza's protests.

"Shhhhh," Grace tried in vain to calm the baby as she crept down the hall to Caemon's room. "Caemon, honey, it's okay. Go back to sleep," she said, hoping he was too sleepy to recognize that the female voice belonged to neither of his moms.

He sat bolt upright. "Where Mommy?" he demanded.

Grace took a deep breath and entered his room. What was she supposed to share with him? Did he know how sick his grandma was? She sat gently on the bed beside him. "Mommy's mom is in the hospital. Mommy and Mama both went to help your Granddad. Do you need to go potty?"

"Mommy." He crossed his arms across his little chest, his eyes brimming with tears.

"Caemon, I can't give you Mommy. Let's lie down and go back to sleep. She'll be here when you wake up."

"Moooommmy," he cried louder. He swung out of bed and padded down the hall, switching to "Mama" as he increased the volume.

Eliza screamed in her ear. "Caemon, I need you to be a big boy for me. Eliza's sad. Can you help me?"

Ignoring her, he ran to the front door. "I go too. I go. I go. I go." He stood by the door sobbing.

"I'm all you've got," Grace said, following him, trying to put her arm around the boy while cradling the board-stiff Eliza. Tears threatened in her own eyes, and she wondered what would happen if she added to the chorus of cries herself.

Caemon moved away from her, pushing his back against the door, as far away from Grace as he could get. "Robyn."

Grace blinked back her surprise and looked at the clock on the counter. Almost ten. Despite the late hour, she was sorely tempted to call Robyn. She saw the boy fist his hands at his side and tried to talk herself out of calling. "It's late, Caemon. Let's crawl into your moms' bed, and I'll lie down with you."

He batted her away. "I want Robyn."

I do too, Grace thought. They eyed each other, and Grace caved. Sending a silent prayer that Robyn wasn't already asleep, she pulled out her cell phone, thankful to have her number handy.

Robyn answered immediately. "*Moshi moshi.*"

"Robyn?"

"Grace?"

Tears sprung to her eyes when Robyn said her name. "Thank you for answering."

"What's with the screaming in the background? Are you okay? Where are you?"

"Kristine swore the kids would stay asleep, and I'd just have to snooze on the couch. Obviously that plan failed. I hate to ask this of you, but Eliza woke up Caemon, and…I don't know what to do…If he can't have his moms, he wants you."

"Me?" she gasped. "What am I going to do?"

"I don't know, but if you would come, you'd at least even out the odds here." She dropped her voice to a whisper. "I think they know I'm outnumbered."

"Okay. Okay." Robyn sounded distracted. "I don't know how helpful I'll be, and it'll be at least fifteen, twenty minutes till I'm there. Will you be okay?"

"I hope. Caemon's just crumpled by the front door. Do I leave him there? Try to move him? I have no idea what to do here."

"I don't know either. Hang tight. I'll be there as fast as I can."

Figuring she wasn't comforting Eliza anyway, she set the baby in a bouncy chair and tried to comfort Caemon. "Robyn's coming. Will you sit with me on the couch until she gets here?"

"Want Robyn now."

"I know," she said, stumped as to what to do while she waited. Her phone rang and she prayed it wasn't Kristine calling to make sure everything was quiet. She could only imagine the panic a mother would feel hearing her children wailing in the background. Luckily, Robyn's name lit up the screen. "Robyn?"

"My friend said the less you engage Caemon, the better."

"What does that mean?"

"She said keeping him where it's dark is best and say as little as you can. Be a robot. Keep telling him I'm coming. She asked if the baby could be hungry."

"I only have one bottle, and she's not supposed to be hungry for another two hours."

"Pacifier?"

"She spits it out."

"Isabel said to do a half squat and on the way up, alternate turning to the right and left. She said it's golden. I'm on my way."

Grace crouched next to Caemon. "Robyn's coming." He kicked at her when she reached out to him. She retreated to the bedroom and found a blanket in his bed. She wrapped it around him and lifted him, carrying the screaming, kicking mass to the couch. "Robyn's coming, and we're waiting here on the couch. Robyn's coming."

He sank down onto the floor, but at least he was on the carpet, so Grace retrieved the baby and tried the bounce-and-sway Robyn had described. Remembering how her own grandfather had always sung "Edelweiss," she began to hum it. Eliza began to relax. Grace bounced and swayed and hummed and counted the minutes until she heard Robyn's car pull up at the curb.

Eliza lay quietly in her arms when she answered the door. Robyn came in without a word, just giving Grace a thumbs-up as she passed and found the crying boy.

"Hey, Caemon. Let's get you to your bed."

The boy stood and flung his arms around Robyn's neck. She picked up his blanket and carried him to his room.

Grace finally slumped into the rocker, her thighs burning from the unanticipated workout, praying its motion would keep the baby calm.

She didn't realize she had fallen asleep herself until she felt a touch on her shoulder. Painfully, she righted her neck, stiff from the angle of the chair. "What time is it?"

"Eleven thirty. Caemon's been out for a while. Want me to put her down?"

Grace yawned. "Is it bad if I keep holding her until it's closer to when she normally eats?"

"You're asking me?" Robyn smiled.

"How'd you get Caemon down?"

Robyn shrugged and lowered herself to the couch. "Just snuggled in next to him and tickled his arm with his blanket.

That seemed to do the trick." She chuckled to herself. "I asked him what he was doing up. You know what he said?"

"What?"

"'Because I a clever, clever boy.'"

Grace couldn't hold back a bark of laughter that startled the baby. "That he is. It got you here. You are so very kind to rescue me."

"What happened?"

"Gloria's mom is back in the hospital. Did you know she has leukemia?"

"Kristine told me she'd relapsed, but we've never talked in depth about it. Is it bad?"

"I think so." Grace's throat closed on her as she tried to relay the information Kristine had given her. "She's been ill for years, fortunately in remission for most of the time. But now she's not responding to anything. Gloria's been at the hospital all day with her mom and dad discussing what options are left. Kristine called me after she got the kids to sleep because she wanted to go be with them." She blinked back the sting of tears.

Robyn scooted forward to perch on the edge of the couch to stroke Grace's shoulder. "I'm sorry," she said.

"I barely know her," Grace said, trying to brush away the crushing feeling in her chest.

"I'm sorry about your mom." Robyn's hand stilled and Grace felt the weight of it and Robyn's words.

Grace buried her face in Eliza's soft swaddling blanket inhaling her soothing baby smell, trying to sidestep Robyn's observation. The baby stirred, and Grace asked Robyn if she would mind pulling the bottle out of the fridge to put in a bowl of warm water. She quickly changed Eliza's diaper and returned to the living room and sat on the couch.

Alone with Eliza in the quiet room, she puzzled at the blanket of grief that enveloped her. What she had assumed was feeling overwhelmed by the crying was really the feeling of her own loss returning as fresh as it had been when Leah called to break the news about their parents.

Robyn had called her friend for advice about the kids. Why hadn't she called her sister to ask what she could do? Only now that she had Tyler back was she finally aware of how her parents' death had fractured every aspect of her family.

Robyn returned with two bottles—milk for the baby and wine for herself and Grace. She wavered when she saw that Grace had switched seats but moved to cover her hesitation by handing over the baby's bottle. She sat to pour red wine into a glass. "Do you want any?"

Grace nodded, accepting the glass after Eliza settled in with her bottle. "How do you do that?"

"What?"

"You knew what was right for Tyler before I could see it. You knew I was upset about my mom before I did."

"Perspective, I guess." She sipped her wine.

Grace waited, sensing from Robyn's quiet that she had more to say.

"And my years in the coast guard. I saw my share of grief. I've seen how a new loss can intensify an old one."

"Maybe a sudden, unexpected loss is easier. You get that call and everything is changed. I can't imagine what it would be like not knowing whether you have a few days or a month, thinking each time you see them might be the last. I wish so badly that I'd been able to say goodbye, but for Gloria…How does she know when it's truly goodbye?"

"It's never easy."

"It feels wrong to sit here feeling jealous…"

"That she has the chance to say goodbye?"

"That she and her mother are so close. I wonder if Tyler hadn't been such a challenge…or if they hadn't gone to bail him out…if they were still here…Before Tyler came to live with me, I could go days without thinking about them. Now…" A gentle sob escaped, and she gulped air trying to quell the ache. "I had no idea I'd miss them more. I thought having Tyler with me would make me angry. I never expected this emptiness."

"It's more difficult to face grief, but it's the only way to make progress. If you turn from it, you let the grief push you and determine your path. It may be harder and more painful to deal with, but you're in control. Even if it doesn't feel like you're going anywhere, you are."

They sat in silence until Eliza drained her bottle and Grace propped her in her lap, tapping her back to help her burp. "I'm so grateful you drove over to help me."

"You sure look like you know what you're doing now," Robyn said.

Grace smiled. "Thank your friend for the bounce-and-sway."

"I will."

"I love babies, so I hope this won't come out sounding terrible, but I will be so glad to hand this little girl back over to her moms."

Robyn laughed appreciatively. "I have to admit I was wondering if you were sitting there wishing for your own baby."

"Not for a second," Grace said, catching Robyn's eye. So many feelings had surfaced that evening, yet she was still surprised by the intimacy she felt with Robyn. "I might be regretting that I didn't spend more time holding my niece and nephew when they were this little, but this doesn't make me want kids at all. You?" She tried to deliver the question casually.

"Nope. I'm too selfish with my time to have my own kids."

"You seem pretty generous with your time to me," Grace replied.

"On my own terms, though. Maybe you hadn't noticed."

Grace had noticed how much of her generosity involved her and her brother and wanted to take advantage of the evening to explore more fully how far that generosity might extend. "I'm going to risk putting this one back in her crib," she whispered.

Inside, her stomach was a storm of butterflies, but she tried to project a soothing calm, willing Eliza to sleep through the transfer to her crib. She silently cheered when Eliza sighed deeply and continued to sleep but stayed a moment more with her hand across the baby's shoulder making sure she was really asleep.

Disappointment flooded through her when she entered the living room to find Robyn standing with Kristine.

"All's quiet just like I left them?" she asked, a twinkle in her eye despite her otherwise weary state.

"Just like you left them," Grace agreed, letting go of her desire to snuggle in next to Robyn on the couch.

"So you called for company, not reinforcements." Kristine looked from one woman to the other.

"I'll never tell," Grace said, picking up her coat.

"How's your mother-in-law?" Robyn asked gently.

"They're talking about transferring her to hospice care."

"Oh, Kristine, I'm so sorry," Grace said.

"That's tough," Robyn agreed.

"I appreciate your help, both of you. I'll get the full story from Caemon in a few hours."

Grace hugged Kristine tight. "Thanks for calling me, and call again if you need anything. Anything at all."

"Tell Gloria we're thinking about her," Robyn said.

Kristine thanked them and saw them to the door.

Grace's mind was spinning. She walked out shoulder to shoulder with Robyn, resisting the urge to take her hand. She then chided herself for even thinking about it given the somber reason for their being there together in the first place.

CHAPTER THIRTY-THREE

Courage

Robyn cursed the short stretch of the path from house to car as she tried to organize her thoughts. She'd just been getting comfortable with Grace when Kristine got home. Kristine with her quirked eyebrow and teasing questions. She was probably watching the two of them from inside, which made Robyn feel like an unsure teenager.

Grace stopped at her car. She looked at the dark house and then back to Robyn. She placed her hand on Robyn's shoulder. "I feel really bad for Kristine and Gloria, but I have to say we managed pretty well."

Robyn flashed a smile. "Yeah," she said, distracted. Though it was after midnight, she didn't want the night to end. Talking about how neither one of them wanted to have a baby made her wonder what other desires they had in common. Right now she very much desired another kiss. She remembered the last one viscerally and regretted presuming that she already knew the kind of person Grace was.

Grace gave Robyn's arm a little squeeze before she let go to open her car door.

"I want..." Robyn stammered.

Grace paused, waiting for Robyn to continue.

"I don't want to go home," she said, feeling like an idiot when the words came out of her mouth. "I know it's late, but I..." Robyn felt like she was floundering in a wild sea hoping Grace would reach in and rescue her, yet Grace kept her hands to herself. Under the soft glow of the streetlamp, she waited. Robyn's insecurities laughed at her for even thinking about asking for what she wanted, noting Grace's flawless complexion, her styled hair and expensive coat.

She wanted to feel Grace's arms around her again, feel their bodies meeting in all the right places and melt into the heat of her kiss, but couldn't see what Grace would see in her, so opposite in poise and confidence.

Pushing past the tides of doubt, she took a tiny step. She reached for Grace. She bent to pull Grace to her, gasping at the satiny warmth of Grace's lips. Grace's hands quickly slipped through Robyn's hair, pulling her closer.

Robyn's arm curled around Grace's hips to anchor her body as the kiss swept her away.

Not letting go of her head, Grace pulled away enough to breathily ask, "You want..."

"More." Robyn sank back into the kiss.

She felt Grace's smile before she broke away again. Tipping her mouth out of reach she asked again, "You want?"

Robyn pulled back enough that she could see Grace's eyes. When she'd said *more*, she was thinking about how much she wanted to touch Grace. More skin. More contact. But she couldn't say that out loud. She should ask for a date, take her out. Her spinning thoughts slammed into the regretful memory of telling the beautiful woman in front of her that she'd already dated her. "I want to say I'm sorry for presuming things about you before I even knew you."

"Your eyes are telling me something very different, but I accept your apology." Grace captured Robyn's sensitive earlobe between her teeth. "What do you really want?"

Robyn inhaled sharply, tipping her chin into the soft warmth of Grace's neck. "For you to follow me home," she whispered. It was easier to say when she couldn't see Grace's reaction.

Grace answered her with a slow, searing kiss. "Drive. I'm right behind you."

CHAPTER THIRTY-FOUR

Touch

Robyn did her best to stretch to her bedside table to pull a stone out of her bowl without jostling the bed. A warm hand slipped around her hip and fanned across her stomach to pull her back into bed.

"You're not going anywhere," Grace mumbled.

"I wasn't even trying." Robyn glanced at her stone and smiled before placing it in the smaller bowl. She rolled back to Grace.

"What was that all about?" Grace propped herself up on her elbow.

"My morning meditation." Robyn took her stone's cue and ran her own palm over Grace's lovely curves, marveling at the beauty of her in the morning light. "I have stones that have words on them. Today I got *Touch*," she said huskily.

"I very much enjoy your touch."

"I'm so glad to hear that." Robyn's hands wandered more freely.

Grace's muscles fluttered under Robyn's attention. "How do I know this isn't some morning-after line you offer all the girls?"

"I never cheat."

Grace took a deep breath, and Robyn sensed her assessing her as well as the statement. A coy smile on her lips, she straddled Robyn to reach for the stone placed in one of the bowls on the small box next to Robyn's bed. It gave Robyn the gift of her full nakedness. Grace ran the pad of her thumb across the lettering on the stone. Robyn ran both hands from Grace's hips across her belly, teasing at the top of Grace's curls with her thumbs and earning her a soft smack from Grace. "Can I try?"

"Sure. Just don't get a little one." Robyn's hands traveled up Grace's belly, admiring her core muscles as she bent to take her own stone. Grace's leaning also afforded Robyn better access to her pale breasts which she brushed with her palms before pushing Grace's waves of hair past her shoulders. She didn't care where her hands were as long as they were somewhere on Grace.

"You just said you don't cheat."

"It's not cheating. It's just that the small ones are *Loss* and *Tears*. Or *God*. I never know what to do when I get *God*."

Grace spun the stone to read her meditation. Robyn watched Grace's expression as she held the stone's word secret from her. "I think you should stop rigging your selection." Seductively, she traced the stone from Robyn's clavicle between her breasts and rested it in Robyn's belly button.

She felt by the way it nestled perfectly that Grace had picked one she would have passed by. Brow furrowed in question, she peeked at the lettering. *Joy*.

"Prophetic," Grace said without any trace of teasing.

Gently, Robyn set Grace's stone next to her own, trying to remember how long her fear of loss and tears had caused her to avoid joy. The two stones would spend the day together, and she willed Grace to stay too. She pulled Grace into a kiss that made her body hum with the memory of their night of exchanged pleasures. As she rolled Grace back into the mess of sheets and blankets, her phone buzzed.

She glanced at the screen and said to Grace, "Kristine."

"Answer it."

Reluctant to interrupt her morning with Grace, she answered nevertheless. "*Moshi moshi.*" She pursed her lips as Kristine quickly updated her on how the kids slept, adding that it would make her life a hundred times easier if she didn't have to feed Bean.

"Consider it done." She smiled apologetically at Grace as she said goodbye.

"What's *moshi moshi*? You said that when I called from Kristine's."

Robyn ran her hand along the curve of Grace's hip. "It's how the Japanese answer their phones. Whenever I called here, my grandmother answered '*moshi moshi.*'"

Grace closed her eyes for a moment. "I like that." She opened her eyes, exploring Robyn's face. "Go."

"You're sure?" Robyn asked. She hated to leave so abruptly, especially with her body begging to linger with Grace's all day long.

"It sounds easier than babysitting." Grace looked at the clock. "And according to Kristine's schedule, you're already late."

Robyn laughed, remembering how she had watched Grace struggle to help her friend at the barn after Eliza was born. "You're welcome to join me."

"Oh, no. I don't see what fun you and Kristine see in the animals. I'm very happy where I am unless you were hoping to sneak me out the back door."

As Robyn backed down the steep ladder to her room, Grace stretched forward on her arms across the mattress. Robyn paused to kiss her once more. "I'd have to sneak you out via the rooftop if that was the case. Stay as long as you like. I'll be at least an hour."

Grace slumped her chin onto her crossed arms watching Robyn on her way down. "In that case, I'll get up in a few and forage for something to eat if that's okay."

"Anything you want." Robyn descended the rest of the way into her room to dress.

"Anything?" She peeked at Robyn alluringly from the loft.

Her question drove Robyn up the steps again where she stole another kiss. "What did you have in mind?"

"Meeting back here. I have to go to work tomorrow, and I haven't had nearly enough of you."

Robyn's head swam with desire and surprise. She couldn't wrap her mind around the fact that Grace was thinking exactly what she had imagined her day to be. A slow smile crept across her face.

"I can see what you're thinking. Go. The faster you go, the faster you're back."

"Agreed," Robyn said, finally wrenching herself away, stumbling as she hastily threw on clothes to get her feeding chores out of the way as soon as possible. She could hear Grace's laughter trail after her as she hit the stairs, taking them two at a time.

CHAPTER THIRTY-FIVE

Grace lay in Robyn's attic loft grinning like a schoolgirl. She closed her eyes and thought about where her morning would have gone had Robyn not had the horses. Exploring her own skin, she thought of how different Robyn's skilled woodworking hands felt against her body, how the lightest of touches made her tingle to her core. And her hands on Robyn's soft skin, how different it felt to traverse the same landmarks on another body taking in the strength of her arms, back, thighs. She needed to get up, get dressed, find something to eat, but all she could do was think about how they had created their own world with their arms around each other.

She skipped her bra, pulling on just her shirt, panties and slacks. Without Robyn to warm her, she shivered outside the covers and wished for a sweatshirt which she found on the last stair when she descended into Robyn's room. Touched, she pulled on both it and the thick socks Robyn had left and crept down the main staircase to the house's first floor.

Someone was in the kitchen bustling about and making Grace feel shy. If it was Jen, she'd have some explaining to do. If it was another tenant she hadn't met... She hated having to face anyone at all in her morning-after glow, and put it off by using the bathroom at the bottom of the stairs first.

Bladder relieved, hands and face washed, she had no more excuses and breezed into the kitchen doing her best to project Robyn's invitation to make herself at home.

"Morning," Jen said without a hint of surprise. "Hungry?"

"I thought I'd make some toast."

"Best to use the loaf right there on the counter." She rummaged in a drawer. "Here's the bread knife. Butter? Jam?"

Grace accepted the knife. "Both, thanks."

"Tea or coffee?"

"You don't have to play hostess," Grace said, feeling like she was intruding.

"It's no problem. I know where everything is."

"This isn't a little weird?"

"It's great. Robyn looked pretty darned happy on her way out of here."

"Can we not talk about this?"

Smiling, Jen set down the butter and jam. "Okay. You want to talk about rehearsal?"

"No. That would be even weirder." The toaster popped, and Grace frowned at the product, toasted only on one side. "Your toaster is broken."

"You gotta flip it around to toast the other side," Jen said. "But count to fifteen and then pop it. Otherwise it'll burn."

Grace flipped the toast and started scanning the open-faced cupboards in search of a teacup.

"Mugs are to the left of the sink."

While Grace extracted a mug from a precariously-jammed shelf full of mugs of all shapes and sizes, Jen popped her toast. "Thanks," she said, accepting that Jen wasn't going to play along with her wanting to be unobtrusive. "Teabags?"

"Second shelf to the left of the mugs. Kettle's already hot."

While she buttered her toast, Grace weighed how impolite it would be to carry her breakfast upstairs to escape Jen's company.

Having brewed two cups of tea, Jen stood poised with her bowl of yogurt and granola. "The sun's out. I'm taking my breakfast out back."

Sucking up her desire to be alone, Grace took her own plate and tea and walked outside. The view from the back porch stopped her short. Whenever she drove to campus, she admired the Humboldt State University buildings nestled in the redwood forest, and that was the scene that greeted Robyn every time she stepped out of her home.

"Nice, isn't it?"

"Redwood forest from the back porch, the bay from your studio: what a place!"

"I know. I may never leave." Jen sat in one of two plastic chairs under a tree. Grace sat next to her.

"Are these fruit trees?"

"This one is a Bing cherry," Jen confirmed. "Another month or so, and we'll be in heaven. Like I said, never leaving!"

"What's in the raised beds?" Grace asked.

Jen launched into a list of what Robyn grew and how generous she was to share so much of her harvest with the tenants, and somehow turned the conversation to music. So when Robyn returned from the stable and found the two of them still together, Grace had entirely forgotten her unease and smiled warmly, welcoming her back.

Robyn walked right to Grace's chair, resting her hand on Grace's shoulder. "Success in the kitchen?"

"With Jen's help," Grace said.

Jen stood. "See you later this week, or...around." She waggled her eyebrows, gathered both of their dishes and disappeared.

Robyn sat in the vacated chair. "Has it been okay?"

"Only a little awkward."

Robyn reached for Grace's hand, resting it on her thigh. "You have on way more clothes than I pictured."

"I'm sure you weren't picturing me in your backyard. I hope you weren't picturing me naked in your backyard," she revised.

"No. I didn't know you'd have breakfast with Jen."

"It seemed rude not to, and it was fine. If we were at my place, we'd have Tyler."

She was just about to ask Robyn about her idea to spend the day in bed when a pale young man in blue surgical scrubs entered the yard through the gate. He wore his short, dark hair spiked off his forehead and a tidy mustache.

He smiled brightly when he saw them. "Nice day for it."

"Isaac, this is Grace. Grace, Isaac."

Isaac's gaze lingered on Grace for longer than she was comfortable. "Enjoy it for me." He climbed the second set of stairs that had puzzled Grace the evening she had found Robyn in her shop.

Robyn squeezed her hand. "Sorry."

Grace wondered if she was sorry for the interruption, for how he'd looked at her or for what his words insinuated. "How many tenants do you have?" she asked.

"One more. Sergio has the room downstairs."

"I didn't even know there was a room downstairs."

"Across from the living room. He keeps his door closed."

"So three tenants." Spending the day with Robyn took on an entirely different feel.

Robyn rubbed the web between Grace's thumb and forefinger. "You're regretting your decision to stay."

Grace appreciated that Robyn wasn't asking, that she could sense the shift in her mood. She took a breath, quieting the disappointment she felt.

"How about we walk up to the redwoods?" Robyn suggested.

"There are trails behind campus aren't there?"

"And the community forest. We can walk from here."

"Like go on a date?"

Robyn swept Grace's hair back to expose her neck, tickling the sensitive skin behind her ear. "Probably a good thing to go on a date before I drag you back to bed, don't you think?"

"Who says you're doing the dragging?" Grace stood and pulled Robyn from her chair and into a kiss.

"Okay. I'll let you take a turn dragging. Does that mean I get you the whole day?"

"I told Tyler I'd be home for lunch, but I didn't make any promises about being home tonight."

"Nice that you can just tell him to fend for himself?"

"Indeed," Grace said, recalling what a relief it had been to walk away from Kristine's little ones the evening before. But even though her brother didn't depend on her like an infant or toddler, she still felt the responsibility of caring for him. That complicated how she'd rather spend her time.

CHAPTER THIRTY-SIX

Confidence

"You don't have to do this."

"I want to see what the fuss is about," Grace said. "And now that I've seen you in your breeches, I'd follow you anywhere."

"Very funny."

"I'm not kidding. Those pants are something else."

She slid her hand along the taut nylon stretch of Robyn's blue riding breeches before Robyn could duck into Bean's stall to hide her embarrassment. Barb had never commented on her body or openly talked about being attracted to her at all. She smiled to herself. Then again, Barb had never seen her in her riding attire. She haltered Bean and led him to the crossties. "Here's your mount."

Not hiding her disapproving scowl Grace crossed her arms. "Why do I have to ride the funny-looking one? Yours is so much prettier."

"Bean is gorgeous. Most people would much rather have the paint than the boring bay."

"But look at his face."

"What?"

"He has funny ears."

"He's a mule, you know? He's supposed to have long ears." Robyn pulled out a curry and brush and made quick work of the grooming, so she could saddle them.

"Kristine owns a mule?" Robyn could hear the dubiousness in Grace's voice.

"Her family breeds them over in Quincy, and their crosses are exceptional. This one is out of a champion barrel racer. You've seen her, right? Kristine said you helped her sell the series of photos she took of Dani riding Bean's dam. We met her at Kristine's birthday."

"Fine. You're so impressed, you ride it."

"You'll change your mind when you see the saddles," Robyn predicted. She finished picking out the animals' hooves and outfitted them with their tack.

"Okay, you're right. I want the big saddle," Grace said after Robyn had finished putting her English saddle on her mare and lugged Kristine's western saddle out of her shed. "Can't you put that on Taj instead?"

"Kristine's saddle is the one set up for Bean. It's got a breast collar and a crupper."

"That means nothing to me," Grace said.

Robyn laughed, taking a moment to admire how nice Grace looked. "Do you know why Kristine lent you her boots and jeans?"

"She said my jeans were supposed to go over the boot, not the other way around."

"But it's also the inseam. On Wranglers, the thinner seam runs along the inside of your leg, not the outside. It's the opposite on your jeans which makes them less comfortable to ride in. The animal has to be comfortable too. This leather bit around the front keeps the saddle from sliding back. And this bit in back, the crupper, keeps if from slipping too far forward. That keeps Bean comfortable."

"Everything you're saying just makes me think that a horse is much easier than a mule."

"Taj has a wider girth than Bean which is one reason Bean's a very comfortable ride. He also has an incredibly smooth gait."

"How do you know all of this?"

"I asked all the questions you're asking, and Kristine made us swap rides one day. Don't worry. I don't think anyone you know will see you."

"If we do, you're responsible for explaining why my mount is superior."

"Deal. You ready to roll?"

"Sure."

They walked to the covered arena, and Robyn checked the saddles one more time before helping Grace from the mounting block into the saddle. She shortened the stirrups, letting her hands wander up Grace's shapely calves as she did so.

"Now I see why you invited me along, not just to show off your fancy pants." Grace smiled, her eyes lingering on Robyn's hands.

Robyn felt her body flush. She pulled on her helmet, swung onto her own mount and directed Grace to follow her around the arena. After circling a few times, she asked Grace if she wanted to try trotting with Bean.

"I like this speed," she replied. "Go ahead and show off. I'll just keep circling."

Robyn nudged Taj into a trot. She serpentined and broke away into smaller circles. Taj was a different creature in the arena than on the trail. She arched her neck and responded to the smallest of cues for each turn and shift in gait.

As they worked, Robyn's mind shifted from the flirtatious exchanges with Grace to her mount's past. She imagined Penelope's workouts, knowing from her trainer that she was an accomplished jumper. Robyn had taken the mare over some simple cross poles but was not experienced enough to work the mare to her full potential.

Alone, she would have worked Taj longer, but knowing how little Grace rode, she cut her ride short, falling in alongside Bean.

"So this is what you do, go around in circles? I can't say I see the draw."

"Kristine hardly ever does any arena work. We ride trails or take the horses to the beach."

"I could maybe wrap my head around a ride on the beach."

"But it's not your first choice for how to relax."

"I'll admit a book and a glass of wine appeals to me more, but I could watch you all day."

Robyn smiled at the reins in her hands, not sure how to respond to Grace's attention. "Let's take them in." As she expected, Grace groaned loudly as she dismounted and gimped beside Robyn as they led the animals back to the stalls.

As Robyn pulled the bridles and saddles off, Grace grabbed her ankles and did several squats. "I've got a great idea. Let's hit those hot tubs at Café Mokka after dinner tonight."

"I have a hot tub at the house," Robyn said.

"Even better!" Grace looked significantly more animated.

"We'll have to do it tomorrow, though. Mine heats by woodstove, so I need the whole afternoon to get it ready."

Grace stared at her. "Then let's go to the ones in town."

"Your muscles will appreciate it more tomorrow anyway." Robyn answered, stepping into the tack room. When she turned around after stowing her saddle, Grace blocked the doorway, hands back on her hips.

"My treat." She didn't move to let Robyn by.

Robyn balked, thrown by how quickly Grace had pegged her discomfort. She and Barb had argued about money so much that the topic seemed like a minefield. "You're not very patient, are you?"

"Not true. I gave you time to figure out you liked me," she teased. She stepped into the dark of the tack room and slid her arms around Robyn's waist. "And I'll tell you right now I like to go out. I love restaurants, theater, seeing music live. I like to spend money, and I can see how that makes you put up your wall." Her hands slid down around Robyn's rear and she leaned in to kiss the spot on Robyn's neck that always made her quiver. "But I live within my means. Don't worry about money. Let me treat."

"Impatient and persuasive."

"Which goes a long way when I'm convincing people to part with their money to support the arts."

"I'd like to see you in action sometime," Robyn said, imagining Grace working her charm.

"Well, you're in luck. I've gotten in touch with Ruth Mountaingrove and she suggested that we talk about her work over dinner. I was going to ask you to be my date."

"I'd love to meet her."

"I'm going to enjoy getting you out."

"Can I say I'll enjoy getting you to stay in?"

Grace smiled radiantly. "I certainly see the merit of staying in."

CHAPTER THIRTY SEVEN

Passion

"Thanks for letting me borrow the truck," Tyler said, holding up the keys.

Robyn cut the power to her lathe and ran her hand over the largest of the nesting bowls she would get out of the huge burl she and Isabel had pulled off the beach. She was close to having the rough spin finished and was pleased not to find any cracks or holes that sometimes plagued the bigger pieces. "Anytime," she said, pocketing them. "Did you have any luck?"

"I picked up a great set for next to nothing. They hardly need any sanding at all. No priming like I've had to do on those first ones from the estate sale."

"Do you want a hand carrying them in?"

"Sure." His eyes sparkled as he turned to walk back out to the street with a definite bounce in his step.

It pleased Robyn to encourage the greenhouse project, and he'd made great progress by visiting the recycling center and hitting more estate sales. With his latest acquisition, he could probably begin the process of framing the house and fitting in the hodgepodge of old windows he'd collected.

"Are you going to work on them tonight?" she asked when they'd carried in the last of the windows.

"No. First thing tomorrow. I…I've got other plans tonight." He glanced away. "I've actually got to get going."

Robyn swung the doors of the garage shut. "I'm calling it a night too." They walked in silence to the house, Robyn turning at the steps to her back door, and Tyler continuing to the gate.

"I do appreciate it," Tyler said just as Robyn was about to step inside.

"You're welcome." She smiled and walked to the kitchen sink to wash her hands. She breathed deeply the smell of something wonderful cooking. The kitchen was cozy from the warmth of the oven, and something both sweet and spicy made her mouth water.

On the walk in front of the kitchen window, Tyler shut the gate and turned toward the street. Something caused a pause in his step. Sergio, a wiry Latino, strode toward the house, glancing briefly at Tyler as they passed. Sergio's expression went from curiosity to annoyance in an instant. Tyler zipped his coat and regained his long stride, stuffing his hands deep in his pockets. Sergio stopped, turning to watch Tyler as he made a left at the sidewalk and headed toward town. He stood rooted until Tyler was out of sight before he shook his head and continued toward the house.

Curious, Robyn turned off the tap. She had no context for the animosity she had read in Sergio, yet the interchange puzzled her. Did Tyler and Sergio know each other?

Reaching for a towel to dry her hands, she stopped at a new shiny steel bucket sitting on her counter. She lifted the lid and found it empty. A pot of chili simmered on the stove.

She reached for a spoon and startled when arms slipped around her middle.

"Sorry I scared you," Grace murmured, pressing her body against Robyn's back.

"I was distracted by all this." She gestured to the stove.

"Hope you don't mind that I took over the kitchen."

"What happened to the scraps?"

"I took them to the compost. And I got you this." She gestured toward the compost bin.

Robyn was mystified. She was the only one who ever tended the compost.

"Is something wrong? Did I overstep?"

Robyn faced Grace and wrapped her arms around her. "No. Not at all. Compost just seems a lot like barn duty which, as I recall, you foisted on me."

"I felt pretty confident the gross stuff would stay at the end of the pitchfork."

"Are you finished with rehearsal already?"

"I had to pull out the corn bread. I didn't know if you'd be in yet. But we just called it a night. We're more than ready for the wedding this weekend." She leaned in and kissed Robyn soundly. "I've been thinking about you," she murmured when she drew away.

Grace's words even more than the kiss sent a shiver of desire through Robyn. "Have you?"

"All day," Grace confirmed. She pulled Robyn's polo from her jeans and slipped her hands underneath to caress Robyn's smooth stomach. "The way I see it, we have two options. The corn bread is ready. We could serve up the chili and sit right down to eat."

"Or?"

"Or we can let the chili continue to simmer while we work up an appetite." The kiss that followed gave a strong hint of what Grace thought was the right answer. When Robyn's feet failed to convey her level of interest, Grace cupped Robyn's breasts, her thumbs teasing the nipples.

The sound of feet on the stairs broke them apart. Grace frowned and refused to let go of Robyn right away. "If it weren't for your having tenants, I'd have my hand down your pants right now to find out how effective that kiss was." For emphasis she gently traced up the seam of Robyn's jeans, following it to her center.

Robyn's heart pounded with desire and amazement. The two of them were still so new as a couple that Grace's advances caught her off guard. Of course, the years of complicated foreplay with Barb had programmed her to think that the kind of kiss Grace had just given her was only appropriate in a bedroom. Sex happened in a bed at bedtime. To suggest something else, especially out loud, would have only served to shut Barb down and put her in a black mood that could last for days.

"Whatever you're thinking...stop." Grace took her hand and led her toward the stairs. She gripped tighter, preventing Robyn's escape, when they met a bright-eyed Jen in the foyer having seen the other musicians out. "Chili's on the stove if you want some."

She offered no more as she took the steps, leading Robyn exactly to where she wanted her. Robyn's head felt full as she welcomed all the new truths of her life. This woman wanted her without question or condition. In Robyn's room, Grace closed the door and made quick work of stripping off her clothes.

Robyn pulled off her polo slowly, mesmerized not only by the beautiful bounty of Grace's skin but also her absolute comfort in her nakedness. She dropped her shirt and reached for Grace.

"Not so fast." Grace clucked her tongue. "You're way behind." She helped by unclasping Robyn's bra, stroking from shoulder to wrist with her fingertips as she removed it.

"I'm always playing catch-up with you."

Grace ran her hands up Robyn's bare chest and lowered her head to suck one nipple as she caressed the other. She unbuttoned Robyn's jeans and pushed them off her hips. "Not this time," she said, backing Robyn to the loft steps. "This time you're first."

Robyn stopped when her naked rear touched the step behind her. She lifted a foot to climb, thinking only about getting to her bed, but Grace stilled her with a hand on her thigh and she realized Grace had no intention of letting her move. Keeping her perched against the step, Grace pulled down Robyn's jeans, her eyes locked with Robyn's. She knelt to free Robyn's legs.

Her hands returned after she discarded the jeans, warm and sure on Robyn's calves.

At Robyn's knees, Grace's hands pivoted, her thumbs now pushing at the insides of Robyn's thighs. Robyn tipped her head back, losing herself in Grace's touch. Grace pushed Robyn's thighs apart and hot breath joined the path to Robyn's core. Robyn shivered as Grace's thumb traced through her wetness, and she was helpless to hold back a groan when Grace followed the path of her thumb with her tongue.

"You are so ready," Grace purred, slipping a finger inside.

Robyn hissed with pleasure as Grace teased her, and she grew hungry for more. In bed, she would have raised her hips to ask, but she'd never been in this position before. She held onto the sides of the steps, testing whether she could lower herself.

"Oh, that's better," Grace said, slipping her left hand around Robyn's ass and entering further with her right.

Robyn opened her mouth to agree, but there were no more words, only hot and wet and deep, her orgasm crashing through her like an unexpected storm. She gave herself over to the waves pounding through her. When she finally stilled, Grace was there in front of her, tracing her body, kissing her with lips heavy with her own scent. "That was a bad plan," she finally managed.

"What was wrong with my plan?" Grace demanded, humor in her voice as she continued to pet Robyn's curves, teasing the curls between her legs.

"My legs are useless now. I can't move."

"I think you can with the right motivation." Grace leaned forward and reached for the stair behind Robyn, her breasts brushing Robyn's face. She found the step behind Robyn's back and raised herself up, offering Robyn her belly.

Robyn realized where the next step would put Grace's body in relationship to her mouth, but instead of pausing and giving Robyn a chance to taste her, Grace shimmied the rest of the way into the loft. Laughing, Robyn spun around and made haste to follow.

"Glad to see I can motivate you." She lay seductively on the mattress, her body an open gift.

Robyn moved between her legs, matching the landscape of her body to Grace's. Grace groaned appreciatively when Robyn found her clit with her own and started to grind. She raised her legs and pulled Robyn closer. Robyn wished she could slip inside Grace, but Grace held on so tightly, all she could do was continue rocking. She lowered her lips to Grace's neck and nipped at Grace's earlobes and neck. Grace's stomach muscles quivered beneath her as she came.

"That hardly seems fair. I didn't even get to touch you."

"But I love where you are." She gripped Robyn's rear more tightly. "I'd love it even more if you were inside of me. Next time maybe we could add a little something."

Robyn lifted her body, so Grace could lower her legs.

"No?" Grace asked hesitantly.

"Yes. Yes, absolutely. I...I'm sorry. I'm just getting used to all this."

Grace shifted to her side and ran her hand along Robyn's hip. "You were in a relationship for years. How is sex something to get used to?"

"I never knew sex could be fun. It was always loaded with all sorts of other emotions, but it was never like this. It was never fun."

Grace's hand stilled. Then tenderly, she traced Robyn's face. Robyn drew back a little, thinking that Grace was going to pity her or worse ask why she never demanded more. Grace surprised her by saying simply, "She was an idiot." Then she added, "and I'm hungry. For more of this, you can be sure, but first food." She threw herself back on the bed dramatically. "If only you didn't have tenants. How can you stand sharing your home with all of these people, not being able to walk to your kitchen naked if you want to?"

"I don't imagine you're walking around your house naked these days."

"No, but that's a recent development." She raised herself up on her elbows. "And not permanent."

"What's he up to tonight anyway? He said that he had plans."

"I don't know. I guess I should give him a call and check in." She sighed deeply and started to sit up.

Robyn stayed her with a hand on her chest, still amazed by how easy it was to touch her. "Stay. I'll grab dinner and bring it up. I'll bring your phone too."

Grace immediately lay back down. "You're a goddess. I promise to make it worth your while."

"I'm sure you will," Robyn bantered, trying unsuccessfully to wipe the huge grin from her face. She took a deep breath to compose herself as she hurriedly threw on her clothes, anxious to hold Grace to her promise.

CHAPTER THIRTY-EIGHT

"Ruth, that's wonderful news. I'm so glad you convinced him to join us," Grace said on the phone, adding another community photographer to her growing list of local artists traveling to the San Francisco Art Exhibition. The college had been reluctant to support her travel request for a trip to the city, but she'd argued convincingly that the talented artists could drum up interest and enrollment for the campus. Dropping Ruth's name as one of the artists she was prepared to bring had helped, and she smiled at the recollection of how pleasant it had been to meet her over a business dinner.

Even better had been Robyn's interest in joining them. She wondered if Ruth might be able to persuade Robyn to join the artists taking their wares to the city. Her cell buzzed insistently in her purse. She stretched to reach her bag to silence it as she fielded Ruth's travel and accommodation questions.

Aaron waved from the door, trying to direct her attention to the flashing light on her phone that told her yet another call demanded her attention. She closed her eyes to give Ruth her full attention as she wrapped up the call.

Eyes still closed, she hit the phone's cradle with her hand and counted to ten knowing that when she released it, she'd have her sister to deal with.

"What kind of bullshit is that leaving a cryptic message and then promptly shutting off your phone? Who does that?" Leah huffed.

"I thought we could talk while I drove into work, but once I got here, I actually had work. It's probably nothing," Grace said, jumping right into the conversation.

"What did he lie about?"

"Being at home. I think."

"What do you mean, you think?" Leah demanded.

"I wasn't at home when I called him. He said he was there, and he was there when I got home, but I was...a little late getting home."

"I can see a band rehearsal going late, but string quartet? You really lose track of time like that with strings?"

Grace bit her lip. Her message had been cryptic because she hadn't told Leah about Robyn.

"Grace?"

"I..." She heard a rap at her door. Kristine waved and then thumbed behind herself, asking if Grace wanted her to leave. Grace stilled her with an outstretched palm that she promptly pressed to her forehead. "I wasn't practicing. Robyn and I..."

"Shit. Robyn's your girlfriend? When were you thinking of sharing that tidbit? How long have you been seeing her?"

"Leah, I know you're not going to believe me, but I've got a professor here who needs to speak with me. Can I call you later? I really just need your take on Tyler."

"The longer it takes to call me, the more personal the questions are going to be."

She clicked off before Grace could argue, and she blushed remembering the details of her night.

"Is everything all right?" Kristine asked.

Replacing the phone in its cradle, Grace gathered her wits. The stress of having responsibility for Tyler, her blossoming romance with Robyn and the big spring show to pull off, she felt like a tangled mess inside. Work. She had to push all of the other things aside and do her job. Snatching up her pen, she said, "Great news from Ruth Mountaingrove. She's convinced one of her sculptor friends to round out our community artists. Do you have the final list of photography students joining us?"

Kristine crossed her arms and quirked her eyebrow as if she were deciding whether to accept Grace's non sequitur. She rolled off the doorjamb and dropped into Grace's office chair, ticking through the list of students she had cleared to go.

Thankful for the distraction, Grace tallied the numbers and dove into the myriad event details. "And remember that I need completed field trip forms from every student attending whether they're driving on their own or taking the..." She visualized the yellow vehicle she had ordered to carry those students lacking transportation. She searched her memory for the word, her brain simply frozen. She hadn't distracted it at all. She had merely overextended it to the point where she stared dumbly at Kristine. Admitting defeat, she rested her head on her desk.

"That was a good run there," Kristine said. "You need to talk about the number of students taking the *bus*, or are you ready to lay out the other stuff?"

"You already know part of it," Grace mumbled into the desk.

"I'm guessing there have been some rolls in the hay. What happened to Robyn not being ready for you?"

"I think your children convinced her otherwise."

"Oh, ho! That night you two watched the kids? Caemon told me Robyn really was there because he asked for her, not because you wanted her company."

"I wanted her there, but I wouldn't have asked. I didn't use your son, I promise. It really was his idea."

"Well?" Kristine said, waiting. "You're killing me."

Grace eyed the doorway not wanting to talk within earshot of Aaron. "How about an early lunch?"

Kristine rubbed her hands together. "I like the way you think. The bagel place?"

"You can't be serious. What if Meg's there."

"Right. Sorry."

"Let's go into Northtown. There's this great funky little place." Grace stood and shrugged into her stylish reversible black and white polka-dot raincoat, having eventually noticed that no one carried an umbrella even though the rain seemed to be constant.

"A place Robyn showed you which happens to be in walking distance."

Grace swung her purse wide, but Kristine's reflexes were too fast. She ducked to avoid the blow. "Not here."

"Yes, ma'am," Kristine said with her most convincing cowgirl drawl.

They walked side by side down the road to a wooden flight of stairs that led to a footbridge spanning Highway 101, a route now very familiar to Grace since Robyn's house was only a few blocks away. She had quickly learned to love walking to work after she'd stayed the night with Robyn.

Kristine broke the silence. "A lot of family drama?"

Grace tipped her head thinking to catch Kristine's eye, but she walked head down, her eyes on her feet, her hands stuffed in her coat pockets. Kristine had acknowledged that she'd gleaned Grace's other distraction, but her posture conveyed that she wasn't trying to intrude. She didn't want to dismiss Kristine's invitation to expand the scope of their friendship but also felt like she needed to keep that aspect of her life close. "My brother's living with me for a while. You get to figure your kids out as they grow. I got thrown into this...I'm still trying to get my bearings."

Kristine chuckled. "I don't think any of the tricks I've learned would be very helpful for a grownup. I assume he's a grownup."

"He's twenty-three, yes."

"Yeah, I don't see you being able to pull off 'Do you want to walk yourself or have Mama carry you.'"

"No, it's been a long time since I could carry Tyler."

They walked in silence, and Grace admired the graffitied underpass, the huge singular eye, the rainbows, every inch covered in caricatures and tags. Approaching voices pulled her attention away from her favorite part of the walk, and she found herself walking straight toward one of Robyn's tenants. Sergio was with a gaggle of drama students and immediately slowed as their eyes met. He looked away, and Grace hoped they could pass without comment. Sharing space with Robyn's tenants unsettled her and she found most encounters with them awkward.

Kristine's voice startled her. "Hey, Martinez."

They both looked at Kristine.

"Oh. Hey Professor Owens." His expression relaxed for a moment before he shyly glanced back at Grace. "Hi...uh..." He waved awkwardly from the hip, added another "hi" and thankfully passed without saying anything else.

"What was that about," Kristine said with amusement.

"I might have seen more...well, we might have seen more than we want...of each other."

Kristine simply raised her eyebrow.

"He is Robyn's tenant. His room is right next to the bathroom..." Grace paused, again considering how much to share. "I think he used my razor."

Kristine doubled over laughing. "Now we get details!" She flung her arm around Grace's shoulder. "This is going to be fun!"

CHAPTER THIRTY-NINE

Believe

Grace sat on her back porch, her back to Robyn, cello between her knees and lost in song. Robyn leaned against the house, watching Grace play, fascinated by the movement of her left hand that produced a rich tremolo for her audience of cows. Three of them were staring at her, one tipped down on its knee to reach under the fence for the long grass that grew on Grace's side. She thought it impolite for the one cow to be foraging instead of watching Grace, appreciating the way her body became part of the music. Grace held her arm extended over the cello after the last long note ended and seemed lost in thought. Robyn hated to break the spell. Even the breeze off the ocean seemed to be rippling the flowing grass in the field beyond Grace's porch as gently as possible. Red curls that had escaped Grace's hairclip gleamed under the setting sun and danced on her shoulder.

"You look like a fairy princess lost in a dream," Robyn finally said.

"Oh!" Grace spun around, her bowing hand pressed to her chest. She glanced at her watch. "You're early."

Robyn gestured to the cows. "If they're expecting another, I'm happy to wait."

"Look at them. Always unimpressed. No matter what I play, they have the same expression, chew with that same bored look."

"I wasn't bored at all. The piece you just played is beautiful. What was it?"

"'The Swan.' I still haven't figured out how to make it soar. When it's done right, it's as graceful as a swan gliding, floating on the surface of the water. But under all that is the powerful energy that goes unseen beneath the water. That's what propels the swan forward, but you're not meant to see it."

"Like 'The Ugly Duckling.' During the winter, he has to keep swimming in circles to keep the pond from freezing, but come spring, what the children see is how graceful and beautiful he is."

"I don't remember that part."

Robyn felt Grace assess her in a new way. "My papa and I found this great volume of Andersen's original tales once." She slipped into a memory of her grandfather explaining used bookstores, how he never went in with an idea of what he wanted, rather waiting to see what the bookstore had for him. Sifting for treasures was how he'd described it.

"Which is still on your bookshelf, and if we were at your place, you'd have your finger on the spine already, wouldn't you?" Grace pushed the endpin into the cello and loosened the bow, a smile playing on her lips.

Robyn agreed. "And I'd find that scene and start reading, and you'd be so charmed by his words, I'd keep reading all the way to the end."

"Next time I'm there, you have to read the whole thing aloud to me. I'd love that."

"Happy to." Robyn followed Grace through the back door and waited for her to stow her cello in its case. "You don't play that piece with the quartet, do you?"

"No. How do you know that?"

A shy smile crept across Robyn's lips. "I sometimes sit in my room and listen to you practice."

"And yet you're always downstairs when we're clearing out." She slipped into Robyn's arms. "Thank you for coming here for dinner tonight."

"I finally get to see your place," Robyn said. Grace stepped away to take dinner out of the oven while Robyn explored the living room, stroking the white leather lounge suite and examining the artfully arranged books and photographs on the thick white floating shelves. Robyn wondered if Tyler had made them. "It suits you."

"How so?"

"Little things, the bright red chairs on the front porch are clearly your accent. You have nice things, and everything matches, like you. I wear clothes. You wear outfits, usually."

Grace gave a throaty laugh. "I thought I was going to have time to change."

Robyn appreciated the faded jeans and new Humboldt State sweatshirt that Grace was wearing. "What you wore the day you came to the barn to take care of Bean wasn't this relaxed."

"So you were watching me." Grace tilted her head.

"Who wouldn't?"

"Exactly why I always take care to look presentable, even if I'm just running to the corner grocery."

"I like this."

"And I, this." Grace ran her fingers along Robyn's shoulders. "You're the one wearing an outfit tonight. Such a lovely sweater, but it would be even better showing off more of you." She eased the zippered front down a few inches.

Robyn was glad for the extra care she had taken in pressing her pants and choosing her sweater. "Isabel bought it for me years ago."

"Tell her I approve of her taste. And I'm guessing you pressed these yourself." She ran her hand down to Robyn's thigh, sparking every nerve ending she touched.

"Military training pays off."

"It certainly does. I like that you dressed up tonight." Grace's eyes sparkled.

"All for you."

Grace nipped Robyn's neck below her ear. "For me to take off," she whispered.

Robyn sucked in a deep breath when Grace's hands touched down and began exploring.

"Please allow me to outline the benefits of not having tenants."

"What about Tyler?"

"Out."

"Will I need to take notes?"

"I have a PowerPoint you can print out later," Grace assured.

* * *

Lying in bed, Grace propped herself up on an elbow. "Hungry?"

"Insatiable."

"For food."

"That is what you promised tonight," Robyn said, though she didn't move, enjoying the weight of Grace's leg draped over her own. She traced the freckles below Grace's collarbone, trying to find a constellation.

Abruptly, Grace sat up and swung over to straddle Robyn. "You said you'd promise to think about the San Francisco Art Exhibition."

"I haven't had a chance to check it out," Robyn said. She'd had plenty of time but had no interest in joining artists from the college and community. While she was thrilled for the opportunity it offered Humboldt County's artists, she had no desire to be seen on a larger scale.

"Here." Grace eased off Robyn and crossed the room to grab her laptop.

Robyn rolled to her side to get a better view of the curves she loved. "You'd be the perfect subject for a sketch class."

Grace sashayed her tush as she quickly navigated the Internet before carrying the computer back to the bed. "The groups of students I've run into in your living room, sometimes it feels like that's what I'm walking into."

Sensing seriousness in Grace's tone, Robyn scrounged her clothes and slipped into them. "I didn't know they bothered you."

"Lucky for you they're theater nerds, not sketch artists," she said, her voice slightly less tight. "Take a look at the Art Exhibition site while I plate dinner." She reached for her jeans and then stopped. "Shall I put on what I was going to wear tonight?" She cocked her hip awaiting Robyn's reply.

"No. Those jeans are incredibly sexy."

With a brisk nod, Grace dressed and left the room.

Unsettled by Grace's shifting mood, Robyn carried the laptop to the table, scrolling through testimonials of artists who attributed the San Francisco Art Exhibition to the launch of their successful careers.

"Take a look at this," Grace said, placing Robyn's plate in front of her and clicking to a photo gallery of lathe-spun wooden bowls. "What do you think?"

The pictures were beautiful, but Robyn preferred to hold a bowl to assess it. So much of its beauty lay in the shape and weight, the feel and finish of the product. "Impressive." She folded the laptop and pulled her plate toward her.

When Grace returned with her own plate, she frowned. "I was going to show you where Ruth's photographs are."

"Now that I know where it is, I'll look it up at home."

Headlights lit up the curtains next to the table, and Robyn leaned over to lift the edge.

"What are you doing?" Grace whispered.

"I just want to see who Tyler's hanging out with. Male? Female? Aren't you curious?"

"Stop. What if he sees you?"

"His head is in the car. He can't see me, and you'll never learn anything if you don't spy a little." When Grace reached across the table and smacked her hand, she dropped the curtain, surprised.

"Who else are you spying on?"

"The baby dyke who has been hanging around the house waiting for Jen's lessons to finish."

"Aren't you the classic Mother Hen."

"It's not like Jen has volunteered anything. She's playing it close to her chest, saying they're just enjoying each others' company."

"Hey sis, Robyn," Tyler interrupted as he beelined to the kitchen to study the contents of the refrigerator.

"There's still some ziti in the pan," Grace offered.

Tyler's eyes lit up. "Can I kill it?"

"Sure."

"Those the guys you met up at the theater?" Robyn asked as casually as she could.

Tyler popped the ziti in its dish into the microwave and poured a large glass of milk.

"How did you already know who was in the car?" Grace asked.

"You guys are spying on me?" Tyler sounded wounded.

"One of my tenants said that he saw you up at the theater. He was surprised to recognize you at the house a few weeks back."

"Oh, yeah. I thought since they make sets up there they might be tossing stuff I could use. I got some good lumber, and they offered to show me around town when I said I just moved here. Any good estate sales coming up?" he said, changing the subject.

"None I'm interested in. My shed's about maxed out on space," Robyn answered, wondering how to bend the topic back to the guys Tyler had met at the theater. "The end of the term is coming up. I'll be hitting the yard sales. Students have to unload the stuff they aren't going to keep in storage over the summer."

"And then sell it back to them in the fall? Sneaky," Tyler said. "But you still have information on sales coming up?"

"There's one at Stansbury Mansion, but they won't be selling anything our speed."

"It sounds interesting, though," he said. "A mansion?"

"I've only been inside once. Years ago it was part of a tour of historic homes. It's quite spectacular. I'd go to get a chance to tour the building but not to bid on anything."

"If the two of you aren't going to be lost in bidding wars, I might even be convinced to come along," Grace said.

"If it's anything like it was when I was a kid, you'll be in heaven. They had some amazing artwork, plus all the furniture matches," Robyn ribbed Grace lightly. Turning the conversation back to Tyler, she asked if he'd contacted the owners of an organic farm out in Blue Lake to see if they'd be interested in his greenhouse.

"Not yet."

"They said they'd have a look as a favor to me," Robyn pressed.

Tyler brought the warmed ziti to the table and shoveled in a bite, puffing past it in an attempt to keep from burning his tongue. He swallowed and gulped his milk. "I'd rather finish up some of the smaller shelves and chairs in time for the fair if you'll still give me a corner of your booth."

Grace smiled at Robyn. "That's generous of you and what good news for me!"

"Why's that?" Robyn asked, frustrated that she hadn't been able to make her point about Tyler needing to follow through with his large-scale project.

"If he's taking up space in your booth, you don't need as much inventory at the fair, so you could have some to put in the Art Exhibition."

The way Tyler nodded encouragingly, Robyn sensed that neither sibling had heard anything she'd said. She remembered Hans Christian Andersen's story again, how the hen and the cat demanded that the ugly duckling purr or lay eggs, refusing to hear that the duckling wants only to swim and dive. She couldn't understand Grace's inability to accept that she was content on her own scale and uncomfortable being pushed beyond it. She didn't want to disappoint Grace, but she certainly didn't want to go to the city either.

CHAPTER FORTY

Robyn and Grace walked arm in arm through the Arcata Plaza, pleasantly full of sushi and conversation and now content in their shared silence and the rhythm of their steps. After climbing the hill, Grace moved her arm around Robyn's waist, pressing her entire side to her lover as they walked, communicating just how much she enjoyed the feel of Robyn's body next to hers. Robyn swung her arm around Grace's shoulder, pulling her snug in agreement.

"Thanks for coming to the reception today."

"You're sure I didn't distract you?"

"No. My mistakes were my own. And you were kind to try to get my mind off them with such a nice dinner."

"It all sounded good to me," Robyn said.

"Not that you're biased," Grace coaxed, stumbling a bit to catch up with Robyn as she stepped into the grass for a few strides to let another pedestrian who was heading into town pass. He glanced at them and offered a friendly smile. Sighing blissfully, Grace followed his progress as he walked away from them. "I love this town."

"Me too. It's always been home. We moved a lot when I was a kid, so the summers here with my grandparents were my consistency."

Sensing Robyn had more to say, Grace remained quiet.

"I'm sure you can imagine the effect couples like us had on the teenaged version of me, and I spent more than one afternoon reading on the second floor of the Tin Can Mailman in the lesbian section."

"Good thing for you that section wasn't right across from the register?"

Robyn laughed and ducked her face down into the high collar of her jacket. She peeked at Grace adding, "Especially since they had a copy of *The Joy of Lesbian Sex.*"

"They did not," Grace exclaimed, extracting herself from Robyn's arms and stopping to study her.

"A very used copy," Robyn admitted, her mouth making the briefest appearance above the zipped up collar before she hid again.

"You know what I don't get?"

Robyn shook her head.

Grace reached out and unzipped the collar to expose Robyn's face. She slid her hands along Robyn's strong jaw. Like she had at Wedding Rock, she buried her hands in Robyn's thick hair and pulled her into a kiss. Unlike that first embrace, Robyn's stiffness immediately melted when their lips met. Aware that they were still on the street, Grace didn't take the kiss as far as she intended to once they were inside the house. "How is it that someone as good at all things physical can be so uncomfortable talking about sex?"

"I want too much," Robyn said.

Grace took Robyn's hand, stroking her palm with her thumb. She loved how frank Robyn always was. Remembering her earnest statement about how she'd already dated the likes of Grace broke her heart. Grace recognized now how Robyn retreated into her shell to escape being hurt. "Whoever told you that was very wrong. I happen to love how much you want me. Let me show you just how much I love it." She started walking again, backward a few steps, so she could keep her eyes on Robyn's, giving her nowhere to hide.

They found the front door locked, and while Robyn was busy with the key, Grace took the opportunity to nibble her earlobe and whisper questions about what she remembered from thumbing through *The Joy of Lesbian Sex*.

She felt eyes on her and pulled away to find Isaac watching them, his arm around a young woman. While she waited for him to speak, his gaze traveled from her to Robyn and then back to Grace, lingering for longer than she felt comfortable. When the hand on his girlfriend's waist slipped down suggestively, Grace elbowed Robyn. Startled, Robyn looked to Grace for an explanation of the jab. Grace redirected Robyn's questioning look with a frosty glare in Isaac's direction.

"My hot water's out." He smirked.

"Sorry about that," Robyn answered. "Probably the pilot. I'll relight it."

"I don't want to interrupt." The look on his face said the opposite. He very much enjoyed interrupting them.

"No problem. It'll just take a minute."

Inside, Robyn apologized and promised to be no more than five minutes before she joined Grace upstairs.

Vowing to let go of the creepy feeling that had encroached on her romantic mood, Grace climbed the stairs replaying the evening before they had been interrupted. She did, indeed, love the town. She loved the local restaurants. She loved spending time with Robyn and wanted to hear more stories about her summers with her grandparents.

Approaching the steps to Robyn's loft, she smiled, wishing she could climb up seductively in front of Robyn. She crawled across the bed and looked at Robyn's stone for the day. *Worrier.* Replacing it, she wondered how often Robyn's stone did in some way match or set the tone for her day. She hadn't seemed worried at dinner. In fact, she deflected Grace's latest invitation to join the good company heading south with humor, and their walk home had not held any of the discomfort Grace felt the first few times she tried to encourage Robyn to explore a bigger market for her work.

She ran her fingers through the cool stones left in the bowl, compelled to take one.

Believe.

The small stone had surprising weight in the middle of her palm. She lay down on the bed and stared at the night sky, *believing* that there was no other place she would rather be. She heard the back door, and her skin tingled in anticipation of Robyn joining her.

Minutes passed, and Robyn did not appear. Perplexed, she shifted around and dropped her head through the hole in the ceiling that led to the loft, listening for the sound of Robyn on the stair. Hearing nothing, she scooted to the edge, resting her feet on the top step trying to decide whether to track her down.

Just as she started down the ladder, Robyn bounded up the stairs from the ground floor. They met at the doorway. "Sorry about that. I'm all yours, now. I promise." She guided Grace back toward the loft as she kissed her.

Grace tried to return to the kiss they'd begun on the sidewalk, remembering how she had thought of where it could have gone had they been inside, yet she couldn't get Isaac out of her head. "I'm sorry," she said, pulling away.

"What is it?"

"I just feel uncomfortable."

"Scoot back. I'll come up."

Grace shook her head and moved to descend the ladder.

Robyn stepped back to accommodate Grace but took hold of her arms, a concerned look on her face. "Grace?"

"Not physically uncomfortable." Grace closed her eyes. "I feel like we have an audience, like Isaac is out there picturing us. He creeps me out."

"Would you rather go to your place? We don't have to stay here."

"Tyler's there. I can't…"

Robyn's expression shifted at the mention of his name, and she stepped away running her hand through her dark hair. She was distracted by something, like her mind was not on the two of them anymore. "What?" Grace asked.

"Nothing."

"Did something happen with Tyler?"

"No. I just...Sergio stopped me on my way up to tell me that a bunch of guys from the theater crew got fired from the set."

"The ones you asked Tyler about when you had dinner at my house?"

"Yes."

Grace propped her hands on her hips. "Why did they get fired?"

"A few weeks ago, Sergio told me that Barbara was having problems with stuff missing from backpacks—books, laptops, stuff she hoped her student workers might have just misplaced rather than it being stolen. Though she suspected some of the building crew, she had no proof. Today, she busted them for being stoned and used that to fire them."

"You knew this and you didn't say anything?"

"I didn't want to betray Tyler's trust!"

"But you agreed that it was important that he have someone watching out for him. I thought you were doing that in letting him use your shop."

"I *am* watching out for him. What do you think I was doing at dinner? If you hadn't been so busy trying to coerce me into your trip down to the city, you might have noticed."

"How was I supposed to know you suspected anything of those young men? Had you shared your concern, we would have been on the same page."

"He's trying to build something new here, not just for himself but with you. I didn't want to get in the middle of that."

"Well, he certainly won't be building anything if he's stealing again," Grace said tightly. "You know what? I'm going to go. I've got to talk to him."

"I'm sorry, Grace. I should have said something before. This isn't how I wanted this evening to end." Robyn stepped forward to hug her.

Awkwardly, Grace returned the hug before slipping away, the sparks she'd felt earlier completely doused.

CHAPTER FORTY-ONE

"Well, what do you think?" Grace asked Kristine during a lunchtime lull at the San Francisco Art Exhibition.

"Are you kidding? This is fantastic. I had to hold a tight rein on myself to keep from barreling over people I've admired for a long while."

"Ruth is in heaven with the attention she's getting. What a crazy coincidence that we approached her for a project and landed this."

"She'd been invited before?"

"They've been trying to get her for years, but she didn't want the work of organizing a trip down here. I was more than happy to involve the campus in the planning and get our students this great exposure. What a success!"

"An amazing success. This is the first free moment we've had. Our students have had such good reception from buyers, and quite a few have made post-graduation contacts that they're really excited about. How are the community artists doing?"

"You mean has your stuff been moving while you've been watching over your students? I still wish you could have brought the rodeo series with you."

"But that's not the Northcoast."

"I know. You made the right call bringing the Woodley Island harbor photos."

"People like boats. Pretty sunsets, reflections. It makes them feel introspective."

"I thought trees sold."

Kristine shrugged. "I thought you had trees covered, but I didn't see any of Robyn's bowls."

"I gave up on that argument. I know her creations would have flown off the table here, but she worried that she wouldn't have enough stock for the North Country Fair if she let any come with me."

"She's not interested in throwing a larger net?"

"Not in the least."

"Seems like she does okay on the smaller scale."

"She does," Grace said, annoyed that Kristine seemed to be supporting Robyn's argument that she didn't need the exposure the trip to the city offered.

"How are things going between you two? I haven't had any time to ride, so I haven't been able to pump her for information."

Grace swatted her without conviction. "I have a sandwich run to make before the next rush. Come along?"

"Sure."

Grace knew Kristine wasn't going to let the subject drop and didn't feel comfortable discussing her dating life in front of the students. As she figured, once they were in the Mini Kristine broached the topic again. "For how great everything seems to be going, you don't seem happy. Are you upset that she's not here?"

"Yes. She should be here. I knew it in Arcata, and seeing the woodworking here…" She maneuvered through the city streets. "Her work is far superior to anything I've seen at this exhibition. I could almost understand when she said she wanted to keep her stock for the North Country Fair, but then she decided to share her space there with Tyler, so it makes no sense for her not to be here."

"You sure you don't need someone with more ambition? Someone who loves the city and the limelight as much as you do?"

"I used to miss the big city." She remembered how Gloria had teased her about her penchant for spending the weekend in San Francisco, taking in the latest shows and galleries, but then she thought about walking through the quiet town next to Robyn and how much like home it felt to her.

"But not anymore?"

"Arcata feels like home. I love the university, and there is so very much about Robyn that feels perfect. But it's tough too. We're not spring chickens like you and Gloria were, ready to strike out on your own and create a life together."

"At least you're both set money-wise, and in the same town. That seems like it would make things a lot easier. For me, moving there felt like a huge risk. I had to worry about whether I'd be able to pull my own weight. I needed to know I'd be able to contribute and not just be a freeloader."

"But like you said, Robyn and I are both financially solvent."

"Having tenants is part of Robyn's livelihood, though."

"Exactly! Part of. As in if I were living there, the money I could contribute would more than compensate what she needs in rental income to maintain a separate household. As it is, I feel like a renter when I'm at her place, like we never have complete privacy." Once it had become clear to her that she was perfectly content being an aunt, she had only ever pictured finding a woman to share her life and home.

"Is it just an issue of money?"

Grace thought of how Jen regarded Robyn as a mother and couldn't imagine asking Robyn to end her lease. "I know it wouldn't go over well if I suggested that we could live the way I want to on my income. She needs to feel self-sufficient, and I know she could be financially independent if she rethought her marketing strategy, but on that we clearly bump heads. I feel stuck. I could see a future with us, but only if we had the house to ourselves. But I don't see her being able to make that shift. I know better than to try to force her to change."

"And you don't know if you could be comfortable there with the current setup?"

"No. The problem is that I'm not."

"I'm sorry, Grace."

"Sorry to dump all of that on you. I know you've got plenty on your plate and don't need to hear about my problems. How is Gloria's mom doing?"

"She's at home, weak but putting up a good front. We're going over as often as we can. I worry about how rambunctious Caemon is, but she says it's more important for him to have real memories of her." Kristine closed her eyes overcome with emotion. "She asked me to take as many pictures as I can, so we won't forget. I keep looking at my images, especially of Gloria's parents together, and I see exactly what I want. That kind of adoration to the very end. It's really something."

"I see that in you and Gloria. And I want it too," Grace whispered.

They found the sandwich shop where she had preordered food for the exhibitors. Grace was relieved to have a diversion from her conversation with Kristine. She'd never have the opportunity to see whether her own parents might have continued to adore each other once their children had left the nest. Grace tended to the bill, convincing the young man behind the counter that he wanted to help carry the order to the car.

Settled into the drive back to the hotel, Kristine noted, "You're as good as Tom Sawyer at getting people to do a job for you. I wish it was as easy to get what you want from the relationship with Robyn. Gloria and I like the two of you so much and were so excited to hear that you'd gotten together. I wish it was all as simple as two people finding each other." Kristine reached out and squeezed Grace's arm.

"When is it ever simple?" Grace tried to make her voice light but couldn't shake the question of her compatibility with Robyn. She knew that they adored each other, but looking into the future, she could not see them coexisting calmly. She couldn't imagine a way past their conflicts. It could be a good thing to discover a deal breaker early on, stop things before she got too attached, she mused. Honestly she feared she was already past that point.

CHAPTER FORTY-TWO

In the dark of Robyn's loft with the night sky above her and Robyn's hands on her in a wonderfully possessive way, Grace could forget that Jen was in her studio. Since she'd returned from the city, Grace had wanted to talk to Robyn about the conversation she'd had with Kristine, but Jen's lingering in the kitchen during dinner had kept her mute on the subject of shared space.

She also thought it inappropriate to mention it as they shed their clothes in Robyn's room, and from there the feel of Robyn's skin next to hers wiped out any coherent thought. Her slow kiss asked if Grace had missed her, and she had. She missed Robyn's undivided attention, the feeling that when she lay under her hand, she was Robyn's whole world.

Never before had she felt as cherished as she did when Robyn traced from her shoulder to her hip with just the right pressure to make every nerve ending in her body come alive. She tingled down to her toes and squirmed, wanting to feel her lover inside. Though she deepened their kiss, suggesting with her tongue what she really desired, Robyn took her time.

Even when she met Grace's center with her mouth, Robyn circled her clit with the tip of her finger instead of entering, which she knew Grace wanted. "You're such a tease," Grace hissed, trying to push Robyn to where she needed her most.

"You like it so much," Robyn murmured. "You are so wet." Still playing with her fingers between Grace's lips, she skirted her tongue up the ridge of Grace's hip, suckling the sensitive dip just below. When her mouth reached Grace's breast, she slowly stroked Grace's clit with her thumb and only when she moved to kiss Grace again did she finally slide past her slippery folds deep within.

Grace felt Robyn everywhere at once, gasping as Robyn pulled out just to enter her again with two fingers. "Yes, yes, yes," Grace encouraged her, trying to get Robyn to increase the tempo.

"Not so patient, are you?" Robyn asked, altering her stroke just as Grace thought she might crest.

"I need you."

"Here?" Robyn said, finally complying with the tempo Grace needed.

"Right there. Oh, don't stop what you're doing." Blood hammered in Grace's ears and the world shook. Her eyes flew open as she realized that the hammering wasn't her own pulse but the house slamming against its foundation. "Robyn?" Fear-induced adrenaline flooded her body.

"You're okay," she answered, not slowing her stroke.

"But…"

Robyn's voice was calm as the contents of the house rattled and shook beneath them. "You're okay. I'm right here."

As the North American plates slipped, jarring the world as they resettled, Grace's orgasm ripped through her. Her own body joined the shaking as she rode out both the earthquake and her pleasure, her hands holding onto Robyn like a lifeline. "You made the earth shake."

"All you," Robyn said, settling in next to Grace to hold her.

Grace clung to her as the house continued to sway. She could still hear the roar of the earthquake rolling through the town. "How…"

"Robyn!"

Robyn's door hit the wall below the loft with a force, startling Grace all over again.

Robyn eased Grace back down onto the bed with a steady palm. "Jen," she said to her tenant. "Not a good time."

"Earthquake!" she panted.

"*We* know," Robyn said. She bent to kiss Grace's ear. "Hang on a sec. Jen is terrified of earthquakes." Realizing all of her clothes were in the room below, she called to Jen. "Toss me my shirt, would you?"

"No, it's okay. I'm sorry," Jen said.

Grace heard the door click shut again. Before she could say a word, Robyn was already on the stairs to her room.

"Be right back, promise."

"You're not leaving." It was a statement, not a question, and she delivered it in her administrative voice.

"I've got to check the gas lines anyway," she said and was gone.

Grace sat up, hugging her knees to her chest. Anger flooded through her. What about her? She was equally rattled by the sizeable quake and felt she deserved to have her lover's comfort. The concerns she'd voiced to Kristine multiplied exponentially.

She scooted from Robyn's bed and down the stairs to collect her clothes. She tried the light but found that the electricity was out. "Great," she mumbled, trying to find her clothes in the dark. She located everything but one sock and decided that was good enough. Dressed, her keys in her hand, she met Robyn coming up the stairs with an electric lantern.

"You're dressed!" she exclaimed.

"I have my own house to check."

"Tyler will call you if there's a problem, won't he?"

"Forgive me if I feel like checking for myself," Grace said icily. She pushed past Robyn and carefully descended the stairs.

Robyn followed. "Grace, I can tell you're angry. Please don't leave right now. Tell me what's bothering you."

Grace spun around. "You need me to tell you what's bothering me?" she said incredulously.

"I had to check the house." Robyn hooked the lantern on the staircase banister and reached for Grace.

"And Jen." Grace stepped away from her.

Robyn crossed her arms defensively. "Jen is your friend too. I don't understand why you're so upset that I would want to make sure she's okay."

Grace looked up the staircase, aware that both Jen and Sergio were very likely listening to everything they said. This incensed her more, that she couldn't even have a lovers' quarrel in private. She turned to the door, but Robyn was there before she had opened it.

"What is it?" she asked. The levelness of her voice conveyed genuine worry.

Tears spilled down Grace's cheeks. "I love you," she whispered.

Robyn cupped Grace's face. "Then why in the world are we down here instead of back in bed?"

Keeping her voice low, Grace said, "Because I don't like sharing you, knowing that your tenants hear everything, that they can interrupt at any time. Any time," she emphasized.

"You want me to get rid of my tenants?" Robyn stepped back as if Grace had struck her.

"I don't see you moving out, so that leaves us here with me worrying about who I'm going to bump into on my way to the bathroom or run into on campus." She stood up straighter with that. "It's not professional."

"If you really love me, you wouldn't try to change me."

"I'm not trying to change you."

"My renters are a huge part of my income!"

"If I lived here, don't you think I'd contribute?"

"I don't want your money," Robyn snapped. "I didn't ask for your fancy compost bin. And what happened to my toaster?"

"The broken one?"

"It wasn't broken."

"I don't think it's unreasonable to want to have toast without having to hover over the machine to make it work."

"So you just threw it away? It still worked."

"Jesus, Robyn. It's out in the shed if you still want it, next to three other toasters that I'm guessing are also semi-functional. That I can't change anything without checking with you first makes me feel like I'm another tenant here."

"Sergio and Jen haven't complained."

"They are renters, Robyn. You're lumping me in with your renters?"

"Of course not, but..." She looked like she was sifting through complaints about Grace that she had tucked away.

"But what? What have I complained about? What else is on your list?" she demanded.

"I don't have a list."

"Oh, I think you do. I am not in the wrong here. You're trying to make me the unreasonable one when all I want is the privacy of a home where we can have sex wherever or whenever we want without worrying about roommates. I'm too old to worry about roommates."

A strong aftershock punctuated her outburst. Robyn reached for the banister and Grace held onto the doorknob, the entryway empty between them. When the earth settled again, Robyn stepped toward Grace who held out her hand to stop her. "Why don't you check on Jen?" She opened the door and slipped out onto the darkened street to her car.

CHAPTER FORTY-THREE

Grace

The springs on Robyn's office chair squeaked as she leaned back. With tufts of stuffing poking through the old leather upholstery it didn't look like much, but she'd never been able to find anything as comfortable as her papa's chair. Papers covered her desk: a stack of bills, statements to file, trash to recycle. She tallied her expenses on a legal pad and just for the sake of argument halved all of them to project what Grace would need to contribute if she moved in.

She had no mortgage to worry about, but she didn't want to trust her coast guard pension to carry her through the end. Each month, she was able to put away much of what she collected in rent. Losing the renters wouldn't hurt her monthly budget, but it would impact her savings, money she would need if Grace ever decided that she didn't want to be with her for the long haul.

Not being legally married to Barb became a blessing when she left. To separate their finances, Robyn only had to open a new bank account, but her leaving had stripped Robyn of the financial security she had felt while they were together. She didn't want to feel that vulnerable again.

Two sets of feet clomped down the stairs: Jen's last pupil leaving with his mother. She could start charging Jen for the studio space, but she hated to bite into what Jen was making. She tipped forward and scrounged in her recycling for a piece of paper with a blank back. How hard would it be to add a separate entrance for the studio and eliminate the traffic through the house? Busy sketching the possibility, she didn't hear Jen until she stood at the doorway.

"Bad time?" she asked.

"No. Great time. What do you think about a separate entrance for the studio? We could run a set of stairs up to the enclosed porch and put an external door to the studio." She turned back to the drawing. "That could be your entry room. You could make a little sitting area there, so the kids coming in wouldn't disturb your lesson. Put in a few chairs, and it would also give the parents a place to sit and wait." She couldn't read the expression on Jen's face. "Bad idea?"

Jen leaned against the bookshelf. "Great idea. I just don't know if you'll want to go to the trouble."

"I thought your lessons were going well. It seems like there's a steady stream of little musicians coming through every day."

"Yeah, the teaching is great," Jen agreed. She wouldn't meet Robyn's eye.

"This is about Grace, isn't it? About the fight we had. Please don't worry about that."

"You're kidding, right? She's totally pissed at me and rightfully so. I should never have gone into your bedroom. I don't know what I was thinking, and I'm so sorry."

"She'll get over it, and if she doesn't..." Robyn took a deep breath remembering the jolt she'd felt when she read the lettering of her lover's name on the stone in her palm that morning. She honestly hoped that Grace would come around and accept Robyn's apology. If she didn't, Robyn had been telling herself that she would be relieved to know they were so incompatible without investing years of their lives into something that would be difficult to dissolve. The problem was that she wasn't convinced. Just the thought of Grace leaving her pressed on her chest like being trapped under a wave— disoriented, desperate for air, without a clue as to whether the surf would let her emerge again.

"You don't mean that," Jen said. "You wouldn't let her get away."

"You're my family. She has no right to ask you to leave."

"So she does want us gone." Jen didn't look hurt.

"She hasn't said that." Robyn left out how they hadn't spoken since.

"If you think about it, what part of this space is hers? I have my room, the studio as my own space. What does she have?"

"Me! My space is our space. I can make room for her, but she has to meet me halfway and see where she's being unreasonable. It's not like she's moving in. That's not what we're talking about here."

"Wouldn't she, eventually? It's not like you'd move, right? So she's got to be wondering whether being with you means living with renters. It's your choice, but if you ask me, if you choose to keep renters instead of her, you're the one losing."

Robyn crossed her arms over her chest, feeling like she was under attack. She had anticipated having Jen on her side, not receiving a lecture about how she was in the wrong.

"I didn't mean to make you defensive. I really just came down to let you know that I'm moving out."

"What!" Robyn's chair snapped back to level position, her feet smacking the floor in front of her.

"I've been seeing someone," Jen said. "We wouldn't have moved in together so soon, but I told her about what happened. She's the one who said that you clearly need your own space, and I agree with her."

"That's for me to decide. I have a room to rent. I'll just put someone else in there. I need the income."

Jen stared at her levelly. "Then I'll keep the studio for my classes and pay you for that. Don't rent out that room, Robyn.

Grace is good for you. She came right out and told you what the issue is, and it's an issue you happen to be able to fix. Easily. You're crazy not to." She pushed away from the bookshelf. "Anyway, I told Tara that I need a week to pack and clean up the room. I hope you'll let me keep doing lessons."

Robyn sat, stunned by Jen's announcement. She thought about her prayer stones and what an answered prayer was: the granting of what one most needed. She reminded herself that she always accepted what she pulled from the bowl. Did that mean Grace was what she needed most?

CHAPTER FORTY-FOUR

Analytical

Tucked under the mare's neck, Robyn stood in Taj's stall. As if she sensed the goodbye in how firmly Robyn held on, Taj swung her muzzle around, wrapping the human in her warmth and comforting horse smell. Responding to the horse hug, Robyn buried her face in Taj's soft coat, wanting to block the beautiful image of her sailing over six-foot jumps with young, talented riders aboard. Sitting ringside, she saw how Taj responded to the challenge, her black-tipped ears perked, neck arched and forelegs tucked tight as she effortlessly cleared fences Robyn would never consider.

Even on a loose rein when the riders cooled her down, Taj had a spring in her gait that Robyn had never felt on the trail. She looked proud and satisfied. Robyn realized she was very likely projecting feelings onto the horse to comfort herself for not buying the mare when Eleanor had called her to say they were ready to sell her.

Tears sprang to her eyes when she remembered the catch in Eleanor's voice when she had called. She knew that letting go of Taj meant letting go of Penelope yet again. She asked for a day to think it over, even though when Eleanor gave her their asking price, she knew she could never justify such a purchase.

It wasn't just the money. Robyn had the savings, but she could not bring herself to tie the animal to mundane rides when she was clearly capable of so much more. In the short term, she had felt good about getting Taj out and keeping her in shape. In the long term, she'd be holding the horse back.

Still, she wanted to ride Taj one more time and took her deep into the redwoods beyond the clear-cut Kristine had shown her the first time she left the barn. She wanted the rhythm of the horse's stride to center her as it had when Barb had left, but instead the ride reinforced her belief that the horse belonged in the ring and was out of place on the trails Robyn loved. They had never been right for each other.

The tears continued, and she did nothing to stop them. Thankful for Taj's patience, she let the sobs come unchecked.

"Robyn?"

Startled, Robyn brushed away her tears, keeping her back to the stall door. When she turned, she saw Kristine and Caemon sharing a look of concern. Feeling exposed, she stepped to the door but did not reach to disengage the lock. Caemon surprised her by tipping forward in his mother's arms over the open window to wrap his arms around Robyn's neck.

Robyn pulled him over and accepted his full body hug. She met Kristine's eyes which were full of pride and love.

"Robyn's sad," Caemon said, pulling back to look into her eyes. He wiped her cheeks with sticky, grubby fingers, smearing her tears around with hands that smelled suspiciously of... blackberry she guessed from his blue-ringed lips. "It's okay. I comfort you."

Rocking back and forth with his weight in her arms, she did feel comforted. "Thanks. That's a really good hug."

"We can muck now? With the tractor?"

"Sure. And you know what? It's a good thing you're here because I have a big favor to ask."

"What?" he asked, his blue eyes full of wonder.

Robyn unlatched the stall and set him down, so she could open her shed and pull out the tractor. "This is actually my last day taking care of Taj." Her chin trembled and she fought from crying again.

"Why?" Caemon looked troubled, and Robyn didn't dare look at Kristine.

"Because I was just borrowing her. Now she has a new owner who is taking her to a different barn."

"And I won't be able to see her anymore? Bean won't see her too?"

"No. You and Bean won't see her anymore. So," Robyn cleared her throat and took a deep breath, "I don't have a place to keep my tractor. Do you think we could put it in your shed?"

"Yeah!" Caemon leapt to the tractor seat and started pedaling, his world set right again. Robyn marveled at the child's resilience.

"You didn't want to buy her?" Kristine asked carefully.

"It's not that I didn't want to. She's just meant for so much more." Again, she avoided looking at Kristine. Robyn hadn't talked to Grace for more than a week. She'd called to apologize once. When Grace didn't return her call, she didn't see a reason to keep calling. When she wanted to talk, Grace knew where to find her.

"She Taj or she Grace is meant for so much more?"

"Taj," Robyn said defensively. "Why would I say that about Grace?"

Kristine shrugged, frustrating Robyn by walking to Taj's stall to offer her a carrot and stroking the pointed white shape on the mare's forehead. Only when she traced the marking with her finger did Robyn connect it to the outline of the Taj Mahal. Grief that she'd never be able to joke with Penelope about how slow she'd been to get it bumped into the hurt that Grace had not returned her phone call. She gritted her teeth, knowing that Kristine had grown silent to force Robyn to talk about Grace.

"I wish a local had bought her. I'll miss seeing her around the barn," Kristine commented, seemingly comfortable with dropping the subject of Grace.

Robyn stewed about what Grace must have told Kristine. Why did she consider that Robyn might be worried about whether she had enough to offer Grace? That she would try to bend her to be someone else had worried Robyn from the start. Somehow she'd let a few intense conversations dissolve her guard.

"I'll miss seeing you around here too."

Kristine kept her eyes on the horse, giving Robyn privacy as she said farewell to Taj. "I'm still happy to help out with Bean if you ever need it. Caemon too," she said, smiling at the boy contentedly loading handfuls of straw into his wagon. "And look, just because I'm not buying her doesn't mean I'm dropping out of riding again. I'm sure I can find something more my speed."

Robyn couldn't really understand the disappointed look on Kristine's face. She closed her eyes and thought like Kristine, replacing the horse with Grace. Her eyes flew open. "You just translated that, didn't you? And in your mind, I just said I'm content to live vicariously through your happy relationship or find a woman who is more like me."

"Having a little more than you can handle makes your heart stretch to match it, don't you think?"

Robyn rubbed her face. "Or gets you bucked off."

"Right. We do tend to remember eating dirt. I get that. Some might go safe after that. Then you're guaranteed not to eat dirt." She stood there stroking the horse long enough that Robyn began to think they were finished talking. But Kristine tipped her attention back to Robyn. "You ever ridden a long way on a dude horse?" she asked.

The question seemed completely random to Robyn, wondering what a dude horse might have to do with her life. "No."

"I used to ride the Sierras all summer long. We had two different strings: one for staff, and another for guests—the dude horses. Every once in a while, I got stuck on a horse meant for unskilled riders." She shook her head. "You spend the whole time trying to push some life into its step, and if you don't, it just stops. Then there are the ones who keep you on your toes.

You can't wait to see where they take you, and every step they seem to be inviting you to see the backcountry in a whole new way. It's breathtaking."

Robyn considered Kristine's words, trying to understand what she was saying.

"I've seen you ride. You underestimate how capable you are. Grace says you're the same with your bowls. We missed you in San Francisco," she added pointedly. "You shouldn't be afraid to put yourself out there." She reached out and rubbed between Robyn's shoulder blades.

"Have you seen her?" Robyn finally gave in.

A sad smile began at one corner of her mouth. "She came over for supper a few nights ago. Didn't say anything about the two of you, but she's off her feed." She tucked her hands into her pockets and took a few steps toward Bean's stall.

"I called her. She hasn't called back."

Kristine raised her hands.

"I know. I don't want to put you in the middle. I just don't know what to do."

"Guess it depends on what you called to say." She turned to Caemon, congratulating him on the load of straw he'd put together while the grownups talked.

Robyn pressed her head to Taj's, thinking about the words she'd left on Grace's phone. She'd said she was sorry, and she was sorry for the fight, but she'd also returned to how unreasonable it was to ask for her to turn her world upside down.

She recalled how easily she and Barb had drifted to separate rooms, and then also remembered how adamantly she had shut down Barb's plans to remodel the kitchen. She bent her head to watch Kristine and Caemon, remembering how she had accurately pointed out the sting of eating dirt. Robyn was scared of eating dirt again, scared of being thrown and getting hurt.

So far, she had kept herself in a safe position by insisting that Grace fit into the home as she had it arranged. She realized how petty it was for her to respond to Grace's purchases the way she had, in fear that Grace was really moving toward a full kitchen overhaul.

She felt a pang thinking about how soon Jen would be out of her room. Even if she did keep the studio with a separate entrance, it was very likely that Robyn would not be seeing her every day as she had for years. She wouldn't be part of her household, her family. Maybe she was right about not putting in another tenant when she left, and then Grace could use that space as her office. Or would she prefer the downstairs room? Robyn suspected that Sergio would not stay over the summer. Typically, she would have run an ad to fill the space again, but now she considered that if she and Grace were serious, she might want a say in what they did with the room.

This was what Kristine meant by asking what she'd called to say. Robyn had been stuck on the present conflict unaware of how it tied into what Grace might see as the future. She thought of the ease with which Jen and Tara decided to live together. Inviting Grace to live with her opened the potential vulnerability she'd experienced with Barb, but exponentially so if she let go of her renters. There'd be no safety net. Tentatively, she felt the toe of her boot slide into the stirrup as she prepared to launch herself back into the saddle for a wholly unpredictable ride.

CHAPTER FORTY-FIVE

Breathe

Robyn stood in her shop, a fine layer of sawdust covering her, the redwood burl salad bowl in her hands smooth from her sanding. She compared it to the other bowls she had been finishing, making sure they presented as a set. Ideally, she could group the five bowls with a larger serving bowl.

Some mineral spirits and a rag brought out the wood's intricate swirling patterns. Though she had no regrets about not taking her stock down to the San Francisco Art Exhibition, Grace's description of the work she had seen there made her regret not going to see it for herself. Occasionally, she perused the local shops that sold elegant redwood products, but mostly she kept to her own booth at the fair, content that she always did the best work she could.

She set down the bowl and sat quietly, wondering if Grace was busy or angry or simply finished with her. After the last quartet rehearsal, she had hoped to intercept her on her way out and was surprised when a woman she didn't recognize walked out with the other violinist and violist. The look on Jen's face told her everything she needed to know. The quartet had lost Grace because of Robyn. She wondered if it was permanent or temporary but did not want to invite more of Jen's judgment by asking.

That night, she had left another message on Grace's phone. She hoped Grace was well and asked if they could talk. Three days had passed. A week and a half in all since their last contact. Grace's silence frustrated Robyn. It felt juvenile to sit wondering what was going on in Grace's head, but she did not want to intrude, hoping that it just meant that Grace needed space. She chose to interpret the quiet as meaning there was still a remnant of hope for them.

Pleased with her progress for the day, she tucked the finished bowls on a shelf and covered them with a soft towel. She heard steps outside the shop, and she felt a rush in her chest remembering how Grace had once found her there. Disappointment swept through her when she turned to find Sergio instead. Fog had blown in from the bay softening the afternoon light and chilling the air.

"I thought you'd want to know that those idiots Barb fired got picked up."

Slowly, Robyn swept dust off her forearms. "Picked up by the police?"

"Sherriff. They broke into a place down on the waterfront in King Salmon."

"Where did you hear this?"

"They called Barbara to tell her they'd recovered her video camera. It has the theater information etched into the side, so they couldn't pawn it."

"This just happened?" Robyn asked, her heart rate picking up. Sergio had told her he'd seen Tyler with the group at the theater around the time when things were going missing. Tyler was smart enough not to get himself tangled up with them, wasn't he?

"Barbara was still talking to them when I left. I just caught the beginning of the conversation and thought you'd want to know." He looked past her into the shop. "Tyler's not around?"

Robyn closed her eyes, praying that he was at home with Grace. She hadn't seen him all day. "No. I was hoping he was doing some prep work for the greenhouse. I'll give him a call. Thanks, Sergio."

"No problem."

Robyn pulled out her cell and called Tyler. No answer. She tapped the phone on her thigh, not wanting to call Grace. Swallowing her discomfort, she hit send on Grace's number, swearing under her breath when it went to voice mail. "Grace, I'm looking for Tyler. Would you just let me know if he's with you? I'd really appreciate it."

She was both relieved and annoyed when her phone rang a couple minutes later since it confirmed that Grace was specifically avoiding her call. To let her know that she wasn't just angling to talk to Grace herself, she launched right into her concern about Tyler. "Sergio just told me that those guys he saw Tyler with in the theater are being held at the sheriff's office. I'd like to think that Tyler's smarter than getting himself involved in a burglary, but I haven't seen him, and he's not answering his cell."

She heard Grace take a deep breath. "I'm still at work, so I don't know if he's home. Let me call the sheriff's office and see if they're holding him."

"Thanks."

"Why are you thanking me for checking on my brother?"

"I thought you'd call me when you know. I was thanking you in advance for keeping me in the loop."

"I'll call you when I have more information," she said in her crisp professional voice.

Robyn hit end but couldn't stop worrying about Tyler so easily. She locked her shop and jogged to the house, grabbing her keys, wallet and a ball cap. By the time Grace called back, she was halfway to Grace's place. She clicked the phone to speaker. "Is he there?"

"They wouldn't tell me anything. The guys they have are all in processing."

"Hang on. I'm almost at your place." She drove in silence wondering what Grace was thinking and how they had reached a place that felt so awkward. She put the truck in neutral, set the brake and grabbed her phone. At the front door she knocked and waited. She knocked again. "Grace, he's not answering. I have a bad feeling about this."

"Now what?"

"I'm going to the sheriff's office. Do you want me to swing by for you?"

"I'll be on the street."

"Bring the number you called." Robyn whipped through the back streets to campus. As she pulled up, she stretched across the cab and rolled down the window. "Can you drive a stick?"

Grace threw up her hands in exasperation. "Of course."

"Good. Come around." Parked, she scooted across the cab. "Take the 101 to Eureka. I'll direct you once we get past the safety corridor." She punched in the number Grace had handed her and interrupted the man who answered the line. "Is Lieutenant Matute in?" Robyn demanded.

Grace looked at Robyn, confused.

Tipping the receiver above her head, she said. "We go back."

"Lieutenant Matute here."

"James, it's Robyn Landy."

"Landy! I heard you retired. How the hell are you?"

"I'd love to catch up with you, but I'm calling for a favor first. I hear you picked up a crew of young men today. I'm worried a friend of mine is caught up with them, and I can't get in touch with him. I'm wondering if you've got him there."

"How'd you hear about it?"

"Your guys called HSU about stolen cameras."

"Ah, yes. The stuff that we found in one suspect's car. I had the deputy call Barbara to see if they were really authorized to have them. Give me a minute to see if we've got your friend. Name?"

"Tyler Warren."

"Let me get the deputy to check."

Robyn relaxed into the seat. "They're checking," she said to Grace.

"You're amazing. Just like that they'll check for you?"

"We worked some disasters together," Robyn said. She looked out the window at the row of eucalyptus trees between the highway and the bay. Listening for James's voice, she tried to keep herself in the present instead of thinking of the cases they had faced together.

"Robyn, he's not here, but we're working on it."

"What do you mean you're working on it?"

"Is there any way you could come in?"

"We're en route, just a few minutes out. Why?"

"I'll update you when you get here."

"What is it?" Grace asked when Robyn ended the call.

"I don't know. Something's up because my friend asked if we could come in. Tyler's not there, but he said they're working on it." She tapped her cell against the palm of her hand.

"Why does he want you?"

"I have no idea. You know as much as I do."

"Thank you for your help," Grace said. "I'm still mad at you, though."

"I gathered." The silence between them felt heavy. "Jen is gone."

"Gone? What?"

"She's still renting the studio space, but she moved out of the room."

"Her choice or yours?"

"I know it would sound better if it had been my idea, but it was her choice. I don't know if that makes a difference. Take a right up here and go three blocks. I haven't listed it. I wanted to talk to you first."

"How about we get to the station and deal with one thing at a time," Grace said, evading Robyn's offering.

Robyn didn't expect one roommate moving out to solve everything, but she had certainly thought that her news would elicit more of a response. She sensed a longer talk coming. Sometimes the lesbian need to talk everything out ad nauseam wiped her out.

CHAPTER FORTY-SIX

Grace was surprised to hear that Tyler had been with the group of young men the sheriff's office had picked up. Since the earthquake, she and Tyler had been spending more time together, and she had seen no signs of him being in trouble. Nothing to suggest he had strayed from his very determined path.

The night she'd left Robyn's so angrily, she'd pulled up at her own place to every light on and Tyler nervously waiting for more aftershocks. Though she knew he'd never admit to wanting her home, the night had turned out to be one of their best. Too wired from the quake and the anticipation of more aftershocks, as well as her fury with Robyn, Grace had set about making a pan of brownies. She and Tyler had polished them off sitting on the back porch listening to the unexpected song of frogs coming from the gully that ran through the pastureland behind their house.

They hadn't talked about anything in particular, which was what stood out so much for Grace. She wasn't trying to guide his choices. She hadn't needed to be in control. They simply riffed on childhood memories which seemed to foster a renewed bond.

Realizing how little attention she'd paid to him since she'd started seeing Robyn, she'd made a real effort to be home from work in time to have dinner together. Each night, he smelled like Robyn's shop—sawdust and sweat—and he seemed pumped about his projects rather than idiotic illegal schemes.

If not for his past, she would have shut down Robyn's goose chase, but she knew from watching her parents' struggle with Tyler that he was capable of slipping up despite his most sincere promises. She just prayed he was smarter now than he had been years ago when he was just a rebellious kid.

At the sheriff's station, she watched as Robyn took the lead, striding through the doors to the counter. "Robyn Landy. Lieutenant Matute is expecting me."

"Have a seat. He said he'd be right with you."

Robyn gestured to the chairs, inviting Grace to sit.

"You have me too worried," she said.

"I'm sorry." Robyn walked to the row of connected chairs and sat, rubbing her face.

"Landy!" Lieutenant Matute's voice filled the foyer as he strode through a door off to the side of the room. He loomed large in a crisp uniform, forest green pants and tan shirt with a star badge above the left breast pocket decorated with an American flag pin. Robyn leapt to her feet and the two shared a back-smacking hug. The officer matched Robyn's stature and coloring but sported a military close haircut and immaculately-trimmed dark beard. "It's been too long," he said, holding her at arm's length.

"If you've got time for chitchat, that means Tyler's not involved with these guys?"

"I'm sorry to say he is, but we've got our boat and the coast guard out on the bay looking for him." He offered a confident smile, rocking to the balls of his feet.

"The coast guard? I don't understand," Grace said.

Lieutenant Matute looked to Grace and back to Robyn.

"Sorry. This is Tyler's sister, Grace Warren."

"Ah, well, apparently one of the boys invited his friends out on the water in his parents' boat. They went down to King Salmon…"

Grace turned questioning eyes to Robyn.

She supplied, "It's south of Eureka, waterfront properties."

The lieutenant confirmed and continued. "We got a call around three. The witness said he'd seen four young men prowling around Stansbury Mansion."

Robyn swore under her breath.

"That's the place you were telling me and Tyler about?"

"Yes. The estate sale is this weekend."

"Probably why they had security on the grounds. When the boys saw them, they fled from the private dock in their boat. The guards gave us a full description, and patrol picked them up at the Woodley Island Marina. They found a bunch of stolen items in their car there along with a few things lifted from Stansbury Mansion. But we only found three guys, one short of the complaint, and all of them high as a kite."

"Tyler wasn't with them?"

"No. We asked them where the fourth guy was. They confirmed that it was Tyler. He was concerned about being picked up, so apparently they dumped him in the water to swim to shore. He has a record?"

"Yes," Grace answered honestly. "He recently moved to Arcata to make a fresh start."

Lieutenant Matute pursed his lips. "I'm not sure how he's involved, but we put our boat on search and rescue and called in the guard."

"If the sheriff's office was already on the scene, I don't understand why you need the coast guard," Grace said.

"We have better boats," Robyn supplied. "Did they send out the BARRACUDA and air support?"

"Coast guard from Eureka Bay responded immediately and is closer to where they dropped him on their way to the marina. The helicopter is on its way from Sector."

"The coast guard has a station near the commercial airport north of Arcata," Robyn explained to Grace.

"They've got it covered, and I'm confident that we'll be hearing from them any minute." To Robyn, he said, "How's retirement? Still can't believe you didn't take the promotion."

"If I'd stayed any longer, the job would have claimed me," Robyn replied.

"I always wondered why you pushed so hard. Most do because they want the next step. I thought that's where you were headed."

"Time to rescue myself," Robyn said. Though Grace would have liked her to elaborate, Robyn characteristically directed the conversation away from herself, asking the lieutenant about his family.

Grace hugged herself as the two caught up, talking about Matute's children, their college and career plans.

"Lieutenant!" The deputy at the desk extended the phone in his hand, a palm covering the receiver. "Coast guard is on the scene but has no visual. They've done a sweep from the station to the marina but haven't spotted him."

Concern clouded Matute's face as he accepted the phone. Panic flashed through Grace's body. Grace couldn't follow anything the lieutenant said. She kept her eyes trained on Robyn, trusting her reaction to reveal what she needed to know about the situation.

"Excuse me. I need to see if we can get any more information about where our suspects dropped Tyler into the water."

"Shouldn't you go with him?" Grace asked Robyn.

"This is James's station. I'm not stepping on his toes," Robyn answered.

"It can't be good that they're calling, that they haven't found him." Robyn didn't answer, giving Grace all the information she needed. She sat again, numb with worry. "What?"

"I'd feel a whole lot better if I knew whether he has a lifejacket."

"He's a strong swimmer," Grace insisted. What she thought would ease the concern in Robyn's eyes had no effect. "That doesn't change anything?"

"This time of year, the water in the bay hovers around fifty degrees. If he has a life jacket, he can maintain his core temperature," Robyn said. "If he's having to tread water, that will take his core temperature down and raise the risk of hypothermia."

"How long does he have without a life jacket?"

"He might have up to four hours with a life jacket."

"That's not what I asked."

Robyn looked at her watch, prompting Grace to look at her own. Ten after four. She looked at Robyn. "Without a life jacket, he probably has a half hour."

Fear sliced through Grace. "A half hour? But your friend said they got a call at three. That was more than an hour ago!"

"You have to stay positive, Grace." Robyn sat down next to her. "We don't know when he entered the water, and my guys aren't going to give up easily. They just want a smart search. The more information they have, the faster they can locate him. They want him out of the water as much as we do."

It felt like forever before Lieutenant Matute returned, motioning to Robyn. "We've got something."

Grace grabbed Robyn's hand. She couldn't be left behind.

"James?" Robyn asked.

He nodded a terse approval and ushered everyone back to the evidence room, explaining that the statement the young men had made on the scene gave them the impression that Tyler had gone overboard close to the marina. "When we informed them that they could face charges for leaving Tyler in the water, they insisted they threw him a life jacket. That's when we learned they had a video clip."

"Video?" Robyn said, doubtfully.

"Lucky for us, one of the idiots whipped out his cell phone. We have it on the monitor now." He nodded to the deputy. Grace struggled to make sense of the grainy gray scene before her. Suddenly, Tyler emerged from the water with a shocked roar.

Grace gasped.

"Better start swimming!" a voice cackled.

"Throw him a life jacket!"

The camera panned as the person filming turned toward the command. The video ended.

Robyn spoke immediately. "What's the time stamp?"

"Fifteen thirty-six."

Grace calculated. "He's been in the water forty minutes, Robyn."

"He could have the jacket...Can you play the clip again?" The deputy complied, and while she watched the screen, everyone else watched her. Grace watched Robyn's eyes as she searched the image. "Again...Stop!" The image froze just after the camera left Tyler. Gray-blue water filled all but the very top of the screen. "James, can you get air patrol on the line?"

"What do you see?" Matute asked, motioning to his sergeant to make the requested call.

Robyn pointed to the top of the screen. "A memorial."

Matute leaned forward, squinting at the barren shoreline. "I see rocks."

"Locals erected a memorial after they lost family when their fishing boat went down by the north spit."

"Dammit," Matute said.

"Is that bad..." Grace started to ask.

Matute held up his hand for silence when the deputy announced that air patrol was on the line. "Captain Eason, I've got Robyn Landy, retired..."

Robyn snatched the phone from him. "Fred. I'm so glad to hear you're out there. I'm looking at some video of the scene and can place Tyler's entry into the water much further south..."

"I don't understand," Grace tried again, overwhelmed by the bustle of activity that followed Robyn's cryptic observation. As Robyn relayed physical landmarks and discussed tidal patterns, the deputy guided Grace to a chair. She watched as they stretched out a nautical chart, Robyn's arms spread wide to hold it in place, the phone on speaker. Though Robyn kept a steady stream of information, Grace heard only a high ringing. Her breath came in short gasps, and she began to feel light-headed.

"Go ahead and lean forward," the deputy advised. "Can you hear me?"

Grace nodded.

"Breathe in through your nose and out through your mouth. Try to stay calm. Do you know how much your brother weighs?"

"Two something. I really have no idea," Grace sobbed.

"It's okay. Ballpark is okay. Do you know his height?"

"Six two. That I know."

"Good. He's my height. You think he's lighter or heavier than I am?"

Grace assessed the young deputy, who had a lot more muscle than Tyler. "A lot lighter."

"That helps a lot. Keep your head down. I need to get those details to the guard."

She did as he said, breathing as the deputy had instructed, wondering why they wanted her brother's height and weight. She closed her eyes, trying to push out the image of Robyn's face when the camera had cut away from Tyler. She wanted to believe that it was going to be okay, but the energy in the room conveyed the seriousness of the situation.

Feeling warm hands on her thigh, she opened her eyes. Robyn crouched beside her and began to rub her back with one hand.

"What was important about the memorial?" Grace asked.

"It places Tyler right at the mouth of the entrance to Humboldt Bay, close enough to shore for me to see that memorial, but with the tide going out he'll be working against the current to reach the coast."

"And the current can pull him out into the ocean?" Robyn's hand stilled, giving Grace her answer. "Why does his weight matter?"

"The mission coordinator has to calculate the survival odds. His height and weight, the temperature of the air and water—all of that go into a program that gives a search timeline."

"What happens if they don't find him?" Grace asked, sitting up. She could not read Robyn's expression. She wore the poker face of an experienced officer.

"They'll suspend the active search."

"And if he is swept out into the ocean?"

"The odds of rescue…"

Grace didn't need Robyn to finish the sentence, knowing that even if Tyler had the life jacket, the odds of finding him in the open ocean were miniscule. She felt a crushing weight, one she knew would compel a mourning family to create a memorial on the shore. "How did you know about the memorial?" she whispered.

"My papa used to take me and Jeff clamming down there. We were always getting bored and wandering off. One time we climbed up on the rocks. When Papa saw where we were, we got a stern talking to about not disrespecting the dead and their grieving families. Jeff shook it off, but it stuck with me. I'd disappointed him."

"You were a child," Grace observed.

Robyn looked away. "There's nothing more we can do here. Let's get over to the hospital and wait for them to bring him in."

"What if they don't find him?"

"This is what the coast guard does, Grace. We rescue people." She wrapped her arm protectively around Grace's shoulder and drew her close. "The important thing is that they are on their way right now. I've pointed them in the right direction. They'll find him."

"She's right," Lieutenant Matute said, joining them.

Grace looked up to see him reading Robyn's arm around her. His countenance shifted as he put together that she was more than Tyler's sister. She felt him weighing whether she was good enough for Robyn. His eyes returned to Robyn and softened.

"We were lucky you were here to help," he said. "We've got it from here."

CHAPTER FORTY-SEVEN

Grace refused to look at Robyn as they drove. "I should call Leah."

"They might have news for us by the time we reach the hospital. Why don't you wait until you have more information?"

"I appreciate the confidence you have in your colleagues..." Grace rested her head on the window. "But I can't seem to muster up your optimism."

Robyn didn't push and they completed the ride in silence.

Grace felt like she should apologize for her pessimism. She knew it seeped from the memory of that life-altering phone call she had received from Leah. She tried to remember how she had known from the minute she'd picked up the phone that something was wrong. What had she read in the silence between her answering and Leah speaking? Not that her sister had been crying. That came later. Grace wondered if she were to call now if her voice would sound the same to Leah. Robyn was right in advising her to wait until they had more information.

Later, she would realize how fortunate she was to have Robyn shuttle her from the station to the hospital and guide her right to the emergency room entrance. She didn't have to think, just follow.

At the counter, she tested her voice. "Do you…" She couldn't even form the question and looked to Robyn for help.

"Has the coast guard called in a rescue from Humboldt Bay? This is Grace Warren. They're searching for her brother, Tyler."

"I can't confirm incoming traumas." The nurse paused, looking sympathetically at both of them. "But we do have an air delivery on its way. If you'd like to go to the front desk and give them your details, I will keep you posted."

"But," Grace interjected.

"HIPAA regulations," the woman insisted.

"We'll get the paperwork started, thanks," Robyn said, steering Grace away. "When my guys called in, they most likely used a radio. They wouldn't be able to say more than race, gender and age. Even if she did have a name, the law is really strict about protecting privacy. Frustrating, I know, but necessary. We'll do the paperwork, and once they match his information to you, they'll be able to release more."

Again, Grace found herself following Robyn, sitting where she suggested and providing the information that Robyn needed to complete the paperwork from the front desk. "I don't know what I'd do without you," Grace said as they walked back to the emergency waiting room. "If I'd gotten here at all, I would have been running into walls and screaming my head off trying to make someone *do* something. Anything. You're so levelheaded." She remembered the calm she had felt radiating from Robyn when she met her at the barn.

"Panic is a natural response, and it's productive if you can channel the energy. You can be faster. Stronger. But you have to stay in control, harness it effectively."

"You seem so in your element here. I'm surprised you retired."

"All those adrenaline rushes take their toll," Robyn answered.

"You told your friend that the job would have taken you. What did you mean by that?"

Robyn took a deep breath before answering. "There were

days that I dreaded going home so much that I let that influence my decisions in the field."

Grace waited for Robyn to explain. When she didn't, she stopped walking. "Influence your decisions how?"

"I didn't care whether I came home or not."

Grace didn't know how to respond. Before she could, the nurse in ER flagged them.

"The coast guard just delivered your brother. They're working to stabilize him, and I'll call you in just as soon as I can."

Grace scanned the room. They'd had a view of the emergency area as they walked from the front desk, but she had seen no gurney, no medical team rushing to his aid. Her body wanted to sag with relief hearing that they had, indeed, brought in her brother, but she couldn't bring herself to believe it without having seen him.

"I don't understand," she said to Robyn. "Is he okay?"

"They most likely brought him in from the helipad. They're going to want to get him stripped down and warmed up with blankets. It's important that they get some fluids into him and bring up his temperature. That's what they're going to be doing right now." Suddenly her face lit up. "Eason!" she called.

The coast guard officer turned toward Robyn's voice. "Landy!" His wide smile flashed straight white teeth.

"Come on," Robyn said, pulling Grace. "He'll be able to give us more information." When they reached the towering man, still decked out in his orange rescue suit and harness, Grace could still see the impression from his goggles on his red face. If the man in front of her had protective gear and still showed the effects of the cold, what did her brother look like?

Robyn spoke first. "This is Tyler's sister. Was he conscious in the water?"

"Just starting to slip. It's a good thing we got there when we did. He had the jacket on, and his face was out of the water. His vitals stayed stable on the way in, and they're setting him up on the IV now." He looked directly at Grace. "It's a tiny space in there, and they're working like crazy. They couldn't wait to get me out of there. It'll probably be fifteen, twenty minutes before they let family in."

Grace gulped back tears. She wanted to see him for herself but understood the need to stay out of their way.

"Fred, I can't thank you enough," Robyn said.

He laughed. "Remember how much you hated the families thanking you? You always came back grumping about how you were just doing your job and how awkward the thank-yous made you feel?"

Robyn punched him. "Point taken. It sucks being on this side."

"I bet. But it's a good thing you were. This guy owes you his life. He a friend of yours?"

Robyn looked at Grace as if she answered the question. Grace could see her doing the math in her head. She cared about Grace, so she cared about Tyler. "He's family," Grace answered, seeing in Robyn's eyes that her words explained their relationship perfectly.

"Family, huh?" Fred said with weight, looking from one woman to the other.

"I'll let her fill you in," Grace said. "I need to find some coffee."

"I'll come with you," Robyn said.

"No. Stay." Grace appreciated Robyn's support but needed to be alone. She had information for her sister now. She should make the call. After she took the chill off, she thought. Following Robyn's directions to the cafeteria, she bought herself a cup of coffee and doctored it at the counter.

Outside, she saw a fountain and lush garden and wove through the tables and chairs to find a door, spotting it around the U-shaped patio. She headed toward it. An elaborate plaque hung in the hallway, announcing the donor who had made the outdoor meditation garden possible.

She remembered the petty officer's words about how her brother was alive because of Robyn. Framed clippings detailed the work the hospital had done to save, repair and rehabilitate a patient who was rescued from a particularly horrific boating accident. Curious about the conditions of the patient's rescue, she passed over the details of what the trauma center had done, looking for more information about the accident itself, strolling slowly toward the doors to the garden. Directly across from the doors were photographs of the young man and the medical staff attached to the copy of the thank-you letter the family had written to the hospital.

The next photograph stopped Grace short.

An official pinned a medal onto a woman in uniform. The text next to the photo read "For Outstanding Acts of Bravery." Though she had already recognized the recipient, her eyes skipped to the name for confirmation.

Chief Petty Officer Robyn Landy.

Grace took a step closer. Though she'd immediately known the woman in the photo was Robyn, she hardly recognized her decked out in her dress uniform. The light blue shirt beneath the dark jacket brought out the startling blue of her eyes. Robyn's eyes in a younger face. A formal and surprisingly guarded face. This Robyn was all professionalism, aloof in polished perfection. Grace recalled how she had told Kristine and Gloria that Robyn had potential. Rough around the edges, she'd said. The Robyn in the photograph was all polish, a version Grace should have found even more attractive.

She carefully read through the bravery citation that had earned Robyn the award. Two young men had been hauled out of a roiling, frigid sea. Their friend was still trapped inside the capsized boat. Without hesitation, Robyn had risked her own life to board it and free the victim. In the details, she recognized Robyn, her selflessness and instinct to put others before herself. The space and encouragement she gave freely to both Jen and Tyler, how easily she provided support for Kristine's family. She gave whatever she could without hesitation.

Robyn had said it was time to rescue herself. She had been brave enough to make the choices that made her happy, yet Grace in her habit of grooming artists for a professional career had only seen what she thought Robyn *could* be. She now understood that if Robyn were to give Grace what she thought she wanted, they would both be unhappy. Grace realized she didn't actually want what she had been asking for.

She chastised herself and reached out to touch her fingers to the frame. Though the image comforted her, she missed the Robyn she knew, modest, unassuming. Something else too. Her eyes roamed the picture, trying to place what else was different. She closed her eyes to call up the Robyn she loved and saw it immediately, the contentment she emanated.

The serenity she appreciated in Robyn came from the life she chose wandering beaches looking for wood to turn on her lathe. Though full of renters, her house was always peaceful. Grace's own house looked exactly like the one she'd had back in Houston. Robyn's felt like Arcata. Grace remembered Gloria's advice to see and enjoy the town she lived in instead of running to the city every weekend. By pushing Robyn to change her home and show her bowls on a larger scale, she was again ignoring the beauty right in front of her.

"Grace?" Robyn's voice broke her thoughts. "I was looking all over the cafeteria."

"You found me," Grace answered.

Neither moved. Robyn stood at the end of the hallway, giving Grace the space she had asked for when she left the emergency room. There was so much that Grace wanted to tell Robyn, that she had found *her* Robyn the day she kissed her on Wedding Rock, that Robyn had helped her find a quiet place inside herself that she had never felt before. She wanted to explain the difference between the photograph and the woman she knew, but also share her awe in how much Robyn had contributed to her brother's rescue. She had so many ideas flying around inside of her head, but all that left her mouth was, "I'm so sorry, Robyn."

"Sorry?" Robyn approached her.

"For not seeing you."

Surprise flashed across her face. She glanced at the wall, and her crestfallen transformation stabbed Grace's heart. "That's not me."

"I know," Grace quickly assured her. She reached for Robyn, her fingers landing on the soft cotton of a wrinkled flannel Robyn had pulled from behind the seat in her truck. Her straight-legged jeans were rolled at the bottom and held sawdust from her day's work, and she wore socks with her Birkenstocks. Grace laughed out loud at the realization that she had fallen in love with a woman who wore her sandals with socks. She drew a frame around Robyn. "This is the Robyn I love."

"But recognition is important to you."

"*You* are important to me. And I'm proud of you and want to show you off. At work, I'm paid to showcase people. I need to leave that energy at work. I love the calm in you. I love the calm I feel when I'm with you."

Robyn considered this a frustratingly long time. "What about my toaster?" she finally said.

"Your toaster I will never love," Grace laughed. She grew serious. "I keep saying I love you, and you're not saying anything."

"I love you, Grace. So much it scares me. What happens if you decide you want someone more spiffy?"

Grace wrapped her arms around Robyn. "Too late. Like I told your friend, we're already a family. Kind of a crazy jumble that..."

"Tyler! He's okay! I came down to tell you they'll let you see him now," Robyn interjected.

"He can wait a few minutes," Grace said, pulling Robyn in for a kiss.

CHAPTER FORTY-EIGHT

Play

"How are you, man?" Robyn asked. Tyler sat at the table with a laptop, and she paused to give him a squeeze around the shoulders. "How'd it go at court yesterday?"

"Good."

Robyn kissed Grace hello.

"I'll be ready in a flash." She dashed into her room to finish getting ready.

"Where are you two off to today?" Tyler asked.

"Corkscrew Tree." Robyn sat and leaned her backpack against her chair.

"I thought you did that last weekend."

"That was Lady Bird Johnson Grove. You're welcome to come along."

He laughed. "No thanks. I've had enough of the local scenery."

"Did they walk?"

"Released on bail. I'm sure their fancy lawyers are working on a plea." He glanced up at her and rubbed his hand from elbow to shoulder. "I still might have to testify, but I really hope it doesn't play out like that." His hands fiddled with Grace's lace tablecloth suggesting he had more to say.

Robyn waited.

"Thanks for believing me about the estate sale."

"Why wouldn't I believe you?"

"I have a record. Anyone else who hears that I was involved will assume that I planned the whole thing."

"Yeah, because you have such an intimate knowledge of the area you'd know the estate sale in King Salmon was accessible by water."

"I thought we were just shooting the shit, you know, but when I mentioned that I had a plan to go to the Stansbury place with you, they got so excited. When they told me it was a shoreline property and said we could take a look, I never thought they'd stop and get out. It didn't seem like the best idea to me, but when we got there…"

"I know. I told you the place is really something. You can just see Lady Stansbury standing out on the widow's walk searching the ocean. It's captivating."

"They said it had been empty for years while the heirs fought about the will and no one would care if we had a look around before the sale. I didn't think it felt right and stayed close to the dock. I wasn't surprised at all when they came running back saying they saw security guys. Back out on the water, I chewed them out. I didn't know about all the stuff up at the university, so I thought it was no big deal anyway. Man, when Jack pulled out an old spyglass that he snagged from the boathouse, I nearly crapped my pants. But I was there with them, you know? That was my choice, so it's all my word against theirs."

"And you were the only one who wasn't stoned, which was very fortunate in your defense. So now you make better choices about who you hang out with. You'll figure it out."

Grace came back with her red curls swept up in a ponytail. She wore a form-fitting T-shirt and stylish cargo pants. Robyn sighed. If she wore cargos, she looked like a guy. When Grace wore cargos, she looked like she had stepped out of a catalog.

"Ready?" Grace asked.

"You bet!" Robyn stood. "Oh. I brought you something." She opened her pack, pulled out a lump of flannel tied with ribbon and handed it to Tyler.

"What's this?"

"A hot thing. It's filled with rice. Heat it up for two minutes in the microwave and set it across your shoulders or put it on your feet. Grace said you were having trouble staying warm."

"Thanks." He unfolded the sock-like thing curiously and slung it over his shoulder.

"Be good," Grace said, kissing him on the head.

Robyn and Grace wove their way up to the interstate and headed north. Grace stretched her arms into the sunlight streaming in on the dash. "Oh, I've missed the sun."

"It does feel nice," Robyn agreed. Just outside of town, she pointed to a huge rock protrusion on the forested hill. "That's Strawberry Rock. It's a good hike."

"But not for today."

"Nope. Another time. I have something else in mind for today."

"Our first kiss," Grace said, taking Robyn's hand as they passed the exit for Patrick's Point. "I was just starting to learn about the great local sights. Imagine my surprise when I found you. You looked so lost that day. Do you remember?"

Robyn remembered exactly how lost she had been on that gray day. How life had seemed so pointless. She met Grace's eyes for a moment. "I was out there thinking about how my relationship had tanked. It's where Barb and I...I don't even know what to call it. I usually just say that's where we got committed." A sly smile crept onto her face.

"What?"

"I just remembered that the stones sent me there that day. I got *Kiss*."

"So you were waiting for me."

"Waiting for you to wake me up like a fairy tale princess."

Grace laughed and rested her head against the back of the seat. "A modern one who rejects being rescued. I imagine that would be difficult for the one used to doing the rescuing."

"It took me a while to figure out I didn't have to do it on my own."

Heading toward summer, the day was bright, affording them a view of the rocky coastline as they followed the twisty road to the corkscrew tree. After they parked, Grace slipped into her Windbreaker, sweeping her ponytail out of the collar. "Now tell me about this one," she said as they fell into step together on the soft forest trail.

"What do you mean?"

"There's always a story. You hiked Tall Trees for years with your papa, but your obaachan preferred Fern Canyon. Your family always went swimming at Willow Creek, but not the beach you took me to."

"No, the nudie one my first girlfriend taught me about. You take good notes." They walked hand in hand through the quiet forest. Vivid green ferns lined the path and seemed to absorb every sound. Within minutes, they were completely wrapped in old-growth forest. "You wouldn't believe me if I told you."

"Try me."

"I've never been here before. I was running out of destinations so I Googled local hikes. This one was on the list, and when I saw pictures, I thought of you."

Grace scrunched her brow and accepted that Robyn was not going to elaborate. They walked in companionable silence, enjoying the serenity of the place until they reached the grand oddly formed tree with four trunks woven together as they stretched to the sky.

"Wow," Grace said. "That's the sexiest tree I've ever seen."

Robyn threw her arms around Grace. "That's exactly what I thought when I saw it, like someone sculpted two people lying with their legs intertwined. You approve of the destination?"

"That and how your mind works."

They climbed the trunk a few feet and peered up the middle of the trees before continuing their hike. "There's another reason I chose this park," Robyn said, pulling Grace to sit on a bench away from the other park visitors. "You know that Sergio moved after graduation."

"Of course," Grace said. "I gave him his very own razor."

"Razor?"

"Since he won't have access to mine anymore."

"That's gross."

"You're telling me," Grace said tersely. "Let's go back to how he's moved out."

Robyn absorbed Grace's need to snark about her former tenant and continued. "Now that it's just me in the main house, I thought maybe you'd like to move in and wind all of our stuff together. Tyler's got a good start on the stairs for the studio entrance, but Jen's students are only there in the afternoons. That gives us total privacy. Isaac has until the end of the summer to find another place. I wondered if maybe you'd be okay with Tyler being in your place at the bottoms on his own for a few months before he takes over that back self-contained unit. Will you stay, not just tonight?"

"That's what you wanted to ask me?"

Robyn felt confused. She'd expected Grace to be excited about the fact that her house was now empty. She'd made sacrifices to make room for Grace, yet now that it was available, Grace didn't seem enthusiastic at all.

"You want us to live together," Grace said flatly.

"Yes, that's what I want. I thought that was the next logical step for us," Robyn responded.

"I see." Grace sunk her hands deep in the pockets of her jacket. "It's a good thing one of us is thinking about the future."

"The future?" The future was exactly what Robyn was thinking about. What part of the conversation had Grace missed to not understand what she was talking about?

"I hope it's not terrible timing…I didn't expect Barbara to come up today…But we have been talking about the future, and I want that to be more than just moving in with you." Grace took a deep breath and slipped her hand from her pocket.

Robyn had never seen Grace uncertain. She'd seen her adamant, angry and perturbed. She'd seen Grace pushed to the edge by Kristine's children and frightened beyond measure when Tyler was missing. Mostly, she'd seen her radiant and confident. The uncertainty threw Robyn, so she was completely unprepared when Grace extended a tiny polished redwood box.

"It's beautiful," Robyn said, running her thumb over its top before pushing the lid back. As she was about to examine the box's construct, she realized its contents.

A silver band.

She tipped it into her palm. "It's heavy," she said.

"Platinum." Grace's confidence returned.

Robyn studied the swirls engraved on it. Robyn opened her mouth to speak, but Grace interrupted, "Don't you dare ask if it was expensive. You're supposed to say whether or not you'll marry me."

"I was getting there."

"I'm forty years old. I don't want to just shack up with someone. I want to start my forever."

"Right to the point, true to your style. Have I told you how much I love your style?"

"No. And you also haven't told me if you'll marry me."

"Yes. Of course I will." Robyn slipped the ring onto her finger and met Grace's eyes. "Yes."

CHAPTER FORTY-NINE

Love

"You totally rigged that," Grace said, placing the cool stone back in Robyn's hand.

"I didn't."

"Just like you didn't pick *Kiss, Passion, Touch or Discovery* on purpose."

"Nope. I told you since you moved in all I get are the good ones, no lie."

"Give me the bowl."

"Once there was a time you'd crawl over me to get it yourself."

"I don't trust you to keep your hands to yourself."

"I guess you think you've figured me out." Robyn handed her the bowl of stones, and Grace ran her fingers through, letting them fall through her fingers before she decided on one. "What did you get?"

Grace turned the stone in her fingers. "*Gratitude.*"

Robyn took the single stone and put it next to hers in the small dish and placed the bowl next to it again. Grace leaned with her, wrapping her arms around Robyn's middle. "I am grateful."

"So am I." Robyn covered Grace's arms with her own before settling back down on the mattress.

Grace took a deep breath and smiled at Robyn. "Listen to that."

"What?" Robyn asked, lifting her head up.

"Silence. I love it."

"Enjoy the next half hour because your brother will be out with the nail gun shortly."

"I never thought I'd bemoan dedication and productivity."

"It's looking fantastic, and I swear he gets three requests for quotes a day just by setting up his workspace out front. He could probably sell his upcycled stuff if he wanted to...though he couldn't possibly get what it's actually worth selling it curbside."

"Don't you dare mock me. I'm a professional, remember?"

"Of course. Ready for some evenly-toasted bread?"

"Again with the mocking."

"I'll stop." Robyn lowered herself down the steps and threw on sweats and an old coast guard undershirt. When Grace joined her, she evaluated her outfit sheepishly. "I should be wearing the PJs you bought me."

"Thanks for thinking of it, but I happen to like the ratty old shirts you wear."

"Really?"

Grace slid a finger into a well-positioned hole in the garment. "I like the access they afford."

Playfully, Robyn pushed Grace away. They descended the stairs and worked on breakfast. Robyn sipped her black coffee, raising her eyebrows at Grace. "That much cream and sugar, I don't know why you bother adding any coffee at all."

"I'd miss the flavor."

"Flavor shmavor. I want the caffeine."

They settled at the table and Robyn organized the morning paper, tossing the ads and sports sections into the recycling. The local and national news she kept, placing the arts and business sections in Grace's spot. Robyn loved the routine they had so easily established. Three bites into her toast, she realized Grace was not reading. "What are you thinking about?"

Grace reached across the table and twisted the ring she'd put on Robyn's finger. "I've been thinking about our wedding."

"Thinking what?"

"Wondering whether the Wedding Rock idea was yours or Barbara's."

Robyn set down her toast. "Why?"

Grace pushed back her shoulders like she was getting ready to present. "Because we have a plan to get married, but we haven't talked about the ceremony."

"What do you picture?"

"You haven't answered my question."

"What do you picture?" Robyn repeated. Though technically, she had not been married to Barb, on some level, she still felt self-conscious about being married a second time. It seemed right to defer to what Grace wanted in a wedding.

"Something grand," Grace began tentatively. "Everyone we know, a minister and a full ceremony. Music, lots of music during the ceremony, and afterward at a huge reception. Catered." She held Robyn's eyes.

Robyn didn't flinch or attempt to stop Grace, so she continued. "A professional photographer. Flowers. I want to carry flowers, and wear a white dress, a wedding dress with a veil and strappy shoes that sparkle."

"That private promise just to each other was Barb's idea. We fought over every single detail. When I realized how much I lost when I compromised, I promised myself never to compromise again." A shadow crept across Grace's face, so Robyn quickly spoke to remove it. "And luckily, I don't have to. I want big too. I want something formal and public and legal. Legal is really important to me."

Grace looked like she was about to launch into a presentation but stopped with a perplexed look. Robyn watched as her words seemed to sink in for Grace. When the pieces fell into place, a radiant smile lit up her face. "It's going to be expensive."

"It's going to be a celebration."

"I was scared that you would only want something small, something intimate."

"Something cheap."

"I wasn't going to say that." Grace wrinkled her nose.

"A wedding is an investment, and I think I've got pretty good odds on this being a wise one."

"I'd say you've got very good odds."

CHAPTER FIFTY

One Year Later

Devotion

"Don't you dare make me late on my wedding day!" Grace growled as her brother's phone clicked to voice mail again. Grace pounded on the kitchen wall, hoping to get an answering knock from her brother whose hallway shared the same wall.

A knock at the front door confused her. She opened the door to find her brother waiting expectantly. "Are you ready yet? Time's-a-wasting!"

"Why weren't you answering your phone?" Grace snatched her purse and ran out the door.

"Sorry. Alison's playing a game on it."

"Keeping Leah happy is important too, I guess. Course I *am* a bride today. Maybe we could remember that?" she said pointedly.

Tyler beamed at her. "It's your turn for it to be all about you."

Grace paused to hug her brother. After putting in the studio stairs he had so much work that he'd enrolled at the community college as a first step toward becoming a licensed contractor. She couldn't remember the last time she had worried about what he was doing.

"You look really beautiful," he said, blushing. "I wish Mom and Dad were here to see you."

Grace nodded, tears threatening. "You're not allowed to mess up my makeup," she said, fanning her face to chase the tears away.

"I'm sorry." They stood together, the moment turning unexpectedly serious. "I really am sorry."

She saw before her the boy who had also lost his parents as well as the man he was today. She'd contributed to who he had become, she realized, she and Robyn together. "I know." She held him tight, knowing how different things would have been without Robyn in their lives. "Now drive, idiot, so Robyn doesn't think I've stood her up."

* * *

Robyn stood in the entryway of the coast guard station, looking out at the brilliant blue sky. Down by the water, her parents and her brother's family together with Major Chief Coughlan explored the rescue boats docked beyond the station.

"I can't believe your whole family made it," Isabel said, straightening the collar unnecessarily on Robyn's dress blues, a deep blue skirt and jacket with her row of medals above the left breast and gold chevrons decorating her sleeves.

"It's the first time I've met my nephew. He's cute, isn't he?"

"Adorable. Do you think your parents will ever move back to the States?"

"No. They want to be near their grandson."

"Did your dad go loco when he found out he's not walking you down the aisle?"

"He understood. It didn't feel right without Grace's dad here."

"Well, you look stunning. Look at you," she said, turning her around to face the row of pictures, current and past coast guard staff. "Ten years, and it doesn't look like a day has passed for you. I can't believe you still fit into this. You look even better in it now."

Robyn stepped across the hall to study her picture. "I looked good in it back then."

"Good, yes. Happy, no. Now you look happy. Your Grace better work hard to keep this smile on your face."

"She does, Isabel. Believe me. She does."

* * *

Robyn stood holding Grace's hands as they waited for Jen's quartet to conclude their processional, overwhelmed by the perfection of the day. A gentle breeze blew in from the Pacific on the cloud-free, blue-skied summer afternoon as the minister offered her words on love and commitment. Robyn knew without doubt that the people who joined them today would be the community of support that the minister emphasized.

Immediate and extended family had traveled great distances. Robyn's former colleagues and Grace's current ones, artist friends and barn friends packed the rows, all there to witness the love she felt for the woman in front of her. Isabel and Kristine stood with them as their best ladies. She knew that they would honor the couple's request to see them through this and many more good days but also be with them to support them through the hard days too.

When the minister called for the rings, Caemon confidently stepped forward to let the brides untie the rings from the pillow. Though they had rehearsed that he would go sit with Gloria for the rest of the ceremony, Caemon insisted that he stay with his friend even when Kristine tried to coax him to stand with her to the side.

Robyn waved her off. Looking into his sparkling blue eyes, she remembered meeting him at the stable and how his joy cut right through her sorrow like the radiant sun that forever has the power to break through clouds to bring warmth and joy.

Reciting the vows they had written together, Grace slipped the platinum band Robyn had been wearing back onto her finger, and Robyn reciprocated with the sparkling gem befitting of her glowing bride. They had eyes only for each other. Robyn felt that although she wore the outfit that had made her father proud, Grace saw the woman she had become after she retired.

Robyn kissed her bride and was surprised when Grace pulled her into an embrace. Her lips hovering just above Robyn's ear, she said, "I still see my Robyn, but you have to know that you look scrumptious in your uniform."

When she let Robyn go, her eyes held the promise of where the uniform was headed the second they were alone together.

Strings sang out, setting them into motion, the notes breezing joyously over them and all those gathered. Holding hands, they exited through the center aisle. The majestic cedars in front of the station stretched their arms above them. Her heart full of joy, Robyn raised her arms in jubilation, never having dreamed such happiness as this could be hers.

Bella Books, Inc.

Women. Books. Even Better Together.

P.O. Box 10543
Tallahassee, FL 32302

Phone: 800-729-4992
www.bellabooks.com